Praise for the Washington Whodunit Series

HOMICIDE IN THE HOUSE

"Shogan's solid second Washington, D.C. (after 2015's *Stabbing in the Senate*) finds congressional staffer Kit Marshall serving as legislative director to North Carolina freshman Representative Maeve Dixon, a middle-of-the-road Democrat.... Shogan does a good job depicting the creaky, squeaky wheels of government, and Marshall plays politics and sleuth with equal dexterity in this capital Capitol Hill mystery."
—Publishers Weekly, April 18, 2016

4 Stars: "The gang is together again in this exceptional murder mystery as Kit, her friend Meg, boyfriend Doug and rescue dog Clarence collectively work to solve the crime. Each distinctive personality shines as they bring the case to a close. Be prepared for another adventure."
—RT Magazine

STABBING IN THE SENATE

"I thoroughly enjoyed reading about the messy political process of creating new policies. Shogan describes the intricacies of policy-making in a way that is related so closely to the mystery, I never felt I was reading a political science lecture. I believe readers who enjoy amateur sleuth mysteries written in the style of Agatha Christie will enjoy this promising debut mystery. "
—Dorothy St. James, author of the White House Gardener Mysteries, for Washington Independent Review of Books

"[*Stabbing in the Senate*] features loads of inside scoop about the workings of Senate offices—complete with all the gossiping, back-stabbing, and procedural maneuvering—plus an appealing young sleuth, sprightly pacing, and an edge-of-your-seat showdown on the Hart-Dirksen underground train. Apart from joining Kit on one of her Hill happy hours, how much more fun could you want?"
—Literary Hill, a Compendium of Readers, Writers, Books & Events

"A fast-paced blend of murder mystery and political intrigue.... *Stabbing in the Senate* is a page-turner that will keep the reader's rapt attention to the very end."
—Wisconsin Bookwatch, Midwest Book Review

"I have to say it is one of the best whodunits I have read this year. Colleen writes with clarity and wit and she knows her subject matter. She has done her research, turned her talent into one of the best new books to be on the 2016 market. *Stabbing in the Senate* is a look at Washington D.C. that is sure to be a memorable, page-turning bestseller. I give this one ten stars."
—Pamela James, Mayhem and Magic Blog

"What do politics, Washington intrigue and an everyone-for-herself outlook on life have in common? They all come together in the suspenseful, thrilling debut novel by Colleen J. Shogan titled *Stabbing in the Senate*.... It's hard to believe this is a debut novel.... Put [Shogan's] book on your shelf or ereader, and her future on your radar."
—LuAnn Braley, Back Porchervations

"A well-written debut novel. The author has been a part of the group of people she writes about, and her personal knowledge shows in her vivid descriptions of people and scenarios.... The

story is filled with twists and turns. Just like the main character, the reader is never quite sure who to trust or who to believe. Kit and Meg, her best friend, are a very likable duo as they try to get to the bottom of things."
—Book Babble

"From the discovery of the body, through pages and chapters of intrigue, to the action-packed reveal and take down of the killer, I was totally engrossed in this stellar mystery."
—Lisa K's Book Reviews

"Full of political intrigue, high-stakes decision makers, twists and turns and red herrings, *Stabbing in the Senate* is a wonderful new cozy. The characters are entertaining and the writing is spot on for a great whodunit. I am not really a fan of politics or D.C. in particular, but the way Colleen J. Shogan presented this story drew me in and kept me excited about it."
—Caro, Open Book Society

"I am not a person who enjoys political novels but this was a pleasant surprise. The mystery, adventure, suspense, and intrigue are not to be missed."
—Penny M., Cozy Mystery Book Reviews

"Amid perpetual rounds of gossip, back-scratching, blame games and cocktails, Colleen Shogan offers an inside look into D.C. politics. A senator is murdered, and members of his staff are simultaneously suspicious, calculating and polite as they scramble for new jobs. Staff must also decide whether to collude on a revisionist history for the maverick's opinions. Everyone is power hungry, but protocol demands that ambitions be kept hidden. Protagonist Kit Marshall is a breath of fresh air in a city of opportunists, and *Stabbing in the Senate* is a smart, snappy whodunit that kept me guessing until the end."
—Susan Froetschel, award-winning author of *Allure of Deceit*

"An interesting snapshot into the world of Senate staffers from a Capitol Hill insider. Political intrigue, mystery, and a rescue beagle named Clarence. What more could you ask for?"
—Tracy Weber, award-winning author of the Downward Dog Mystery Series

"In this smart, fast-paced mystery, Colleen Shogan gives a fascinating look at Washington, D.C., politics through a Senate staffer's eyes. She kept me turning pages until the surprising reveal at the very end."
—Mary Marks, author of the Martha Rose quilting mysteries

"A taut mystery, set in the halls of the Senate, a backdrop Shogan knows well. It kept me guessing until the end!"
—Carlene O'Neil, author of Cypress Cove Mystery series

"*Stabbing in the Senate* is filled with memorable characters and finds you rooting for Kit Marshall, an honest, smart and funny young woman, navigating a complicated city fueled by politics."
—Purva Rawal, health care consultant and former Senate staffer

"Shogan does a good job of describing the work of a staffer—unsurprising, since she herself was one in a former life. Also believable is Kit Marshall's confusion in being thrust into the role of suspect.... *Stabbing in the Senate* is a quick read, perfect for those commutes on the Red Line."
—The Hill is Home Blog

"I was so intrigued with the story and wrapped up in all the possible suspects that I wasn't sure who the guilty party was until very late in the story. I liked Kit. She was a character who was easy to relate to and she made for a good amateur sleuth."
—Brooke Blogs

Homicide in the House

Homicide in the House

A Washington Whodunit

COLLEEN J. SHOGAN

Seattle, WA

Camel Press
PO Box 70515
Seattle, WA 98127

For more information go to: www.camelpress.com
www.colleenshogan.com

This is a work of fiction. Names, characters, places, brands, media, and incidents are either the product of the author's imagination or are used fictitiously.

Cover design by Sabrina Sun

Homicide in the House

ISBN: 978-1-60381-333-4 (Trade Paper)
ISBN: 978-1-60381-334-1 (eBook)

Library of Congress Control Number: 2016933263

Printed in the United States of America

Acknowledgments

AFTER LUMBERING ABOUT the deserted Madison Building at the Library of Congress for three weeks during the fall of 2013, I decided the sequel to *Stabbing in the Senate* would take place during a government shutdown. Capitol Hill assumed an unsettled eeriness during the closure. Hallways were quiet, restrooms shuttered, and all public events were canceled. A high degree of political tension layered on top of the gloomy and desolate setting provided a perfect backdrop for the second book in the Washington Whodunit series.

Thank you to my agent Dawn Dowdle and the talented publishing and editorial staff at Camel Press, Catherine Treadgold and Jennifer McCord. My social media "fans" read excerpts of this book on Facebook and provided helpful feedback, particularly when I described familiar scenes in the House of Representatives. While working on the plot, I shared several twists and turns with my colleagues at the Library of Congress, who were always willing to listen enthusiastically and patiently. Thank you to several House of Representatives employees who provided key pieces of information about congressional operations. Your input made this book possible.

Finally, without the support of my family, particularly my husband, I would have never been able to finish another mystery novel while balancing the demands of everyday life.

Capitol Hill provides a great backdrop for telling entertaining stories. That said, all characters appearing in this work are fictitious. Any resemblance to real persons, living or dead, is purely coincidental.

Chapter One

THE DIGITAL CLOCK blinked an irritating red, glaring "11:59" in block numerals. The wait was nearly over. Every television news station had displayed the number of days, hours, minutes, and seconds remaining until the inevitable federal government shutdown. We'd peered over the cliff, and apparently, it was time to jump.

"Kit, did you approve my quote for the press release?" The high-pitched voice of my boss, Representative Maeve Dixon from the great Southern state of North Carolina, jolted me out of my brief reverie. The clock now radiated "12:01." Armageddon had officially arrived.

"Yes, Maeve. I approved your comment a few hours ago. I like the part about you standing with the people of North Carolina against the politicians who caused this mess. It's always good to run against Washington." I mustered a small smile and added, "Especially when it's shuttered."

"I can't imagine the quote will put me in good stead with my fellow colleagues in Congress, but what choice do I have?"

Representative Dixon, who insisted I call her Maeve, was right. She had been elected to the House by the narrowest of margins a little over a year ago, and it being February, she'd face reelection in nine months. Homespun constituents closely monitored her political posturing. On the other hand, the leadership of her party in Congress would also look to Maeve, who was young and energetic, to carry the day when the politics surrounding the shutdown ripened on the airwaves and Twitter-sphere. We were heading into uncharted waters. Maeve was a middle-of-the-road Democrat new to Congress and I had never dealt with such a monumental catastrophe. But as her legislative director, it was my job to know everything about the ensuing crisis.

A cacophony of telephone rings resembling a bad handbell choir served as background music. It was all hands on deck in the Dixon office. We'd been barraged with calls from constituents for several hours now, with questions ranging from Maeve's position on the shutdown to whether they could still visit the Smithsonian next week during February's Presidents' Day holiday. The negative answer to the latter question was usually met with a litany of loud expletives, routinely resulting in our interns holding the telephone receivers at least six inches from their ears.

"Kit, I asked you a question. Do I have any other options?"

I looked directly at Maeve, whose long brown hair had been drawn into a hastily assembled late-night bun. Her athletic body assumed a slumped posture, no doubt the result from tiresome workdays with no recent opportunities to relieve stress at the gym. I thought her earlier question was rhetorical, but I should have known better. Maeve was literal and straightforward. She'd completed military tours of duty in both Iraq and Afghanistan. If she asked a question, she expected a direct answer.

"Not right now, ma'am. We should move forward with the plan we discussed. Let's not deviate until we know how long this shutdown might last."

When it became clear that Congress might not come to

a resolution on the federal budget before funding ran out, Maeve and I had devised a plan for how she'd handle the crisis. She needed to walk a fine line. Our party was pushing a spending bottom line that was too high. On the other hand, the Republicans wanted to cut every social program known to mankind. Maeve couldn't stand wholeheartedly behind her party's leadership because it would kill her with the more conservative constituents in her congressional district. But if she spoke too loudly against mainstream Democrats, they would make her pay when the crisis was over.

Keeping her head down wasn't an option, either. As she'd told me many times, she'd done enough of that during her military service. For her, being labeled a backbencher for the rest of her congressional career was tantamount to a political death sentence.

Behind me, a deep voice said, "I agree with Kit. Let's stay the course." I turned around to face my immediate supervisor, Dan, the chief of staff. A few years younger than me, Dan was a nice guy who meant well. Unfortunately, the kind words ended there. He came to Washington with Maeve and knew her congressional district like the back of his hand. But he understood almost nothing about policy and Congress. It was a constant battle to educate him about how politicians operated and the distinct culture of Capitol Hill. I was a newbie to the House of Representatives, but at least I knew how a bill became a law. Dan struggled with the most basic *Schoolhouse Rock* version of events.

Dan looked as if his brain had been wiped clean. His eyes were round with panic. He hadn't bargained for a government shutdown when he left North Carolina for Washington. He moved closer so that Maeve couldn't hear his whispered question.

"What should we do next?"

"Dan, doesn't it make sense to issue the press release?" I used my regular speaking voice. Maeve should know her top aide had no clue about handling a political crisis.

"Right. I'll make sure that gets done."

He sped down the hallway toward his small private office. I hoped he knew how to email the release to our important press contacts, but I had my doubts. Yesterday, I overheard him ask his iPhone, "Siri, what is a government shutdown?" I pretended I hadn't overheard. Ignorance is bliss, especially in Washington D.C.

All staffers in the Dixon office were working tonight, but tomorrow would be an entirely different story. A government shutdown meant no money was available to keep government programs or buildings operational. That included paying government employees. Each member of Congress had to determine how to keep his or her office functional during the shutdown. Maeve decided that Dan and I would report for work. Everyone else would remain at home unless absolutely needed. Despite the winter darkness, that meant long workdays were ahead, unless Congress resolved the dispute over government funding levels quickly. With deeply entrenched views on both sides of the aisle, it was unlikely that this fiasco would be short-lived.

My desk phone buzzed. Recognizing my live-in boyfriend's cell number, I answered it.

"You're still at work?"

"Good evening to you, Doug. Happy government shutdown."

"Sorry," he muttered. "I wanted to check because I'm headed to bed soon. Are you going to stay there all night?"

"No, I'm going to leave as soon as Maeve decides to call it a day. I'll see you soon."

"Okay, great. Bye." A click was followed by a dial tone.

The conversation with Doug was par for the course—lately, at least. I'd been at my job with Maeve for six months now. Working for a newly elected freshman member of Congress had proven more time consuming than my previous position with elder statesman Senator Lyndon Langsford. After my former boss's murder, which I helped the police solve, I interviewed for numerous jobs in Congress. My best friend Meg had accepted a job working in the House of Representatives. When the opportunity to work as a senior legislative staffer for Maeve presented itself, I eagerly applied.

I'd anticipated a steep learning curve. After all, the House and the Senate function as separate political institutions with totally disparate traditions and norms. What I had not anticipated was how much work it was to staff a member of Congress who was just starting her political career rather than approaching the end of it. As a military veteran with no track record, she had to consider every vote she made and position she took with the utmost care. Her constituents in North Carolina were watching her every move. She represented a "swing district," which meant her seat frequently changed hands between the two political parties due to the evenly divided voting electorate who resided there. Doug hadn't quite adjusted to my new 24/7 responsibilities. He was a history professor at Georgetown, and between my work and his attempt to finish yet another book, our recent time together had been limited to hastily shared late-night dinners or abbreviated, stilted phone calls.

His increasing detachment should have been causing me considerable concern, but this wasn't the time to focus on it. I glanced at my email inbox. The messages were already piling up. There were several from top staff in the Speaker's office. Maeve couldn't ignore those emails. Not only was the Speaker the leader of the entire House, he was also her party's head honcho. An almost equal number of emails came from the Minority Leader's entourage across the aisle, who knew that Maeve had tough decisions ahead, pitting her district's beliefs against her partisan loyalties. The game was on. Both parties wanted a piece of Maeve Dixon during the shutdown.

An email from Meg popped up. Ignoring the rest of my inbox, I eagerly clicked on it. Meg's new position as an investigator for a House committee focused on oversight had been time-consuming, as well. Our days of carefree happy hours had dwindled. We were lucky if we found time to share frozen yogurt in the House cafeteria.

Can you believe this is happening??? she wrote. *Are you excepted? If so, let's try to meet for lunch.* :) *Meg*

"Excepted" was slang for an "excepted federal employee." That meant that even though the government had no money to pay salaries, you still had to report for work.

My spirits lifted after reading Meg's email. At least I wouldn't have to suffer through this mess alone. I hit reply.

I'll be here. See you at Tortilla Coast at noon. I suggested her favorite restaurant near the House office buildings. Some things never changed. Though you wouldn't know it from looking at her, Meg still had an appetite to match her ambition.

It was nearly one o'clock in the morning, and thankfully the phones had quieted. I clicked off my computer and walked toward Maeve's office. As I approached the open door, I was struck by how loudly she was speaking.

Dan was standing next to my boss, who was seated at her desk with the phone at her ear. He was sweating profusely, and when he saw me, he grabbed a tissue and blotted at his forehead and cheeks. Maeve was having an argument. Only one hour into the shutdown and the shenanigans were in full swing.

"You know the shutdown puts me in a difficult position," she yelled. "The Speaker understands that. He told me yesterday he'd rather have me in Congress next year than count on my solidarity with the party."

Who was on the other end of the line? Maybe the Majority Leader of the House, the Speaker's second-in-command? Or the Democratic party whip, who had the unenviable job of trying to make sure everyone on our side of the aisle stuck together on the problematic floor votes ahead?

I mouthed silently to Dan, "Who is it?"

He shook his head. *No idea*. Why was I surprised?

I grabbed a blank Post-it note from Maeve's desk and wrote: *Who's on the line*?

Whoever it was, his voice was getting louder. Maeve held the receiver away from her ear to avoid being deafened. She punched the "mute" button on the phone and covered the receiver with her hand, just in case.

"Jack Drysdale."

That explained why Maeve was getting an earful. Drysdale was the Speaker's top aide and Washington politico extraordinaire. Just shy of fifty, he'd been working on the Hill for two decades and had finally ascended to the most powerful staff position in the House of Representatives. I knew him only by reputation. Even senior legislative staffers like myself were never in the same room as him. He was the Speaker's eyes and ears, and when he didn't like what he was seeing and hearing, he made your life a living hell.

Jack must have come up for air, because it was now Maeve's turn to get a word in edgewise. "I can't give you my answer now. I told the Speaker I need to take the temperature in my district. Like I said earlier, my chief of staff will be in direct contact with our North Carolina office. After he gives me a report, I'll be in a better position to tell you what's possible."

Drysdale must have said something that upset Maeve, because she frowned and then promptly gave the middle finger to the phone receiver.

"If you don't want to deal with Dan, then you can communicate with my legislative director, Kit Marshall." A brief pause as she listened to his response.

"Yes, that's Kit Marshall. She can run point for me on the policy decisions related to the shutdown. Touch base with her tomorrow and we'll go from there." She slammed the phone down with no pretense of a polite farewell.

Maeve pressed her fingertips to her forehead to forestall the inevitable headache. "That man is insufferable. I don't understand how the Speaker of the House stands him."

Dan shifted his weight from one foot to the other nervously. "Did he say something about me?"

Maeve grabbed a bottle of water on her desk and chugged several gulps. "He doesn't want to deal with you on the specifics of the shutdown."

I was embarrassed for Dan, who fiddled with his glasses and said, "Did he say why?"

Maeve looked directly at Dan before answering. Was she going to try to soften the blow? I held my breath, praying that she wouldn't make an awkward situation worse.

In her infinite wisdom, my boss must have decided to take the high road. "He knows you're going to be spending all your time on the phone with our district director and the press in North Carolina to figure out the political thinking there. That's why I told him to communicate with Kit on the details of the Speaker's proposal to end this mess."

I exhaled in relief. I doubted that Drysdale had been so diplomatic. Dan's reputation as a lightweight was well known. Maeve's ability to think on her feet and bend the truth was impressive, especially for a novice politician.

She sat down at her desk. "I can't think straight. Let's call it a night and come back fresh in the morning."

I glanced at my watch. It was 1:30. How fresh would I be after four hours of sleep? I'd have to take what I could get until Congress solved this mess.

After gathering my belongings, I took the elevator to the ground floor and walked mechanically to the southeast exit, which was closest to the Capitol South Metro station. The busy station entrance was quiet, with no one entering or leaving. Then it dawned on me that it was well after midnight and I had missed the last train. I pressed the Uber app on my iPhone, and in three minutes, my own personal taxi was on the way.

While I waited for my ride, I walked west on C Street so I could catch a glimpse of the Capitol at night between the Cannon and Longworth House Office Buildings. New Jersey

Avenue provided the perfect view. The February night was cold and clear. The Capitol's iron dome stared back at me peacefully, but the tranquil silence was deceiving. Starting tomorrow, a battle would ensue within those walls. Instinct told me some unlucky politicos wouldn't survive the fight. As I climbed into my cab, I had no idea how accurate my premonition would turn out to be.

Chapter Two

The snooze alarm on my iPhone had already gone off twice. It was time to face the music. I silenced my favorite wake-up song, "Rainbow Connection," and threw the covers aside. According to Kermit, rainbows had nothing to hide. The same thing couldn't be said of angry politicians fighting over the federal budget.

As soon as I got out of the bed, our overweight beagle-mix rescue mutt jumped up and took my place. As a history professor, Doug usually slept later than me. Clarence might think Doug couldn't tell the difference between his two bedmates, or maybe the dog just liked curling up in a pre-warmed location. Either way, once I vacated the bed, my spot was taken.

After making myself a venti-sized latte in our complicated high-end espresso machine, I took a shower and dressed quickly. With no time to wash it, I had to wet and blow-dry my shoulder-length straight dark hair to make it behave. I was even paler than usual due to lack of sleep, and my normally plump cheeks looked almost gaunt. As someone who was always gaining and losing the same five pounds, I hoped that meant I'd lost some weight.

It was already half past seven. Not good. No doubt many congressional staff had never gone to bed, and others had already descended upon Capitol Hill. I clicked on the television in the living room to assess the damage.

While listening to the cable news reports, I began scrolling through the messages on my iPhone. Many staffers had worked through the night. Emails had arrived at all hours and were piling up. Numerous bright blue dots next to the unread messages stared at me in a long, vertical column. After determining who sent the emails, I knew there would be no swiping and deleting. These missives had come from important Capitol Hill staffers and could not be answered without careful consideration.

Doug stirred inside the bedroom. I'd had no time to walk Clarence this morning, so hopefully he was getting motivated to take him outside.

"Hey," I called out, "every channel is talking about the government shutdown. I need to head into work right now."

Doug flipped over onto his back and ran his fingers through his messy, thick brown hair. Blindly he reached for his glasses, sitting on the nightstand. He put them on and yawned loudly.

"What did you just say? I'm just waking up."

I sighed. I didn't have time for a long conversation. "The government is shuttered. I'm heading to the office because I'm running point for my boss."

"Well, good morning to you, too," Doug grumbled.

I ignored his snarky comment. "Can you take Clarence out? I'm already an hour behind schedule. There are at least a dozen emails I'll have to answer on the subway."

Doug shifted on the bed and rolled Clarence onto his side. As Doug scratched his pink belly, Clarence entered a trance-like state of ecstasy. Our dog, always passive in the morning, particularly liked being rubbed on his underside.

"That's fine, I don't have a class until this afternoon. Clarence and I know how to fend for ourselves these days, don't we, buddy?" Clarence growled softly.

This time I took the bait. "Doug, the entire federal government is closed. I work for Congress, who decided shutting down the government was preferable to agreeing on a budget. That means I need to get to work."

Doug waved his hand at me in a halfhearted attempt at dismissal. "Congress wasn't always the problem, you know. It used to function just fine."

As a historian, Doug could make comments like this and rattle off a hundred different anecdotes to back them up. Best not to argue with him when I had no time to spare. Besides, I wasn't ignorant when it came to congressional history. "I'm not dealing with Henry Clay these days. Not everyone is a great compromiser. I'll keep you posted about tonight."

Doug didn't reply, so I hustled out of the bedroom, grabbed my purse, and left the condo. He certainly hadn't won any sunshine awards for his attitude this morning. It was true I hadn't spent much time with him and Clarence lately, but this was Washington D.C., and I was trying to climb the ladder on Capitol Hill. Doug's job as a tenured Georgetown professor was far less stressful. He taught classes and wrote books. He was busy at times, like when he was trying to meet a publisher's deadline or preparing to teach a new course. But for the most part, his schedule was predictable. Mine was the opposite. Until a few months ago, our divergent lifestyles had always seemed complementary. Lately, I wasn't so sure. I still enjoyed spending time with Doug. Since accepting this new job in the House, those carefree opportunities had almost disappeared.

I reached the eerily desolate Metro. At the height of rush hour, the long platform that lined the subway tunnel had fewer than ten people waiting for the next train from suburban Virginia into the District of Columbia. This was the reality of the shutdown. Only a miniscule portion of federal workers faced the commute into work today. Everyone else was sitting in their pajamas or robes, watching Kathie Lee and Hoda get tipsy while sipping a cup of coffee and munching on homemade waffles … or at least that's what I would be eating.

I shoved the image of leisurely furloughed life out of my mind. The shutdown was no vacation for the office of Maeve Dixon. In fact, it was precisely the opposite. It gave Maeve the opportunity to show her constituents, and maybe the whole country, that she was a rising star in American politics. My job was to make sure she was front and center when every important decision and deal transpired.

With renewed resolve, I triaged the growing list of emails requiring immediate attention. There were several messages called "Dear Colleague" letters about various legislative proposals that had been filed last night to "solve" the shutdown. After scanning those, I saved them in an email folder but did nothing further. Time would tell which bills received attention from the party leadership or the media. Those would be the solutions Maeve might want to support.

One message caught my attention. It was from Jack Drysdale, the Speaker's top staffer who had called Maeve last night. Drysdale didn't miss anything. He had obviously made note of my name when Maeve told him I would serve as her lead person on the various policy proposals to end the crisis. I'd never met Drysdale, so this email might present an opportunity to build a valuable political relationship.

Drysdale had a reputation for terseness. His message indicated the scuttlebutt was rooted in reality, *Speaker wants to meet with Rep. Dixon at 2pm. Members Only meeting but come so we can talk. JD.*

We had been summoned to the Speaker's lair in the Capitol. The first order of business upon arriving at work would be to make sure that Maeve had no conflict for two o'clock. I had lunch with Meg at noon, but that left plenty of time to make the afternoon appointment. I'd think about strategy for the meeting once I had time to consider how Maeve should play her cards.

The next message that caught my attention was from another VIP staffer on the Hill. The name "JUDY TALENT" stood out prominently on my list of unread iPhone emails. Judy was in the same position as Jack Drysdale, but one rung lower. She was the top aide for the Majority Leader in the House. I scanned Judy's email. She didn't request a meeting but wanted to "touch base" to make sure Maeve was "on message" for the shutdown. Who was running the show for our party, Jack or Judy? Both deserved responses, and I needed to email them pronto.

After the subway arrived at the Capitol South Metro station, I rode the long escalator to exit and was greeted by a freezing blast of arctic air. Why did wind tunnels persist in subway stations? I tightened the scarf around my neck and shoved gloved hands in my pockets. At least the shutdown hadn't taken place in a nice weather month. That would have only intensified my envy of my furloughed federal brethren.

Capitol South was more conveniently situated than my previous Senate Metro station. The House of Representatives office buildings were located less than a block away from the subway, a suburban commuter's dream. Only two minutes after leaving Capitol South, I ascended the concrete staircase to enter the Cannon House Office Building. Usually, a line snaked outside the doors, particularly during the popular tourist months. Today there was no line, and I marched right up to the heavy door. I gave it a good tug, but the door didn't budge. Cupping my hands around my eyes, I peered through the dark glass doors. The entrance was usually filled with Capitol Hill Police officers screening visitors and staff through metal detectors. Then I saw the sign proclaiming this ingress closed "due to the government shutdown." So much for convenient access to the office. I hiked down the stairs and headed up First Street toward Independence Avenue.

The Cannon Building was the oldest congressional office

structure in the entire Capitol complex. On a typical working day, its entire 800,000 square feet were occupied with elected members of Congress, their staffs, tourists, lobbyists, and other visitors who came to Washington D.C. to plead their case to the nation's legislature. After I entered the building through the security checkpoint, I stared down the long hallway, flanked with numerous congressional offices on both sides. Rather than resounding with the chattering of staff and the click-clack of high heels pounding on the ornate floor, the corridor was silent. Two staffers stood outside one of the offices, their heads huddled close together in a seemingly private conversation, no doubt trading secrets about how Congress was going to dig itself out of the mess it had created by shutting down the government. Other than that, the corridor was jarringly empty.

A similarly uncomfortable silence greeted me inside our office suite. No perky intern acknowledged my arrival, and the flat screen television that entertained visitors in the waiting room was turned off.

I slowly opened the door that led to our workstations and the chief of staff's small private office. Peeking around the corner, I said tentatively, "Dan, are you here? Representative Dixon?"

No response, but someone had to be here. I had walked right into the office suite without using my key. After placing my purse on my desk, I turned on my computer. Before I started answering emails, didn't it make sense to figure out who was inside the office?

Dan's door was closed. I knocked softly, but he didn't reply. There was a low humming sound coming from inside.

Ummmm. Ummmm. Ummmm. It repeated itself several times.

This was officially weird. There was no way I could start working without identifying that noise. The last time I barged into an office unannounced, I had discovered the body of my former boss, Lyndon Langsford, who had been stabbed inside his Senate office. Did I want to go down that road again? That was a ridiculous notion. What were the chances of something like that happening twice?

I grasped the knob, twisted it, and pushed open the door. Dan was sitting at his desk with his shoes off and his legs crossed, sporting bulky earphones and a blindfold. My presence had gone completely unnoticed. His arms were outstretched and his hands were turned upwards, as if he was summoning a higher power. Completely oblivious, he continued humming, or whatever that sound was.

I decided to wait another fifteen minutes. Perhaps he'd be done by then. When I returned, I cleared my throat to get his attention. The "ummmms" grew louder.

I walked over to Dan and lifted one of the coverings away from his right ear. "Earth to Dan. Are you almost finished?"

Perhaps my response was foolhardy; after all, Dan was my boss. But did he realize the clock was ticking, and every minute this crisis lasted could negatively impact Maeve's approval rating?

My intrusion must have surprised him, because he almost levitated off his chair. He hastily removed his eye mask and earphones. "Jeez, Kit, why did you do that? I was in the middle of my meditation."

"I'm sorry I ruined your flow, or your buzz, or whatever. But Maeve needs to make decisions, and she won't want to issue an edict without finding out how her constituents perceive the shutdown. Have you called our district director in North Carolina yet?"

"I was going to do that right after my morning chant." He stashed his earphones and eye shield inside a desk drawer.

I didn't have any more time for Dan. "Let me know what you find out. In the meantime, the Speaker wants to see Maeve at two o'clock this afternoon. I need to confirm the appointment and make sure she's ready."

Dan seemed surprised by this revelation, but he didn't say anything else. I interpreted his silence as approval of my plan and marched out of his office. I almost ran into Maeve, who was taking off her coat and heading into her private sanctuary. By now I was certain Dan was out of his league. It was up to me to get Maeve through this calamity without suffering a major political setback.

Chapter Three

My stomach always seemed to know what time it was. When it rumbled, I knew it was time for lunch. The office was now under some semblance of control. Dan was scheduled for numerous phone calls with the congressional district, Maeve was reviewing a Congressional Research Service report in preparation for her meeting this afternoon with the Speaker, and I had confirmed the appointment with Jack Drysdale. Sneaking out now meant I could enjoy a quick lunch with Meg, no doubt the highlight of my day.

After exiting the Cannon Building, I retraced my steps toward the Capitol South Metro station and approached Tortilla Coast, a popular watering hole for House members, staff, and lobbyists. It was never empty, even when Congress wasn't around. Today was no exception. Faced with limited options in the cafeteria, Capitol Hill staffers forced to work during the shutdown were all congregating at the Coast. If we couldn't sit at home with a warm mug of hot chocolate, at least we could sip yummy margaritas.

As I made a beeline for the entrance, I heard a familiar voice over my shoulder.

"Howdy, stranger!"

Meg appeared out of nowhere and immediately stretched out her arms for a big hug. We'd worked together for four years in the Senate and during our tour of duty had become best friends.

"You look terrific, as always." That wasn't merely a polite comment. Meg was stylish, attractive, and smart. In Washington D.C., having all three of those qualities definitely gave her an edge.

Meg ran her fingers through her short blond bob and waved her hand to dismiss my comment. Her manicured fingernails and recent highlights indicated she hadn't let the threat of the salary hiatus during the federal government shutdown interrupt her beauty regimen.

"Are you ready to eat?" Meg headed through the doors to the restaurant and asked the hostess to seat us. Meg had a voracious appetite and good genes. The latter prevented her from gaining an ounce, no matter how much she ate.

We plopped ourselves down in a booth and the waitress delivered a basket full of warm tortilla chips, the watering hole's signature offering.

The minute the basket was on the table, Meg dove into the chips. "Can we have some Sunset queso to go with this?" The waitress looked amused at Meg's immediate request, but she nodded and scuttled off to place our appetizer order.

It was often hard to get a word in edgewise with Meg. I waited until she had stuffed her mouth with a big chip saturated in yellow cheesy dip mixed with jalapeños. Asking all my questions at once might prove the best strategy. "Why are you working during the shutdown? When is this going to end? And oh, how's Kyle?"

Kyle was Meg's clean-cut boyfriend from the other side of the political aisle. He used to work in the House of Representatives but now was a chief of staff in the Senate. We'd met him last year while informally investigating the murder of our boss.

Meg swallowed and took a big gulp of water. "Actually, those three questions are related."

Before she could elaborate, our waitress came over to take our lunch order. Given my constant battle with the bulge, I usually stuck to a bowl of soup when I indulged in lunch at the Coast. But this was no ordinary day. Who knew how late I would have to stay tonight? "I need some shutdown comfort food. I'll have the chicken fajitas."

Meg studied the menu. "Kit, you are absolutely right. I'd like to build my own burrito with steak, guacamole, and tomatillo sauce." She handed the menu to the waitress and smiled. Her order was met with another brief stare of disbelief from our server, who undoubtedly wondered how svelte Meg could ingest a monster burrito after having inhaled a basket of chips and creamy queso.

"I'm going to have to eat lunch and run because my boss has an appointment with the Speaker in an hour. Give me the lowdown on what's happening."

"Like I was saying, your questions are tied together. I'm working during the shutdown because the committee is crashing on a big hearing involving government waste." She lowered her voice and leaned in close. "We think the White House might have tried to cover up questionable expenditures from several executive branch departments."

Meg worked for an oversight committee in the House of Representatives who kept a close eye on government spending and procedures. While our party controlled the House of Representatives, the Republicans had the White House. Divided government made the politics on her committee particularly contentious. With less than a year until the next election, Meg and her colleagues were under considerable pressure to scrutinize the current administration.

I moved in closer to the table so we could keep our conversation discreet. Washington D.C. was full of snoops who liked to listen to the private conversations taking place in adjacent restaurant booths. "When are you going to bring this scandal to light?"

Meg shrugged. "It depends how much we can dig up during the shutdown. The chairman would like to go public as soon as the government reopens, if that's possible."

We ended our conversation as our waitress approached with our lunches. My fajitas sizzled as she placed them in front of me, and Meg's burrito could have fed an army. Less than five seconds later, we had both dug into our meals. Too bad stress didn't burn calories, because if it did, calories consumed during a government shutdown wouldn't really count.

After several big bites, time was growing short. I needed to talk to Maeve before we walked over to the Speaker's office, so I had to wrap up lunch with my best pal. "You didn't answer my other two questions."

Meg smiled with her mouth full. After swallowing, she said, "Sorry. Didn't you ask how long this shutdown was going to last?"

I nodded. Meg usually had good information because of her various committee staff contacts.

"I don't think you want to know the answer to that question. My sources are telling me this isn't going to be a brief one. The sides are far apart, and neither party thinks it's to their advantage to give in."

"Do you mean several days?" How could we possibly keep the office running with just Dan and me? He didn't carry his share of the workload under normal circumstances. The intensity of a shutdown would amplify the problem.

"No, Kit. You're not getting it. I mean weeks."

I choked on the big bite of chicken I had just put in my mouth.

"Are you okay? Jeez, have some water." Meg handed me a full glass.

Sputtering, I took a gulp and then wiped my mouth quickly with a napkin. "Weeks? Are you serious?"

"Of course. It takes Congress days just to take the political temperature of the country. Then it's at least another week to start coming up with a compromise. After that, who knows how long it will take to broker the actual deal? Remember, the president and Congress don't exactly see eye to eye these days." Meg seemed unaffected by this prospect. She calmly sliced up another large bite of burrito.

"Doesn't this situation bother you?"

"It's annoying. None of us will get paid as long as this debacle continues. But we have most of our staff onsite during the shutdown, so it's business as usual. The commute's a lot better, isn't it?"

"I guess that's one way of looking at it," I muttered. I couldn't get over the reality of trying to run the office for an extended period with only Dan's help. Had Doug stocked up on some nice Virginia wine varietals? For sanity's sake, I hoped so.

I'd put a sizable dent in my fajitas, and it was time for me to head back to the office. I stood up, opened my purse, and counted out the appropriate amount of money to cover my meal. "Do you mind paying the check? I need to run."

"Sure. But didn't you have another question?"

"It was about your significant other. How is he?" Meg had dated Kyle for six months, which was a long time for her to remain attached to one guy.

"He's fine."

I raised my eyebrows at her terse response. Since we saw each other infrequently these days, Meg was usually eager to go into detail. Most of the time, she offered too many specifics. It was possible to over-share, and Meg and I had different ideas about where to draw the line.

"Just fine?"

She sighed. "It's related to everything we've been talking about. I really enjoy dating Kyle, but he's from the other political party."

"I know. But that's never been a problem before. This town

is filled with political party odd couples." Mary Matalin and James Carville were the most famous, but countless others existed.

"Until this investigation started. Kyle heard about it, and he's really upset we might uncover something about the president. He thinks it's pure politics and not substantive." Divided government, perhaps not viewed negatively by our founding fathers, caused considerable political heartache in Washington these days.

Meg paused a moment, and then she blurted out in a too -loud voice, "He even asked me to delay the investigation!" She put down her fork and rubbed her temples.

"He can't ask you not to do your job. That doesn't seem fair." I sat again in the booth. Meg needed my full attention—at least for three more minutes.

She moved her fingers from massaging her temples to rubbing her eyes. "I feel like we're at a crossroads. If I dive into this investigation, I'm not sure our relationship will survive."

I reached across the table, took hold of her hands, and gave them a reassuring squeeze. "Meg, listen to me. We've been through a lot together, and I'll be here for you if this doesn't work out. But you need to make this decision. I'd want to be sure Kyle is really issuing an ultimatum. I don't know him well, but that approach doesn't seem like his style."

She nodded and wiped away a tear. I had never seen Meg cry over a relationship. It was shocking. She usually got rid of guys at the slightest pretext—such as when they didn't order the type of wine she liked.

"Thanks. I'll keep you posted. Maybe it will work itself out."

I got up to leave again, but she caught me before I could go. "Wait. We talked about me, but what about you? Is Doug any closer to making you an honest woman?"

I gritted my teeth. Meg was just being friendly but had managed to aggravate my Achilles' heel. I raised my left hand and shook it in front of her. "Nothing to report. No diamond here." I didn't add that recent events hadn't been conducive to domestic bliss.

She shook her head in apparent disbelief. "He'd better get moving, or someone else is going to beat him to the punch."

Leave it to Meg to have the last word. With that pronouncement, I hauled my unbetrothed body back to the United States Capitol to deal with the Speaker of the House.

Chapter Four

By the time I reached the office, I'd already decided how Maeve should handle the meeting with the Speaker. She had to listen to the man's spiel; after all, he was the most powerful member of Congress. But she shouldn't commit to supporting his proposal to end the shutdown, at least not yet. The longer she held out, the more likely the Speaker might be inclined to sweeten the pot. If pressed, she could easily claim her constituents in North Carolina didn't completely support the Speaker's plan, whatever it was.

My phone was ringing as I reached my desk. I didn't recognize the number, but given the crazy political situation, anyone might be calling to lobby Maeve Dixon. On-the-fence votes were rare in the House of Representatives, and Maeve qualified as such. I snagged the receiver after placing my handbag on my desk and removing my gloves.

"Kit Marshall speaking, can I help you?"

"Hello, Kit. This is Gary from Capitol Hill Media and Consulting. I'm calling about Clarence and the Capitol Canine contest."

Talk about a miscalculation. This wasn't exactly a call from a Beltway power player. I chuckled. "Sorry. We're in shutdown mode around here and I wasn't expecting your call. I completely forgot about Capitol Canine."

"Totally understandable, given the political circumstances these days. I hope Clarence is still ready for the competition."

I hesitated. Capitol Canine was an online contest in which members of Congress and Capitol Hill staff posted photos of their dogs with quirky bios. Internet voting determined the winners.

"Are you still going forward with the contest, despite the shutdown?"

"We thought about postponing it, but we decided that Washington needed an uplifting contest like Capitol Canine to distract itself from the shutdown. Besides, most federal employees are furloughed, so they have plenty of time to browse the web and vote."

"I'd l-like to do it," I stammered, "but it's a really busy time, and—"

Gary cut me off. "You don't have to do much. We already have the paragraph about Clarence and his photo. I just need final permission to post it so we can start the voting tonight."

"I had planned to lobby my friends to vote for Clarence. I just don't have the time to do that now. Maybe Clarence should take a pass this time around."

Gary's voice grew impatient. "According to the contest rules, if Clarence withdraws, he will not be eligible for the contest in future years. Is that what you want?"

I was caught off guard by Gary's ultimatum. Did Clarence deserve a lifetime ban from Capitol Canine? I looked at the framed photograph I kept of him on my desk. His large brown beagle mutt eyes pleaded for a chance to win the top dog title.

"Okay, you got me. I'll keep Clarence in the contest."

Gary's voice brightened. "Terrific. The voting starts this evening and lasts for forty-eight hours. Don't forget about the party two nights from now to reveal the big winner. Good luck!"

I hung up, wondering if I had a death wish. How was I going to make sure Clarence garnered a respectable number of votes in the contest and help my boss solve the shutdown crisis?

I didn't have much time to ponder my predicament before Maeve appeared. "Kit, are you ready to join me for the briefing with the Speaker?"

"Yes, ma'am."

She tapped her watch. "We only have ten minutes to get to the Capitol. We have to go now."

"Absolutely, Congresswoman." When Maeve was annoyed, it was better to call her by her title than her first name. I grabbed my notebook, iPhone, and congressional identification badge.

On the walk to the Capitol through the underground tunnel, I briefed Maeve on the proposed strategy for the meeting. She agreed it was best to play it cool for now. I reminded her this was a member-only briefing. No staff, including myself, would be in the room. To my knowledge, Maeve had never met with the Speaker one-on-one before today. I snuck a look at her. Her long hair was perfectly styled, likely the result of a professional blowout at a salon. That wasn't a bad idea for such an important day. She wore a tailored black power suit and had chosen a fitted white blouse with a crisp collar. Her only jewelry was delicate diamond-stud earrings. Like me, Maeve was an unmarried woman navigating the nation's capital, although I doubted she'd remain single for long. Ten years my senior, she was a hot commodity on the D.C. dating market. K Street power brokers, prominent lawyers, and wealthy businessmen had thrown their hats in the ring for a chance to spend a visible evening with Maeve Dixon.

We turned the corner in National Statuary Hall and approached the Speaker's lair. Other offices in Congress had gatekeepers, but they were located inside the actual suites. The Speaker stationed his gatekeeper in the hallway outside the series of rooms he and his staff occupied. Capitol Hill Police provided security at all times, ostensibly supplying actual firepower to support the staffer who worked the entrance desk.

Previously, I had only stolen a furtive glance down this corridor. The imposing "SPEAKER OF THE HOUSE" title appeared above the doorway. The only people allowed to enter were those who had business with the Speaker, and I had never been summoned before today. Crystal chandeliers hung from the ceiling, and ornate wood furniture added to the regality. The appearance of the Speaker's antechamber projected a singular message. The person who occupied this real estate was the epitome of power and authority.

The guy at the desk immediately recognized Maeve. After all, he worked for the Speaker. It was his job to recognize members of Congress, particularly those in the same party. After appropriate greetings, he asked her to take a seat while he confirmed the Speaker was ready to see her.

He peered at me from under his glasses. "Staff is not permitted to attend this meeting."

"I know. Jack Drysdale said that he wanted to speak with me while Representative Dixon meets with the Speaker." I returned his steely gaze with one of my own. He was leadership staff, a coveted position in the House of Representatives pecking order. That didn't mean he had the right to treat me like the hired help.

He grumbled in response, but I saw him start to type something. No doubt, he was sending an instant message to Jack to confirm my story. I took a seat next to Maeve on the ornate bench. We waited in silence, shifting uncomfortably on the ceremonial furniture as the minutes droned on.

Finally, the gatekeeper told Maeve she could head to the Speaker's office for her meeting. Out of pure habit, I stood up when Maeve was summoned. He quickly motioned for me to sit until Jack graced me with his presence. This had better be worth it. I was used to waiting for members of Congress, but staff usually treated each other with a modicum of respect.

Ten minutes later, Drysdale turned the corner and strode

down the hallway. I easily recognized him from all the times I had seen his photo in Capitol Hill newspapers. In his late forties, Jack was one of those politicos whose looks had improved with age. His brown hair was slicked back in a *GQ*-inspired coiffure that matched his fitted wool designer suit. I guessed Burberry, but perhaps it was Paul Smith London? Either way, Jack Drysdale was the most supremely confident man I'd ever seen in my five years of Hill experience. I couldn't stop staring.

I stood up as he approached and thankfully the gatekeeper refrained from instructing me otherwise. Jack flashed a thousand-watt smile as he extended his hand. It was like shaking hands with Bruce Wayne. "Kit, I'm pleased to meet you."

"Likewise." I shook his hand politely. I needed to play it cool. By virtue of his position and undeniable sex appeal, Drysdale was a man used to getting what he wanted. Right now, Maeve wasn't for sale.

"Why don't we chat in my office? It's on this corridor. The meeting between our bosses shouldn't take long."

Jack evidently believed that Maeve would succumb swiftly to the Speaker's proposal. No need to disabuse him. I dutifully followed him down the hallway and entered an office suite. Several people were waiting in the anteroom as we breezed past. With one dismissive glance, Jack waved them off. "Don't worry. They're just Hill reporters. We're doing a quick pen and pad session with them in a few minutes."

Jack motioned for me to take a seat in his private office, which though voluminous resembled the workspace of a typical rank-and-file House member. The formal settee was no more comfortable than the bench in the corridor. Maybe the Speaker's office believed a sore behind encouraged shorter meetings and made visitors more inclined to acquiesce. Admiring the marble fireplace and mantle behind his desk, I could picture Jack donning a smoking jacket and offering me a brandy. But his face was all business.

"I'm not going to beat around the bush here. The Speaker needs Representative Dixon's vote for his budget deal. It's imperative the party caucus stick together. If we can count on her vote, then we can figure out how to make it worth her while in the long run."

I shifted slightly in an effort to look more at ease. "Do you know the details of the Speaker's proposed deal? The level of funding for various programs will matter to her and the constituents in the district."

Drysdale chuckled. "I'm not your details person. If you want to talk policy, I can put you in touch with the people writing the legislation." He leaned across his desk and added, "But let's get real here. The details don't matter. This is a political decision, plain and simple. We need Maeve Dixon's support."

His face was less than a foot away. I suddenly had newfound respect for the politicians back in the day who were the infamous recipients of the "treatment" from Lyndon Baines Johnson. I leaned back on the settee, but that monstrosity was too heavy to budge an inch.

"Believe me, Representative Dixon wants to be helpful. Right now, she can't commit to a course of action."

Drysdale fixed me with a hard stare. The frustration on his face implied he didn't appreciate a noncommittal answer from a low-level congressional staffer. But after a few seconds, he relented. With a friendly grin, he asked, "Isn't your dog in the Capitol Canine contest?"

He'd caught me off guard with such an abrupt change in mood and topic. I narrowed my eyes in distrust. "Yes. His name is Clarence."

"I love dogs, and I'm sure you want Clarence to do well in the contest. You know, my dog won Capitol Canine a few years ago."

"I didn't know that. Congratulations." Where was this headed?

"Capitol Canine is about who you know. And I know a ton

of people who would be happy to vote for Clarence. Maybe we can become better friends if we join forces?" He followed up his offer with a sexy wink.

Had I just been propositioned to sell my boss's vote for a Clarence victory in the Capitol Canine contest? A direct approach was often best. "Are you trying to trade support for the Speaker's shutdown plan for votes in a dog popularity contest?"

"Don't be so literal, Kit. We're colleagues, and I'm simply trying to help you out."

After a long moment of silence, I decided to throw him a bone—no pun intended. "Maybe I can give you an answer on the Speaker's proposal in a week? I'll have to check with my chief of staff about the conversations he's having with the voters in the district."

Apparently, Jack didn't appreciate my version of a compromise. The sexy Bruce Wayne smile disappeared instantly, and his face contorted in anger. Raising his voice, he growled, "Check with your chief of staff? This is useless. I need to make sure the Speaker seals this deal."

Jack stormed out of the office, and I followed him down the corridor until he entered the Speaker's private suite. I was gutsy, but marching uninvited into the supreme leader's office space was beyond my pay grade.

I didn't want to return to the uncomfortable wooden bench in the hallway with the gatekeeper wondering why Drysdale had dismissed me. Instead, I took a seat next to the reporters in the outside waiting room. I had a clear view of the Speaker's suite across the hallway so I'd see Maeve when she emerged from her meeting. I'd stuck to our plan. Had Maeve held firm? I'd find out soon enough.

Smartphones are great time wasters. I fiddled with various apps as I waited. The next level of "Angry Birds" was within my grasp when I heard footsteps and voices across the hallway. I got up and stood in the doorway to greet my boss.

From the look on her face, she was not pleased. She charged like a linebacker to the exit of the Speaker's lair with Jack Drysdale on her heels.

"Stop, Congresswoman Dixon. You're not listening to reason!" From behind, Drysdale placed his hand on Maeve's left shoulder in an attempt to prevent her from leaving the suite.

Maeve had impressive reflexes. She turned her body toward him and grabbed his wrist with her right hand. "Don't touch me! Is this how the Speaker's staff treat members of the House?" Her voice was loud and filled with vitriol.

The gaggle of reporters who had been relaxing inside the anteroom trailed behind me. This was better than a boring pen and pad session. One of them murmured, "I think that's Dixon from North Carolina."

This was not a good development, but Maeve didn't know that the press had a front-row seat to her altercation.

Maeve clutched Drysdale's wrist for several seconds until she let it go. Apparently her physical assault didn't intimidate him. He ran ahead and stopped directly in front of her.

Stretching his arms out wide to slow her down, Jack made his last stand. "I apologize. I shouldn't have done that. Please come back in the office so we can sort this out. You're a valuable part of this caucus and the Speaker wants to work with you on this deal."

Maeve shook her head. "You guys in House leadership are typical politicians. You can't take no for an answer. I'm not ready to make a decision. Now get out of my way."

Unmoving, Drysdale locked eyes with Maeve. She didn't look away and squared her shoulders. I could almost feel the tension around me as the reporters anxiously waited for the outcome. What was Maeve going to do? Knee him in the groin if he didn't back down?

After a moment that seemed like an eternity, Drysdale gave in and stepped aside. I breathed a deep sigh of relief and hurried into the hallway to catch up with her. As we exited the corridor, I glanced back to the doorway where I'd been standing. Every reporter was on his or her phone, ostensibly calling in the most salacious story of the shutdown thus far. A junior member of Congress and the Speaker's top aide had nearly come to blows in the Capitol. A high school reporter could make that story fly.

As soon as we turned the corner and left the Speaker's passageway, the interrogation began. "What happened in the meeting? Were you really going to fight Jack Drysdale?"

"I'd rather not talk about it."

"But we're going to have to talk about it. A bunch of reporters were waiting across the hallway for a briefing from the Speaker's office on the shutdown. They saw everything that happened between you and Drysdale."

Maeve stopped abruptly and turned to face me. "You mean to tell me you knew there were reporters around and didn't stop me?"

I put my hands on my hips and looked directly into my boss's eyes. She meant business, but the feeling was mutual. "I didn't have the opportunity. Even if I had signaled, you never glanced in my direction. Besides, if I had intervened, it would have made matters worse."

Maeve didn't reply immediately, hopefully reflecting on the situation. "I see your point. If you'd interrupted me, then the story becomes about both of us ganging up on Jack Drysdale, the Speaker's media darling."

I breathed a sigh of relief and gave Maeve a restrained smile. "Well, he is handsome."

Maeve seemed to consider my comment, and then she returned the grin. "Yes, he certainly is. But that's not going to help me when this story breaks."

I didn't want to tell Maeve that in all likelihood it had already broken. "Let's get back to the office and strategize with Dan." The words "strategize" and "Dan" didn't belong in the same sentence, but at this point, he was the only ally I had.

We picked up the pace and returned to the Cannon Building ten minutes later. Upon our arrival, my suspicions were confirmed. Every Capitol Hill media outlet was already reporting the altercation between Maeve and Jack Drysdale. Phones were ringing off the hook, and after Dan had answered one call without knowing how to respond, he'd ignored the remainder of the inquiries. With our press secretary on furlough, we needed to spring into action.

Maeve and I quickly explained the situation to Dan. His pasty face, already devoid of color due to the winter doldrums, somehow paled visibly.

We needed a plan, and we needed it fast. There was no time to call in reinforcements. Even if we could, furloughed employees weren't allowed to perform government business during the shutdown under penalty of law. When the Capitol Hill Police investigated me as the lead suspect in my former boss's murder last year, visions of orange jumpsuits had flooded my consciousness. I didn't need a repeat for violating the Antideficiency Act, for sure.

Dan and Maeve both sat in silence. They needed me to help them through this maelstrom. It was time to let my political instincts take over. In situations like this, thinking too much could potentially lead to an overwrought decision and an unnecessarily complicated strategy.

I took a deep breath. "Dan, you and I are going to man the phones." I turned toward my computer and visited several key websites to assess the damage. "This isn't as bad as you think. It's the usual suspects. *Roll Call*, *Politico*, the *Hill*, the *Examiner*, and the *Daily Caller* have the story. But the *Washington Post* and the *New York Times* aren't reporting it. It's a Beltway story, and that means it'll last one day. Tops."

Maeve and Dan sat in rapt attention. I was no Bob Woodward, or even Carl Bernstein, but I had worked in Congress for almost five years now. That tenure had afforded me a modicum of media savvy. After racking my brain, I continued, "We need to decide how to respond. Maeve, we could blame Drysdale and say he bullied you, but he's a favorite amongst the Capitol Hill crowd. I don't think they'd buy it."

Maeve nodded. "Agreed."

"So we avoid that angle and simply say you and the Speaker haven't come to an agreement yet on a budget deal. We address the substance, not the petty fight. That way, you take advantage of the situation and make your position clear, and we don't muck around in the dirty details."

As a GWOT (D.C. lingo for "global war on terrorism") veteran, Maeve rarely beat around the bush. "I like it. Let's do it." With that pronouncement, she returned to her office.

I turned to Dan. "Do you think you can handle talking to the press about this? If we split up the calls, it will go a lot faster."

"I can do it." He didn't sound confident, but he was the boss. If he said he could do it, then I wasn't going to override his decision.

We listened to the voicemail messages left by reporters on the main line, made a list of calls we needed to return, and got to work. By five o'clock, we had spoken to every reporter seeking a comment and successfully spun the story to focus on Maeve's policy position on the shutdown.

I hung up the phone for the last time and rubbed my eyes. Today's fire drill had inspired a newfound respect for press secretaries. After finishing his final call, Dan pronounced, "That wasn't too bad!"

"Really? I have a splitting headache and my ear is sore from two straight hours of badgering from Capitol Hill reporters."

"Look on the bright side. It's over, and after tomorrow, this story will be old news."

I exhaled with a mixture of exasperation and weariness. "This *story* will be old news," I said, "but we just created a new story for enterprising reporters. Maeve is now front and center on the shutdown. Every journalist out there is going to follow her position like a hawk. We'd better start preparing a more detailed policy explanation for her tomorrow."

Dan's expression was blank. Clearly he had never considered the consequences of our press strategy. It had been necessary to divert attention away from Maeve's altercation with Jack, but by venturing down that path, we'd handed the media an entirely new line of inquiry for the coming days.

I hoped that Dan's silence meant he was digesting my revelation. He finally spoke. "No sense worrying today about something we can't solve until tomorrow. That's my motto! If you need me, I'll be in my office for my evening chant." Dan bounced toward his office and closed the door behind him.

I shook my head in disbelief. My last boss in Senator Langsford's office had been an inspiration. Matt coached us when we faced difficult choices, provided words of wisdom at opportune moments, and tried to impart lasting knowledge about Congress and the legislative process. Now my immediate supervisor depended on me for his survival. This gave new meaning to the term "managing up."

I glanced at the time—just after five o'clock. A quick scan of my inbox confirmed that nothing required my immediate attention. I'd meant what I said about the piercing headache. Luckily, I found two over-the-counter painkillers in my purse, which I swallowed with a gulp of water. Could I go home? Interrupting Dan's nighttime mantra recitation was out of the question, but Maeve's door was open. I marched toward her office.

"Congresswoman, do you mind if I call it a day? Nothing requires my immediate attention, and we finished the media calls a few minutes ago."

Maeve was ensconced in reading the local North Carolina news online. She glanced away from her computer and said, "Sure, I'd take advantage of the downtime now. When the bills providing specifics on the budget start to emerge, we'll be staying late to pore over the details."

Inwardly, I groaned. Today's press incident was going to look like child's play before this fiasco was solved and we were back to normal.

"Yes, ma'am. I will do that. Are you headed home soon?"

Maeve shook her head. "No, I just received a request to serve as the presiding officer on the House floor tonight. I thought it would be a good opportunity to gain visibility with the district. Also, after the way I manhandled Jack Drysdale, some time in the chair might help repair my standing with the Speaker, right?" She grinned wryly.

Members of the majority party in the House of Representatives took turns serving as the presiding officer of floor debate. Freshmen spent more time "in the chair" than senior legislators. It gave them prime coverage on C-SPAN and also provided them with an opportunity to learn how bills were considered and debated. It was largely a ceremonial function, but an important role since the presiding officer controlled the flow of debate on the House floor, announced the result of roll call votes, and maintained decorum at all times. The latter was achieved by banging the Speaker's gavel until the members present in the chamber hushed up or at least reduced their chatter to a dull roar.

"Absolutely, I agree. Are you sure you don't need me to stay until you're finished presiding on the floor?" A sense of duty as a staffer obligated me to ask.

She waved her hand in dismissal. "Of course not. You know the parliamentarian tells me exactly what to say as presiding officer. You earned an early departure this evening. Thanks for coming up with a strategy to minimize the press damage. I know Dan appreciates it." She gave me a knowing wink.

Two winks in one day. This was a new record for my Capitol Hill career. No reason to push my luck. I hastily said good night and headed out of the office.

The subway was busier than this morning. However, my

fellow riders weren't wearing work attire. Most were in jeans or other casual clothes. Undoubtedly, they were federal employees on furlough who had decided to enjoy a night out on the town. With another day out of the office virtually guaranteed for tomorrow, why not? Luckily, the pain relievers had taken care of my earlier headache, but the pulsating sting was replaced with pangs of jealousy as plans for late-night movies and barhopping unfolded around me.

I closed my eyes until the subway arrived at my stop in the Virginia suburb of Arlington. At least Doug couldn't complain about my lateness tonight. A cold wind encouraged me to hustle the several blocks to our condo building. After exiting the elevator on the fourth floor, I braced myself before putting my key in the lock. Clarence the Wonder Mutt sensed when an opportunity for escape might present itself. He positioned himself perfectly in the entryway, waiting for the precise moment when the door opened. When it did, he pounced, showing impressive agility for a chunky canine. In three seconds flat, he could race to the end of the hallway, violating numerous condo rules in the process.

I slowly turned the knob and pulled the door toward me. Sure enough, Clarence's floppy ears and adorable snout poked out. Many evenings, Clarence caught me off guard, but tonight, I was prepared for his shenanigans. As he made a break for it, I stretched my lower leg and foot to block him. He looked up with an expression reminiscent of the famous "guilty dog" YouTube video. I nudged him back inside the condo and shut the door behind us.

Doug didn't appear immediately, which wasn't unusual. After his classes at Georgetown finished for the day, he frequently spent the remaining hours working in his office at our condo. He was currently working on yet another book about early American history. His previous two tomes had focused on the Virginia dynasty of presidents and the inaugural Supreme Court. Closer to my ken, this one aspired to be the most comprehensive historical account of the first Congress of the United States.

I wandered toward the back of our abode and Doug's scholarly lair. He was sitting in front of his iMac with at least a dozen books surrounding him. Several were open with earmarked pages. Piles of photocopied pages, which appeared to be excerpts from the *Congressional Record*, were squeezed into the spaces not occupied by books. Most scholars took advantage of note-taking software that organized sources, both documents and electronic. Despite his relative youth—particularly in comparison to other accomplished historians—Doug had never adopted modern methods of conducting research. He worked exclusively with books and paper, employing his own systematic approach to collecting information. Most of the time, I thought his professorial proclivities were endearing. However, there were times when he frustrated the hell out of me. He was so lost in this newest venture that he seemed to forget I existed.

Almost a minute passed before Doug acknowledged my presence. But when I cleared my throat, he turned around immediately. "I didn't know you were home from work. Weren't you expecting to be late tonight?"

So much for an enthusiastic greeting. "That's what I expected, but Maeve was asked to serve as the presiding officer on the House floor tonight, so I got a reprieve. Besides, I had a difficult day." I told Doug about the encounter with Jack Drysdale.

"How long do you think this shutdown business is going to drag on?"

"I had lunch with Meg and she wasn't optimistic."

Doug frowned and adjusted his glasses, which had fallen lower on his nose. "Did you know the First Congress established the State Department, the Department of War, and the Department of the Treasury in five weeks?"

"I had no idea."

"I find it fascinating that these novice legislators, who knew almost nothing about representative democracy in practice, were able to accomplish so much of consequence in such a short period of time."

This was Doug's way of taking a shot at the current Congress. "Did you ever think that the reason they were so successful was that they didn't know any better?"

"That reasoning doesn't make much sense, Kit."

"Try working for Congress and you'll get my drift. Dealing with two hundred twenty-five years of precedent, law, and custom isn't exactly easy, either."

Doug must have failed to muster a clever retort. He turned back toward his computer and resumed typing.

I headed to the kitchen and poured myself a tall glass of diet tonic. Then I carefully measured a serving of Bombay Sapphire using my favorite sterling silver shot glass and tossed it into the drink along with a few slices of lime. Selecting one of my favorite ceramic swizzle sticks, I slowly stirred the concoction. A strong G&T was typically summer fare, but the events of the day warranted an exception. If I had known what tomorrow had in store for me, I wouldn't have stopped at just one.

Chapter Five

The iPhone alarm buzzed at six. I was in a deep sleep but somehow located the device to silence it. After forcing myself to get out of bed, I performed my morning ritual of walking Clarence and then taking a hasty shower. My reward for getting up on time was a few precious extra minutes to make a frothy cappuccino from our espresso machine. The coffee beans with their hint of chocolate gave off an aroma reminiscent of freshly baked brownies. I was sipping my mocha masterpiece when Doug walked into our small kitchen.

"Something smells great in here."

"If it's the morning, I'm making waffles!" I smiled. Doug usually could identify my movie quotes.

"Since there's no waffles being made, I have to assume you're quoting Donkey from *Shrek*."

"You got it. However, I could make you a cappuccino with these tasty espresso beans."

"Sure, sounds good." He gave me a gentle kiss on the forehead and then retreated to the living room with his iPad to check the morning news.

Over the grind of the beans, I asked, "Can you look at

the Capitol Canine site to see how Clarence is doing in the contest?"

"What are you talking about?"

"Remember, we entered Clarence in that online contest for the top dog on Capitol Hill?"

"How could I forget?" Doug muttered under his breath.

A few moments later, Doug returned to the kitchen. "Clarence is doing quite well. He's got over a thousand votes and he's in first place."

I almost dropped the cappuccino I had made for Doug. "That doesn't make sense. With everything that happened yesterday, I didn't have any time to email friends to remind them to vote for Clarence. I meant to put it on social media but I forgot. How did he get all these votes?"

Doug shrugged and passed me the iPad. I looked at Clarence's profile. Sure, he was cute. His face was a mixture of tan, black, and white fur and he had big brown eyes with adorable floppy ears. He looked like a cross between a beagle and a rottweiler, with a Jack Russell thrown in for good measure. However, good looks only get you so far in Washington—even if you're a dog. Something else was up.

"I wonder if Jack Drysdale persuaded his contacts to vote for Clarence. Maybe to try to win me over so Maeve wouldn't hold a grudge after the altercation yesterday?"

"If that's the case, it's one of the craziest things I've heard since moving to D.C. Would he really think you could be bribed with votes on Capitol Canine?"

Doug was right. It was a little nutty, but if the former Virginia governor could be bought for a Rolex watch and a joyride in a Ferrari, maybe Drysdale thought a few votes for Capitol Canine would do the trick.

"I'll try to figure it out. Can you persuade your colleagues at Georgetown to vote for Clarence?"

Doug appeared skeptical. "I don't think academics would understand why it's important for our dog to win a Capitol Hill popularity contest."

"Well, I don't have a lot of time during the shutdown to drum up support for him. You can't help out?"

He'd returned to reading the news on his device. Without looking up, Doug said, "He seems to be doing okay without our help, right?"

Doug's blasé attitude annoyed me. I was poised to respond with a clever retort, but my iPhone indicated I'd received a text message.

I grabbed the phone off the countertop, put in my security code, and touched the green Messages app. *Come to Cannon rotunda immediately. I'm in trouble.* I double-checked the sender. It was Maeve.

I typed back a reply: *On my way. What's wrong?*

No more time to think about dog contests or coffee. Time to bust a move and get to Capitol Hill pronto. "Doug, Maeve needs my help. Gotta run. See you tonight."

Doug didn't look up from his iPad. "Good luck."

I checked my phone as I headed downstairs. No reply yet from Maeve. It was a quarter past seven. How had she managed to involve herself in another crisis before sunrise?

After exiting our condo building, I quickly evaluated my transportation options. Should I take the subway or find a cab? Using my phone, I located the nearest Uber driver. Ten minutes away. By the time I waited for the driver to arrive, I'd be halfway to the Hill on the Metro. Maeve hadn't returned my text. What did she mean by "in trouble" exactly? Without knowing the severity of the situation, the Metro was an acceptable choice.

Absent the big commuter crowds to slow the boarding of trains, I arrived at Capitol South twenty-five minutes later. Maeve hadn't replied. Perhaps the "trouble" had already blown over. Just in case she still needed help, I headed directly to the Cannon rotunda without stopping at the office. Reporters usually camped out inside the rotunda to shoot live cable television hits from Capitol Hill. It wasn't as grandiose as the Capitol rotunda, but its Corinthian architecture with imposing columns did provide a stately backdrop for the camera.

I exited the elevator and walked past the famous Cannon Caucus Room, which hosted the House Un-American Committee hearings decades ago. Hearing Maeve's voice in the distance, I followed the narrow hallway circling the rotunda. After rounding the bend, I found my boss. She wasn't alone. Next to her was Detective O'Halloran of the Capitol Hill Police. Jack Drysdale was between them, but the Speaker's top aide wasn't looking so handsome this morning. Blood flowed from his head onto the pristine marble floor. If he'd generated Clarence's Capitol Canine votes, there wouldn't be any more favors coming my way. Jack Drysdale was dead.

Chapter Six

Maeve took one look at me and almost leapt into my arms. I'd never seen her so discombobulated. "Thank God you're here. What took you so long?"

"I'm sorry. I had no idea. You didn't answer when I asked what the problem was."

She leaned close to me. "I couldn't very well text you what happened," she whispered. "I'm the lead suspect."

"You're *what*?" My voice was ten times louder than hers, but I couldn't hide my reaction.

She grabbed my arm and pulled me near. "Keep quiet. This cop just arrived, and believe me, it doesn't look good."

I lowered my voice. "Don't worry. Let me talk to him. I know Detective O'Halloran."

I couldn't tell if the look on Maeve's face expressed astonishment or utter bewilderment. It didn't matter. I raised a finger to my lips, indicating she should stay quiet while I spoke with O'Halloran.

The detective and I had become acquaintances last year when Meg and I solved the murder of our former Senate boss. O'Halloran had originally pegged me as the chief suspect for the crime, but eventually appreciated my amateur assistance after I stumbled upon several key clues.

The beefy middle-aged detective was deep in conversation with several uniformed officers who had begun to secure the perimeter. If I'd arrived any later, this area would have been sealed off. As I approached, I gave him a friendly wave. "Detective O'Halloran, remember me? It's Kit Marshall."

O'Halloran stopped talking to his colleagues. He extended his hand and I shook it politely. "Ms. Marshall, how could I forget? The better question is why you've shown up again at the scene of a murder in the United States Capitol complex."

There was no good explanation for that question, except I'd somehow managed to find trouble again. I shrugged. "I'm here because my boss, Representative Maeve Dixon, messaged me this morning to meet her in the Cannon rotunda."

O'Halloran perked up. "Dixon texted you to come here? What time?"

I opened the Messages app on my iPhone. "I got the text at seven-oh-three this morning."

O'Halloran rubbed his chin as he considered my answer. "Very interesting."

"Do you mind telling me what's so interesting besides the dead body on the floor?"

O'Halloran motioned to follow him a few steps away from the growing cadre of Capitol Hill police officers. Maeve was standing silently by herself, her head buried in her smartphone. She was likely trying to determine if news of the murder had broken yet. No reporters were on the scene, but they'd figure it out soon enough, especially when the police told them they couldn't set up for their live television shots in the rotunda today.

"Listen, I don't know how you've gotten yourself involved in another murder, but you might want to consider a different line of employment."

"I know this is a strange coincidence, but why would I do that?"

"Because I don't think you're going to have your Hill job for much longer. Your boss is our top suspect for the murder of Jack Drysdale."

I looked directly into O'Halloran's eyes. "We've been down this road before, Detective. I was your number one suspect when you investigated Lyndon Langsford's murder. Look how that turned out."

O'Halloran returned my gaze. "You're correct. But this one's different. You didn't have a motive to kill Langsford, which bothered me from the beginning. I don't have that problem with this one." He motioned toward Jack's lifeless body. "Your boss nearly came to blows yesterday with the victim, and every newspaper on Capitol Hill reported the incident." To emphasize his point, he brandished yesterday's *Roll Call* story on his smartphone.

O'Halloran worked quicker than I remembered. He'd already fingered Maeve as a suspect with a credible motive. But she wasn't the only person in D.C. who had a beef with Drysdale. "Isn't it a big leap to assume Representative Dixon killed Jack because she got into an argument with him yesterday? If I murdered every person I disagreed with on Capitol Hill, I'd have a rap sheet a mile long." There was nothing wrong with injecting a bit of humor. I gave O'Halloran a small grin.

He didn't return the smile. "It's not just motive. A police officer saw Maeve Dixon hovering over the body a few minutes before seven this morning."

The morning's events started to make more sense. I glanced in Maeve's direction. The worried expression on her face indicated she understood the gravity of the situation. "That could be purely circumstantial. Maeve might have noticed Jack's body as she walked past the Cannon Caucus Room. Any good citizen with a conscience would investigate if someone was lying on the floor."

O'Halloran shook his head. "Sorry. It doesn't add up. Your boss has an office on the first floor of this building. Why would she be on the third floor so early in the morning?"

He had me there, but there was no need to let him know it. "She's a military veteran, Detective. She doesn't believe in sleeping late. She might have been stretching her legs or looking for an available restroom. During the shutdown, they don't open them up on every floor."

O'Halloran raised his eyebrows. "Last time I checked, members of Congress had private bathrooms in their office suites. I've been on the Capitol Hill Police force for over twenty years. You're going to have to try harder to pull the wool over my eyes, Ms. Marshall."

O'Halloran was at the top of his game. He seemed more confident than when he'd investigated the murder of my former boss. Better to change the subject and get as much information as possible from him. I tried to get a peek at the body, but now a bevy of forensic investigators surrounded Drysdale. There'd been a gash on his head, indicating that some sort of physical assault had killed him.

"Do you have a murder weapon, Detective?"

"I shouldn't be sharing this information with you, but we won't be able to keep a lid on this detail for long, once the media sharks get hold of this story. It appears that Mr. Drysdale was bludgeoned with the Speaker's gavel."

I swallowed hard. It was best to watch my tongue here. O'Halloran could nail Maeve with motive and opportunity. Did he know she also had access to the weapon the night before when she presided over the House of Representatives?

"That's certainly an unusual w-weapon," I stammered.

"I agree, Ms. Marshall. Not too many people have access to the gavel used on the floor of the House. I imagine it will narrow our suspect pool considerably." He paused for a moment, deep in thought. "Tell me something. Don't members of Congress have access to the gavel when they sit in for the Speaker during debate on the House floor?"

O'Halloran knew the answer to that question. He wanted

to emphasize a point. I answered him as casually as possible, "Sure. But all members of the majority party preside over the House floor from time to time."

He rubbed his chin again. "That's right. I'm sure it won't be hard to see who was in the chair yesterday evening, after your boss's fight with Jack Drysdale in the Speaker's office. Don't you agree?"

I gulped again. *Yikes.* O'Halloran had the trifecta. He'd established a plausible motive, confirmed she had the opportunity to kill Jack, and soon enough, he'd tie her to the murder weapon. My heart started to beat faster, and my mind raced with suspicious thoughts. Had Maeve slipped her trolley and killed Jack Drysdale? Sure, my boss was a handful, but I didn't peg her as a killer.

It was time to end this conversation and switch into damage control mode. I ignored O'Halloran's question. "Thanks for your time, Detective. I'm sure we'll be in touch in the coming days."

"I'm not sure about that, but I can guarantee your boss will be hearing from me soon."

Ominous words. I trotted toward Maeve, who was chewing on her thumbnail. Before this morning, I'd never seen her so ruffled. Her air of apprehension had intensified in the past ten minutes since I arrived on the scene.

I wanted to throttle Maeve for getting herself into this predicament, but this wasn't my best pal Meg. Maeve Dixon was still my boss, and I had to treat her accordingly. In a halfhearted attempt to calm myself, I counted silently to ten before speaking.

"Congresswoman, I talked to Detective O'Halloran from the Capitol Hill Police. He said that an officer found you standing over the body around seven this morning. Can I ask what you were doing by the rotunda at that hour?"

"I woke up early this morning and planned to squeeze in a workout in the House gym. On my way there, I got a text message from Dan."

She retrieved her phone from her purse and entered her security code. Maeve turned the phone so I could read the message: *Jack Drysdale wants to meet you at the Cannon rotunda at 7 this am. He wants to talk about a deal.*

"Instead of heading to the gym, I decided to see what Drysdale had to offer. I got here a few minutes before seven and didn't see him anywhere. I walked past the caucus room, and then I saw him on the floor. I ran over because I thought he'd had a heart attack." She paused for a moment, clearly distraught. "I couldn't stop looking at the terrible wound on his head. There was a bloody gavel next to his body."

"Maeve, this is important. Did you touch anything?"

She shook her head vigorously. "No! I swear I didn't. It was surreal. I'm not sure how long I stared at the body. The next thing I remember is a police officer grabbed me by the arm and asked me what happened." She rubbed her temples vigorously with her fingers.

"There's something not right about this story. Why would Jack Drysdale text Dan and not me?"

Maeve frowned. "I have no idea."

"Remember, Jack said he didn't want to deal with Dan on the shutdown. He asked for another name, and you gave him mine."

"That does seem strange," Maeve said slowly.

"What it means is that Jack didn't communicate with Dan this morning. Someone else texted Dan so you'd show up at the rotunda at precisely seven this morning. Someone who wanted you to discover the body."

Maeve gasped. "You mean I was set up?"

"That appears to be the case. Your fight with Drysdale yesterday was the perfect frame for the murderer. You played right into his hands." I corrected myself quickly, "Or her hands." Last year I'd learned the hard way that with the proper motivation, both men and women could transform into killers.

"The police told me to wait while they figure out what they

need from me. After I texted you, I called a lawyer in town and he said he would meet me at the police station if I'm called in for questioning."

That was a good move. It was flattering that Maeve contacted me first after she discovered the body, but I wasn't a legal eagle. If she became the prime suspect, she would need the best defense lawyer in Washington D.C.

"Let me find out what's going to happen next."

Maeve nodded. O'Halloran might take another question from me. After that, his patience would likely wear thin.

He was consulting another plainclothes police officer adjacent to the crime scene. "Detective, can I ask you one more favor?"

O'Halloran put his hand up to silence me. After he finished his conversation, he turned in my direction. "Why not? Would you like a bagel and coffee, too?"

Actually, a bagel and coffee sounded terrific. I restrained myself from asking him for toasted sesame with light cream cheese and a cup of java served light and sweet. One look told me a sarcastic retort would get my butt tossed out of the rotunda area. I was already pushing the envelope with my police comrade.

"Detective, my boss wants to know if her presence will be required at the Capitol Hill Police station today? If so, legal counsel will meet her there."

From the look of concentration on his face, I guessed that O'Halloran was carefully evaluating his answer. He might have wanted to haul Maeve to the precinct for a full-scale interrogation, but the threat of her lawyering up gave him considerable pause. He was also dealing with a member of Congress. Bringing her in officially if he wasn't absolutely certain about her status as a suspect might cause him more political trouble than she was worth at this point.

My gamble paid off. "We can have an officer conduct an interview here." Then he added, "For now. That doesn't mean we won't want to schedule a more formal Q&A at the station later on."

I breathed a sigh of relief. At least Maeve would be spared the indignity of a potential mug shot today. Her face relaxed when I told her she'd avoided an imminent trip to the pokey. However, her relief didn't stop her from barking orders. "Kit, you need to return to the office and bring Dan up to speed. I might be tied up here for a while. Get prepared for the press inquiries." She glanced about furtively. "We're not going to be able to keep a lid on my involvement. We'll need a plan."

I held my tongue, but I knew firsthand the pressure Detective O'Halloran was feeling to solve the homicide of a congressional staffer. Maeve would need more than a well-devised press plan. She'd better have Perry Mason on speed dial.

This wasn't the time or place to advise Maeve about murder investigations. I'd debrief her later in the privacy of the office and ask a few questions of my own. Number one in my mind concerned the Speaker's gavel. How in the hell did it travel from the House floor to the Cannon rotunda? The gavel was a monumental symbol of the institution. Given its unique status in the House, figuring out the path of the murder weapon would likely point to the person responsible for this horrible crime.

No amount of meditation was going to prepare Dan for this news. I hustled downstairs and found him trying to operate the fax machine. Given the morning's events, I skipped telling him that no one communicated via fax anymore.

After I told him what had happened, he buried his head in his hands and started to shake uncontrollably. His hands flew to his brown mane, and a moment later, the tugging commenced. As I watched in amazement, I realized the origin of the idiom "tearing your hair out."

I was about to suggest he needed to get a grip when the shaking and yanking suddenly stopped. His eyes were semi-crazed and intensely focused. He pointed directly at me. "You. I have the answer. You can fix this."

"Have you had a mental breakdown? Do I need to call the Employee Assistance Program for help?" EAP provided counseling to congressional staff. I hoped they made emergency office visits.

Dan ignored my question. "When I hired you, someone in House leadership told me that you solved your former boss's murder in the Senate. I couldn't believe it so I searched on the Internet and found the news stories."

"That was a completely different situation. I knew the suspects because they were associates of my boss. I was an insider. I only met Jack Drysdale yesterday, remember?"

"You have to solve this murder to clear Maeve." Dan looked at me with pleading eyes. A few tears glistened in the corners. "I left North Carolina to move to Washington D.C. for this job. No one else is going to hire me if she's accused of murder. It's not like I've exactly impressed everyone here. I haven't had a chance to prove myself yet!" Dan's tirade culminated in a high-pitched squeak.

I had to calm him down. I eased him into a chair next to my desk and put a hand on his shoulder in an attempt at a comforting gesture. "Look, I've been in a similar situation. I'm sure the police are going to solve this murder. Detective O'Halloran's not a bad cop." The last part was true. O'Halloran was an admirable public servant. His investigatory skills hadn't impressed me last year, but maybe he'd learned a few tricks since then.

Dan was a political ingénue, yet he wasn't completely clueless. "If this detective is so great, why didn't he solve the murder in the Senate?"

I sighed. "Dan, I'd like to help Maeve out. I already recovered once on Capitol Hill from being labeled a murder suspect. I'm not sure having a boss accused of murder is much better. But what I said a few minutes ago still stands. I don't know the players in Jack's world. How would I come up with a list of suspects to investigate?"

Dan stood up and towered over me. "That's not my problem. You need to figure out who killed Jack Drysdale. I don't care if you help the police or pull a Jessica Fletcher. Your job depends on it. Don't worry about the press calls. I'll take care of them. Just focus on clearing Maeve Dixon's name."

"Dan, you're being completely unreasonable—"

He cut me off. "I'm the chief of staff here. I don't assert myself too often, but I mean business. Either start sleuthing or find another job. Pronto."

As I stared into Dan's implacable gaze, I recalled the catchy 1990s Paula Cole tune. Never mind the cowboys. Where had all the chakras gone?

Chapter Seven

I TURNED ON my computer and consumed the headlines. Sure enough, the police hadn't been able to keep a lid on Jack Drysdale's murder. The Washington-based news outlets were reporting that a high-level staffer had become the first victim of the shutdown. One particularly salacious paper boasted the headline "Shutdown Slaughter." Despite its macabre tone, I appreciated the admirable alliteration, no pun intended.

The media hadn't yet confirmed Jack was the victim, but a treasure trove of stories about him already existed online. My ignorance of Drysdale's world was as thorough as I claimed. Luckily, Jack had never turned down an interview or press profile, especially when he was climbing the Hill ladder to his last position in the Speaker's office. Although I didn't live completely inside his world of political insider intrigue, maybe I could figure out the big players with enough Google searches.

I stretched out my arms and my fingers flew across the keyboard. This type of research wasn't as difficult as Doug's academic inquiries. At times, he spent all day searching for an obscure historical document, ledger, or letter. More often than not, he came up empty-handed. In stark contrast, when

I entered "JACK DRYSDALE CONGRESS" into the search engine, over a thousand hits came up.

Would this take hours? I scanned article after article in various Capitol Hill newspapers. Slowly, a clear profile of Jack Drysdale emerged, along with a few tantalizing personal tidbits. Drysdale's congressional career had spanned two decades, he'd worked under numerous political bosses. Slowly and methodically, Jack had crisscrossed the Hill, working for increasingly powerful members of Congress. Finally, two years ago, he'd picked the winning horse when his boss was elected Speaker of the House and Jack became the most influential staffer in Congress.

Along the way he'd certainly ruffled a lot of feathers. Two recent conflicts in particular had received considerable press coverage. According to newspaper and blog accounts, Jack had developed a vicious rivalry with Judy Talent, another top staffer who currently worked for the House Majority Leader. Apparently Judy and Jack had risen on the Hill on parallel career tracks. Both were gifted, respected, and ambitious. Jack had managed to end up with the Speaker while Judy's boss was the second-in-command.

With Jack out of the picture permanently, wouldn't Judy be a prime candidate to take his job in the Speaker's office? Judy had emailed me shortly after the shutdown, requesting we keep in touch about various solutions. Given what I'd just read about her rocky relationship with Jack, a chat with Judy seemed like a good place to start. I replied to her email and asked if she had free time tomorrow to discuss the Majority Leader's plans for ending the shutdown.

The other promising lead involved the House Sergeant at Arms office. A series of articles described the ongoing disagreement between the Speaker's office and the Sergeant at Arms concerning security in the House. As the head law enforcement officer in the House, the Sergeant at Arms was responsible for maintaining safety and order. With threats issued every day to destroy the Capitol complex, both from domestic and international sources, the Sergeant at Arms had a tough job. Recently, he had issued a proposal to increase security protocols for the House of Representatives and its office buildings, which would have made it more cumbersome for visitors and tourists to traverse the hallways. Representing the Speaker's interests, Jack had strongly opposed the suggested changes. A man named Gareth Pressler, a senior aide for the Sergeant at Arms, had criticized Drysdale in several news stories. The latest story in the saga caught my eye, headlined "SPEAKER SERGEANT WAR." In the article, Pressler and Drysdale had traded barbs, each accusing the other of undermining congressional operations.

I grabbed my trusty notebook and jotted down the most relevant information about Pressler and his conflict with Jack. I'd never interacted with the House Sergeant at Arms office. Without a solid contact or a good excuse for a meeting, tracking down this lead could prove challenging.

Enough surfing the web. How else could I gather information about the complex world of Jack Drysdale? A lightbulb switched on in my brain and I immediately picked up my phone to dial one of the few House extensions I'd committed to memory.

A familiar voice chirped in my ear. "Hello, Meg Peters, House Oversight."

"It's Kit. Have you heard the news yet?"

"If you're referring to Jack Drysdale's murder, of course. Everyone is buzzing about it."

I lowered my voice. Even though Dan had commanded me to investigate, I didn't trust him. "Did you know my boss found Jack's body?"

Unfortunately, my news had the opposite auditory effect on Meg. She might as well be speaking into a megaphone. "Who did you say found Jack?" she bellowed.

"Can you please not announce it to the rest of your office? It hasn't reached the press quite yet and we're trying to keep it on the down low." Capitol Hill staff rarely had private offices. Meg was no exception.

"Sure, I'm sorry," she whispered. Now I could barely hear her.

"Dan wants me to investigate the murder so I can clear Maeve as a suspect. But I don't know anything about Jack Drysdale and his crowd."

"Did you know Drysdale recently got married?"

"No. Who's the lucky lady?"

"Wrong gender, Kit. Jack was gay. After the District of Columbia legalized same-sex marriage, he and his longtime partner Jordan Macintyre got hitched."

"It's sad that Jack died so soon after getting married."

"Maybe not. I heard a rumor that Macintyre was up to his eyeballs in debt. He owned a restaurant that went under. Now he's going to inherit a lot of money from Jack."

Not a bad motive for murder. I'd add Jordan to my growing list of suspects. I could always count on Meg for an accurate download of Capitol Hill gossip. Her knowledge of the cocktail circuit was almost as vast as Doug's scholarly expertise in American history. Both served a worthy purpose inside the Beltway.

"Thanks for the tip. You're not free for lunch today, are you?" Meg had been a resourceful ally last summer when we tracked down Senator Langsford's killer.

"I wish. We're up to our eyeballs researching this White House investigation."

"Did you make any progress with your significant other?"

Meg sighed. "Not really. He knows we're moving forward with the hearings."

Meg was in a pickle, and I didn't envy her situation with Kyle. "Just hang in there," I said. "I bet things will resolve on their own. If not, several glasses of Prosecco might help." Meg's favorite bubbly drink usually lifted her mood.

"More like the whole bottle."

I said goodbye to Meg and thanked her again for the juicy tip about Drysdale. I'd have to figure out a way to learn more about their relationship and his husband's financial difficulties. That was going to require serious ingenuity since I'd never met Jordan Macintyre.

In the tradition of *Casablanca*'s infamous Captain Renault, who else could help me round up the usual suspects? Doug didn't know much about Hill politics, but he deserved a call. Even if he'd read about Jack's death online, he wouldn't know about my boss discovering the body. My fingers hesitated over the phone's keypad. Although my boyfriend had been relieved when the culprits were caught last summer in the Senate, he'd never wanted me to engage in novice sleuthing. Doug wasn't going to embrace a repeat performance of Kit Marshall, amateur detective extraordinaire.

I commanded my digits to dial the familiar cellphone number. Maybe Doug was busy and a long voicemail would suffice. "Doug, this is Kit. Just wanted to let you know that another murderer is loose on Capitol Hill and I'll be nosing around to solve the crime. Don't wait up!"

Just as I chuckled at my fantasy message, I heard Doug's voice on the line. "Hello. Hello? Kit, is that you?"

"Sorry. I thought it might go to voicemail."

"Should I not pick up the next time you call?"

"Never mind. Did you hear about the homicide in the House today?"

"I saw a headline in the *Washington Post* about a Speaker's aide who was found dead. Did you know him?"

"That's not an easy question to answer."

"I don't understand," Doug said, his exasperation already evident.

"I just met him yesterday. He's the guy Maeve almost got into a shoving match with outside the Speaker's office."

There was silence on the line. Now the wheels of Doug's

brain were spinning. No point in turning back now, so I kept talking. "Maeve found Jack's body this morning. She had the opportunity to kill him, motive for the crime, and access to the murder weapon."

More silence.

"Doug, are you still on the line?"

His response was clipped. "I'm here. I heard what you said."

I tried to hide the annoyance in my response. "Don't you have anything to say?"

"Quite frankly, I'm speechless. How could you possibly be involved in another murder on Capitol Hill?"

"Beats me. It's not as though I'm looking for these crimes. They find me."

"I suppose you're angling for a reprisal of your Nancy Drew role?"

Since my ordeal in the Senate, Doug had taken to calling me by the names of female amateur sleuths. He preferred Trixie Belden, young Miss Marple, and Veronica Mars. Nancy Drew was a new one.

"If so, does that make you Ned Nickerson?" Two could play at this game.

"I imagine it does."

"It might be a short-lived romance. I'm not sure I have many clues to solve this one. I hardly knew Jack, and even if I can identify the main suspects, they're not people I associate with on a regular basis." To put his mind at ease, I needed to make Doug understand how remotely I was situated to solve the crime.

"You should talk to one of my former students who works in the House press gallery. She might be able to tell you about Jack's world. She frequently mentioned dealing with high-level staffers and their egos."

My eyebrows shot up. The purpose of my phone call had purely been to provide information. I never expected Doug would offer to assist my investigation. "I'm surprised you're helping me develop a lead. Did you change your mind about my sleuthing?"

"I still think it's dangerous and you should leave it to the police. But I know you're going to poke around no matter what I say. Her name is Melinda. Just tell her I sent you."

There was no sense in arguing with Doug about the perils of snooping. He had a valid point. Last time I barely escaped the killer after a scary chase along a deserted underground passage in the Senate. I ended our conversation after a quick goodbye and a promise to exercise caution.

Maeve still hadn't returned to the office, so I clicked on my email inbox. There were several messages about proposed legislation to end the shutdown and notifications about staff meetings to negotiate other proposals. Nothing about Maeve being a suspect or involved in Jack's murder.

Just as I read the last email, the door connecting the outside waiting area to the staff office space opened. Maeve looked as though she'd seen better days. In contrast to yesterday, she was a mess. Her disheveled hair and wrinkled suit matched the strained expression of defeat on her face. A few years ago, someone had approached her in North Carolina and convinced her it would be a good idea if she ran for Congress. Did Maeve regret that decision? Was the strain of another rigorous campaign, a government shutdown, and a felony murder charge worth the privilege to represent over seven hundred thousand disaffected constituents?

This wasn't a good time to wax philosophical with Congresswoman Dixon. Instead, I needed facts. "What happened with the police?"

Dan must have heard Maeve's arrival. After one glance at her uncharacteristically ruffled appearance, he furrowed his brow in concern. "Is everything okay? You look a little—"

Maeve cut him off. "I know, I know. I look terrible. It's been a tough day, all right?"

Dan fawned over Maeve as if she were a wounded puppy.

After she sat down, he delivered a glass of water and her favorite nutrition bar. Despite the stress, Maeve didn't deviate from her sacrosanct low-fat, low-carb, low-sugar diet. Her willpower dwarfed mine. One bad meeting and I reached for dark chocolate and a bottle of wine with no second thoughts.

Maeve took a long drink and then launched into her own interrogation. Turning toward Dan, she asked, "Why did you send me to the rotunda this morning?"

His face twitched. "I got a call early this morning on my cellphone. It was Jack Drysdale, and he said he wanted to meet you at seven to talk about a deal on the shutdown. He apologized for everything that happened yesterday so I told him I'd get you there."

Maeve sighed. "How did you know it was Jack Drysdale?"

Dan shifted his weight from one leg to another. "I assumed it was Drysdale. Why wouldn't I?"

She continued peppering Dan with questions. "Did you recognize the number? Or his voice?"

Dan shook his head. "No, but Drysdale had never called me before."

Maeve kept her head cradled in her right hand, as if the stress of the day had made it impossible to keep herself upright. Despite her skewed posture, she fired more inquiries at Dan, who had now turned from flustered pink to a darker crimson shade of trepidation.

"Do you realize this was a setup? The person you spoke with murdered Jack Drysdale. He called you so I would appear conveniently at the scene of the crime. Do you understand the ramifications of what you did, Dan?"

The poor guy visibly flinched when Maeve screamed his name at the end of her tirade. The scene gave me a small sense of satisfaction. Dan had proven barely competent since I'd been working in the office, yet Maeve always gave him a pass. His cluelessness had finally manifested in a screwup of epic proportions. However, any selfish smugness on my part was soon put aside given the horrendous seriousness of the situation. Both of our necks were on the chopping block.

It was time for cooler heads to prevail. "Can I see your phone?" I asked.

Dan handed over his iPhone. I navigated to the "recent calls" directory and found the incoming call at 6:03 this morning. After the D.C. area code, the first three numbers were 225. That was important.

"This extension means the call was made from a phone somewhere in the House. We might be in luck." I dialed the House of Representatives operator and gave her the number from Dan's phone. After listening to her response, I thanked her and hung up.

"The number is from a phone in the Capitol Visitor Center. It's located within an information desk inside the CVC. Anyone who has Capitol complex access could have used it to make the call."

Maeve rolled her eyes. "So much for that lead."

"Not so fast. We know the call was placed around six. The only people allowed in the building that early are members, congressional staff, and journalists with all-access badges."

Maeve stood up. "Terrific. We've just narrowed down the suspect pool to ten thousand people."

As she walked toward her office, I yelled after her, "Not really. A lot of the staff has been furloughed!"

Chapter Eight

If Dan had been a dog, he would have put his tail between his legs and run. Despite his humanity, Dan's body language mimicked the universal sign of canine defeat. With a sulking posture, he returned to his office and closed the door, likely lighting a double dose of incense to combat the negative vibes sent his way by our boss.

Several online news sources confirmed that Jack's murder was the trending story in the local media, but so far, Maeve's name hadn't appeared in connection to the crime. O'Halloran was undoubtedly responsible for the tight lips. The less they said, the more evidence the police could gather without reporters breathing down their necks. Unfortunately, in this instance, the cops were marshaling resources to build a case against my boss.

With the police focused on Maeve, who would search for the real killer? The crime wasn't going to solve itself. If I wanted to find the person responsible for Jack Drysdale's demise, I'd have to do some serious pound-the-pavement snooping. Sitting on my duff was nothing but a waste of time. Dan's directive wasn't my primary motivator. If Maeve was convicted, Dan was irrelevant. We'd both be collecting unemployment.

The phone call to Dan's cell was an important clue. That had been a clever ploy, pure and simple. Why would Jack Drysdale place a call from a phone in the Capitol Visitor Center to Dan? He'd met me the day before and had personally requested I work on the shutdown for the congresswoman. If he needed to speak to Maeve early in the morning about a proposal, he would have called my line. Furthermore, unless his own phone was lost, he would have used his cell to call, email, or text—not some random phone in the tourist enclave of the United States Capitol.

No doubt about it. Maeve had been set up. The criminal was a crafty one. He or she had capitalized on Maeve's altercation with Drysdale, seeing her as the perfect suspect. The perp had figured out how to get Drysdale and Maeve in the same location. After he or she murdered Jack, Maeve would come across the scene and suspicion would fall on her. Using the Speaker's gavel was a nice touch, especially since Maeve had served as presiding officer the night before during the House of Representatives debate.

I glanced at my email inbox. Judy Talent hadn't replied. I had no connection whatsoever to the widower Jordan Macintyre or Gareth Pressler from the Sergeant at Arms office. That left me with one option: Doug's former student. A speedy survey of the House employee directory online turned up a Melinda Gomez. Bingo. I dialed her extension and prayed she'd pick up.

"House press gallery, Assistant Superintendent Gomez speaking."

The formality of her announcement caught me off guard. I stuttered for a second and then words flew out of my mouth in a rush. "I'm Kit Marshall and my boyfriend Doug Hollingsworth suggested I call you. He was your professor at Georgetown and thought you might be able to help."

The line was silent. "This is a House extension, right? Do you work for Congress?"

My opening gambit hadn't included that important information. If I planned to reprise my sleuthing, I'd better get a grip. "Yes, I'm sorry. Let me start over. I work for Congresswoman Maeve Dixon from North Carolina. Doug, I mean Professor Hollingsworth, suggested I call you to talk about Jack Drysdale." I always forgot to use Doug's academic title when speaking with his undergraduate minions.

There was another pause. The Drysdale request had likely thrown her for a loop. She lowered her voice to a whisper. "We're not supposed to say much to reporters about the murder."

"I understand, but I don't want to give information to the press. I need to gather information about Jack so I can figure out who killed him."

"Now I know who you are. I was interning in the press gallery last year when you solved that stabbing in the Senate. There was a rumor at Georgetown that Professor Hollingsworth was somehow connected to the investigation, but no one knew how."

Never a fan of notoriety, Doug had tried to bury that connection as deep as possible. "That's me. This time, I need a little assistance coming up with a list of suspects. You see a lot from your perch. Maybe you can help?"

She chuckled. "I do see a lot, it's true." Melinda was referring to the location of the press gallery, which overlooked the House floor.

"I bet you do. What do you say?" I glanced at my watch. Melinda hadn't been working in the House very long. Most young staffers were recent college grads motivated by the free food and drinks provided at the many receptions hosted by lobbyists and trade organizations every day on the Hill. The time for lunch had come and gone, but maybe Melinda hadn't eaten yet or would succumb to a tempting offer.

It was worth a shot. "Can I buy you a snack at the Creamery?" By far the best eating establishment in the House, the Creamery served coffee and ice cream to members and staff with cravings for caffeine, sugar, or both.

"I really shouldn't leave, given everything that's happened today and the continuing interest in the shutdown." She paused. "But I'm pretty hungry. I suppose a few minutes won't hurt."

The offer of free food had resonated. Melinda was a woman after my own heart. I'd have to thank Doug tonight for making the connection.

"Terrific. I'll see you there in ten minutes."

Should I tell Maeve or Dan where I was headed? The doors to both of their private offices were shut. I decided against it. If they needed to reach me, they could call my iPhone. The Creamery was located next to the main House cafeteria in the adjacent Longworth Building. I descended to the basement of Cannon and crossed through the underground level of the rotunda, which displayed a huge plaster model of the Capitol commissioned by the powerful Speaker Joe Cannon in 1903. Despite his autocratic rule, the extension of the Capitol envisioned by Cannon and reflected in the sculptor's model hadn't been completed until 1962.

With Congress, some things never change. It takes forever to make a difference around here.

The looming Capitol model was a constant reminder that congressional achievements were measured not in days, months, or even years, but decades.

After sliding into a seat at the Creamery, I realized I had no way of recognizing Melinda. Steady streams of House staffers paraded through the eatery at every moment, scarfing up the coffee and ice cream treats. A few moments later, a young woman in her early twenties entered. She appeared to be Hispanic and wore stylish dark-rimmed glasses that screamed "smart, yet fashionable." She looked tentatively around the establishment. This had to be Melinda Gomez, or at least the odds were good. Given Dan's mistake earlier today, I'd better check for myself. I got up and walked toward her, extending my hand. With a questioning rise in my voice, I said, "Melinda?" At the same time, I stole a hard glance at the official House identification badge she wore around her neck. It was hard to see the entire name on the tag, but I could definitely make out a capital "M" followed by a last name starting with a "G." Pay dirt.

She returned my question with a shy smile. "Are you Professor Hollingsworth's girlfriend?"

I cringed slightly at her description of me. The feminist in me screamed, "No, I'm Kit Marshall, House staffer extraordinaire!"

I stifled my insecurity, but Melinda must have noticed me wince because she added, "I'm sorry, I just forgot your name from our phone call."

Her explanation erased my tense reaction to her initial greeting. "That's okay. Yes, I'm Kit Marshall. It's nice to meet you. Would you like some ice cream?"

Melinda laughed and responded enthusiastically. "Actually, I would *love* ice cream."

We placed our orders and sat down. I hadn't eaten lunch, so ice cream didn't constitute a terrible indulgence. Rationalizing was a dieter's bête noire, but right now a good lead on Jack's murder was a bigger priority than a trim waist. Maybe Melinda had missed lunch, too. She licked at her ice cream cone as though we were battling ninety-five-degree heat in the middle of summer.

She didn't have much time to spend with me. I set my cup of chocolate chip aside so I could begin my friendly interrogation. "Is there chatter in the press gallery about who killed Jack?"

Melinda stopped inhaling her cone for a moment to utter one word. "Sure."

Obviously, I needed to lead more with my questions. Even though Melinda was a newbie press staffer, she had apparently learned the cardinal rule of D.C. media relations: never volunteer additional information.

Flattery often worked. “The police are the formal investigators, but we know the press really drives these stories. What’s the chatter on the likely suspects?”

Melinda had just stuffed the last piece of cone into her mouth. She put her finger up to indicate she had to finish chewing before answering. After a big swallow, she wiped her mouth with a napkin. She’d clearly enjoyed the ice cream. Now would she return the favor?

“It’s a little early for speculating, but everyone in the press gallery is chattering about Hill Rat.”

Hill Rat was an anonymous blogger who wrote scathing posts about Congress. Nothing was off limits for Hill Rat. He or she wrote about members of Congress, staffers, Capitol Hill rumors, political intrigue, internecine fighting, romantic gossip, and policy deals. Hill Rat never had anything good to say about Congress or the people who worked there. The blog, though written by an obvious narcissist, drew heavy online traffic from the Beltway crowd. Denizens of Capitol Hill both feared and desired a mention in Hill Rat’s reports. A mention from Hill Rat was almost always unfavorable, but it also meant you mattered. Only the main players appeared in Hill Rat’s blog, even though the acerbic observations never portrayed our city’s most prominent citizens in a flattering light. Lending to Hill Rat’s fame was his or her clandestine identity. Journalists joked the identity of Hill Rat remained the best secret in D.C. since Watergate’s Deep Throat.

Although I’d read Rat’s most infamous entries, I wasn’t a devotee. The writing was witty but the condescending tone rubbed me the wrong way. Washington had its share of snobby, self-indulgent blockheads who deserved Hill Rat’s drubbings. Alongside the numbskulls, however, were hardworking bleeding-heart staffers who arrived at work each day with the goal of making the country a better place to live. Sometimes Washingtonians didn’t fit neatly in either of those categories. Hill Rat either ignored or failed to appreciate the shades of gray motivating daily decision-making in our nation's capital city.

"Do you mean reporters consider Hill Rat a bona fide suspect?"

Melinda smiled. "That's a good question. Hill Rat focused on Jack Drysdale in several posts a few months back. He or she even wrote about his spouse Jordan's failed business venture." That explained how Meg knew about this tidbit. She was a dedicated Hill Rat reader.

Contemplating Melinda's response, I rubbed my chin. "But why would Hill Rat kill Jack? It seemed like he enjoyed writing about him. I'd think bloggers would want their subjects alive and kicking so they could keep writing salacious stories."

Melinda pushed her chair back, indicating our conversation was nearing the end. "That's true, but Jack wasn't one of Hill Rat's typical victims. After the blog about Jordan, Jack vowed to get even."

We both stood up and started walking to the Creamery's exit. "How so?"

Melinda hung her purse on her shoulder and turned toward the hallway. "Jack promised reporters that he was going to discover Hill Rat's true identity."

I raced to catch up with Melinda before she left. "You think Hill Rat might have killed Jack before he could reveal his name? Or her name?"

Melinda stopped walking and turned to face me. "Jack said he'd expose Hill Rat, even if it was the last thing he did."

Chapter Nine

After parting ways with Melinda, I strolled at a leisurely pace back to the Cannon Building. The ice cream had proven a valuable investment. Hill Rat's anonymity allowed him or her to script scintillating observations about D.C. power players without repercussions. Furthermore, since Hill Rat's identity was a mystery, no one knew when to shut up. Hill Rat could be any astute observer with access to the Capitol Hill crowd. But Hill Rat's cachet would be destroyed if he or she could no longer operate as an anonymous ghost. Jack had threatened exposure, and surely Hill Rat knew that Drysdale always made good on his threats.

I returned to the office, which was as quiet as when I left. A hasty check of the relevant media outlets confirmed what I already guessed. Maeve Dixon hadn't been named as an official suspect, and her involvement in Drysdale's murder hadn't been revealed. There was little hope we could keep her name out of the press much longer. Even if Maeve could avoid an official interrogation, the police would have to eventually disclose that she'd discovered the body. It was half past four. Sighing, I hauled myself to Dan's office. I couldn't assume Dan understood our relatively peaceful office existence subsisted on borrowed time.

Dan's door was ajar. I knocked lightly and heard him say, "Kit, is that you?"

I took his question as an invitation to enter. Dan was sitting at his computer, apparently at work. At least he hadn't reverted to an emergency meditation session involving self-inflicted acupuncture.

"Where did you go? You haven't been at your desk."

I sat down in the chair opposite him. "You told me to investigate, so that's what I've been doing."

His eyes lit up. "Did you figure out who killed Jack Drysdale?" Dan leaned forward, eager for my response.

"No," I said slowly. Dan must not have read the Hardy Boys growing up. Or perhaps he watched too much *CSI* and expected murders to be solved in sixty minutes or less.

Dan's face fell. "Oh. How long do you think it's going to take?"

"I'm going to be honest with you, Dan. I have no idea. I've got a couple suspects identified but it's not going to be easy. I'm not exactly friends with the people in Jack's political and social circles."

Dan lowered his voice. "You'd better keep digging. Maeve's in there," he pointed toward her office, "with her legal counsel."

Maeve hadn't wasted any time. "Do you know the specifics of their conversation?"

"I think he's trying to outline her options."

Options? That sounded ominous. "What do you mean?"

"I wasn't invited to listen. But I did linger outside her office for a minute or two," Dan admitted sheepishly.

"You eavesdropped. It's hardly a crime in light of our current situation. What did you hear?"

"I couldn't make out everything, but I did hear the word 'resignation' several times."

I swallowed hard. "As in her resignation from Congress?"

"What else could it be? Like I said, she told me the lawyer was going to cover every alternative."

This situation was headed from bad to worse. Even if Maeve wasn't arrested, she might want to avoid a media maelstrom concerning her involvement in Drysdale's murder. Sidestepping the whole mess could include ditching her political career. Meg's wisdom about working for a freshman member of Congress rang loud and clear in my brain. She'd said something akin to "opportunity of a lifetime" since I'd help "shape her political trajectory." Unless Jack's real killer was exposed, Maeve's congressional career was headed in the notorious rather than noteworthy direction.

I glanced at my iPhone and noticed a new email message. I clicked on the mail icon. Judy Talent from the Majority Leader's office had responded to my message. Dan must have noticed my surprised reaction. "What is it? Has the news hit the press?"

"Calm down. That's not it. I requested a meeting with Judy Talent and she just replied to my email."

Dan's voice squeaked like an adolescent's. "Why did you do that? I told you solving this murder and clearing Maeve was your number one priority."

Dan's annoying persistence had pushed my patience to the limit. "I had an ulterior motive, Dan."

He looked perplexed, as if I had announced the landing of aliens on the Cannon Building's roof. Some people needed every move spelled out for them. "I used the excuse to discuss the shutdown so I could find out if she knows anything about Jack's murder."

"Wow! That's really clever of you," Dan said with enthusiasm.

Not really. "I'd better get cracking then. Is there anything else you'd like me to do before heading home tonight?"

Dan shook his head. "I'll wait to talk to Maeve, but I don't think there's anything else we can do. Let's just hope the police don't mention her involvement."

As far as that front went, the sands of the hourglass had

almost run out. *No need to worry Dan. Why soil the reality of the blissfully ignorant?*

I returned to my desk and replied to Judy's email. She'd suggested the possibility of lunch. That would be ideal, since I'd likely get more out of Judy during a meal than a hurried office meeting. But Judy probably didn't have a lot of time for eating these days. An idea popped into my head and I started typing: *Judy, how about lunch at We The Pizza at noon?*

We The Pizza was a popular Capitol Hill restaurant situated only three blocks from the Cannon Building and the Capitol. Owned by celebrity *Top Chef* star Spike Mendelsohn, the pizzeria offered one of the best "quick" options for lunch on the Hill. With the shutdown, the typical long lunch line would be nonexistent. We could order, grab a seat, and eat within thirty minutes.

I was ready to shut down my computer for the night when another email popped up. Judy had answered, so I clicked on her reply. *See you there. Get ready to talk shutdown solutions.*

Sure, we could do that. But we were also going to talk a little murder, too. I clicked off my terminal and grabbed my purse. It was almost impossible to think about the case while stewing inside the office. I needed to clear my head and plan my next move.

I hustled out of the office and made my way down the empty hallway toward the only Cannon Building door that remained open for egress. As I prepared to leave, I spotted a short, mousy-haired man in a Brooks Brothers suit gathering his laptop briefcase, *Wall Street Journal*, and smartphone from the conveyor belt that scanned all personal items brought into the congressional complex. His head was turned away as he focused on retrieving his various possessions. Even though I couldn't see his face clearly, I knew who it was.

"Trevor? Is that you?"

Startled, he raised his head and peered at me from behind his horn-rimmed glasses. Yep, that was Trevor. I'd recognize that stare in my sleep.

"Kit Marshall. What a delight."

Trevor and I had been colleagues in the Senate for several years. We had never been friends, even though our cubicles had been right next to each other. Trevor wasn't the most pleasant person in the world, but when Senator Langsford was murdered, he'd supported my attempt to solve the crime. Congeniality and a basic degree of human empathy eluded Trevor. Yet his intelligence and quick thinking had proven invaluable as Meg and I sorted through the suspects last summer.

Judging by his professional appearance and expensive attire, Trevor had done well for himself. He'd accepted a position as a lobbyist for a big military contractor after the governor named Senator Langsford's successor. "Are you still working for Carter Power?"

Trevor straightened his tie and smoothed his suit jacket. "Yes, of course. I heard you had secured employment with the newly elected Maeve Dixon?"

"That's right. I'm her LD these days." LD was Hill lingo for "legislative director."

"Another challenging position. She barely won her election, as I recall."

Leave it to Trevor to point out the shortcomings. "Right again. That's one of the reasons I took the job. I wanted to work for a House member who wasn't going to follow the party line. It makes life more interesting."

Trevor chuckled. "You could put it that way. If you consider reduced job security an acceptable work challenge."

I clenched my fist around my purse. Trevor had the uncanny ability to twist my own words against me. Two could play at this game. After all, Trevor wasn't a congressional staffer anymore. He worked off the Hill as a lobbyist. That meant he should be begging me for information and access.

"How's working on K Street? Is it everything you'd dreamed it would be?"

Trevor's face clouded over. I'd hit a nerve. "It has its perks." He sniffed defensively. "For one thing, I'm finally able to dress the way a true professional should." He gave me a brief up-and-down glance, an unspoken criticism of my unfashionable attire. Hill staff didn't make big salaries, so most of my suits came from the sales rack.

No way I was letting him off the hook. "Besides the money, what do you like about the job?"

Trevor wasn't one for small talk. A direct question often elicited a straight answer. After a brief pause, he spoke slowly. "If I can be honest with you, it's not as challenging as I would have hoped. It's more about schmoozing with the right people all over town, including the Hill. So I've been working on my relationship skills."

My eyes must have bulged out of my head. Trevor was as smart as a whip, but he wasn't Mr. Congeniality. I choked out, "How's that going?"

He straightened up. "Actually, not badly. I'm meeting the right people, going to the important social functions, and learning what I need to know, plus a lot more. I can't complain."

If Trevor could charm the pants off the Beltway crowd, there was hope for me to become a swimsuit model. "That's really impressive, Trevor. I'm proud of you."

"It's hardly worthy of commendation. But that's enough about me. How are you adjusting to life in the House of Representatives?"

Trevor really had learned some basic social skills since his time in the Senate. He'd never asked me one question about myself in the four years we shared a workspace.

"It's been harder than I thought working for a first-term House member. There's so much to do, and each vote really matters for her record. Still, I've been enjoying it … until this week, that is."

"Yes, I know the shutdown has congressional offices scrambling."

Maybe Trevor would help me again. Running into him could be a lucky break. "It's not just the shutdown. Did you hear about the murder of Jack Drysdale today?"

"I read about it in the *Washington Post*. I didn't know him well. I'd only met him a handful of times."

Good. Trevor knew him better than I did. I gave him a sideways glance. "I may need to repeat my role as a homicide detective."

Trevor did a double take. I'd captured his attention. "Kit, why on earth would you get mixed up in Drysdale's murder investigation? You don't have any close ties to the Speaker's office."

I let slide Trevor's snide comment about my lowly status in the House's pecking order. Sighing, I moved a step closer. Even though the Cannon Building was deserted, the walls had ears. I couldn't afford to let this information slip into the wrong hands.

I leaned in to whisper, "My boss might be involved."

Trevor's eyes narrowed in circumspection. He moved six inches forward to nearly close the gap between us. "Might? Either she is or she isn't."

Trevor was like many Washington type A personalities. Literal. Organized. Impatient. Demanding. For these folks, it was a strain to understand ambiguity. Beating around the bush wouldn't get me anywhere with him.

"Maeve Dixon discovered the body this morning, Trevor."

My words hung in silence. Trevor was rarely shocked by anything, but his immediate reaction indicated my revelation had thrown him for a loop.

After a long moment, Trevor said, "I assume she's a suspect?"

I reminded Trevor about her encounter the day before with Jack Drysdale. He nodded, clearly aware of the public tiff.

I leaned against the wall in the hallway, needing the support. It had been a long day, and mental exhaustion was setting in. "You can see my predicament, right?"

Trevor smiled tightly. "The situation is a bit different than last year, but an urgency exists nonetheless. Believe me, I have great respect for Detective O'Halloran and the entire Capitol Hill Police force. If you don't solve this crime swiftly, they might end up blaming the obvious suspect." As if I needed clarification, he added, "Your boss, of course."

"The problem is I don't know the suspects as intimately as I did before." I outlined the short list I had developed today after my discreet inquiries.

After Trevor listened to my list, he rubbed his chin thoughtfully. "I know several people you've mentioned. Who do you need to meet tomorrow?"

My intuition had proven correct. Trevor wanted to assist. Probably he would leap at any opportunity to reenter the Capitol Hill orbit. I mentally clicked through the suspects I'd identified. "I have no connection to Gareth Pressler in the Sergeant at Arms office. I also don't know Jack's husband. Now I guess he's a widower." Just pronouncing the word was depressing, even though I wasn't acquainted with him.

"I can help you with Pressler. I know a guy who works in the Sergeant's office and reports to Pressler. His name is Trent Roscoe and I can get you a few minutes with him tomorrow."

What a relief. Running into Trevor had been a godsend. "Thanks, Trevor. I appreciate it."

He pressed his lips together and gave me a curt bow. "At your service." After a moment, he added, "By the way, what is the status of your relationship with your inamorato? I believe his name is Doug, is it not?"

Trevor's formal way of speaking used to irk me, but now I accepted it as part of his eccentric personality. It was almost as though Trevor was a vampire, born in a different era. I pushed that thought aside. Maybe I'd read one too many fantasy e-book trilogies. Trevor had nothing in common with Edward Cullen.

"We're still living together in Arlington."

Trevor exhibited numerous personality defects, but he

was no dummy. "I assume you have not formalized your relationship?" He looked pointedly at my left hand.

Reflexively, I touched my ring finger. *Damn Trevor.* He always knew how to get my goat. My annoyance obvious, I replied, "No, but we're very happy together."

"I see. Well, I think you will enjoy your meeting tomorrow with Trent. Look for an email to confirm it in the morning. Have a good evening, Kit Marshall."

Trevor didn't wear a cape, but if he did, he would have swirled it around him and disappeared in a cloud of smoke. Instead, he made a beeline down the long congressional office hallway behind us, headed for destinations unknown. I admired his long strides and swift pace, wishing I could demonstrate the same self-assurance.

What did he mean about my meeting tomorrow with Trent? That was mysterious. I dismissed his comment as typical Trevor. There was no point in trying to figure out the enigma.

On impulse, I grabbed my iPhone and shot off a text to Meg: *Drink? Leaving now.* I'd give her three minutes to answer. If not, I'd head home and catch up with her later.

My phone chimed to indicate an iMessage: *Italian happy hour?*

I wrote back immediately: *See you there.*

We didn't need to confirm the location. We only frequented one place with cheap drinks and food. Two blocks away from the House office buildings, Sonoma was convenient. As a bonus, it added a touch of class to our Hill outings. The dinner offerings could be pricey, but their Italian happy hour featured inexpensive wines and tasty small plates. The key for Meg was the sparkling wine, her libation of choice when stressed out. To be fair, bubbly was Meg's preferred drink even if she was just plain thirsty.

In five minutes, I was inside Sonoma and heading upstairs. The open seating and upstairs bar hosted the boisterous happy hours. This evening, only two clusters of patrons were enjoying drinks and nibbles. Pretty soon, the District's small businesses would add themselves to the growing list of victims turned upside down by the federal government's shuttering.

I sat in the corner of the lounge area. At least we could talk privately. Due to her busy work schedule, Meg's free time was limited. I wanted to make good use of the unexpected opportunity.

Meg glided into the room and saw me instantly. She signaled a "hello" with a brief waggle of her hand and bustled over to the overstuffed sofa. Meg's fashionable style was evident even in the dead of winter. She wore a fitted red peacoat accented with a dark black belt and sported a trendy crochet flower hat that sat slightly off-center on her head. All this along with tight black riding pants and leather gloves. Meg had been my best friend for years. We'd survived political campaigns together, the tribulations of being overworked and underpaid congressional staffers, and even a high-profile murder investigation. One would think that through it all, Meg's sense of style might have rubbed off on me, even via osmosis (if that was biologically possible). But it hadn't. As much as I tried, I simply couldn't adapt Meg's fashion sense to my body and coloring. Whenever I tried, it just looked wrong.

"Did you order me a glass of sparkling wine yet?"

No hello or perfunctory salutations for Meg. She meant business. "Not yet, I just got here myself." I motioned for the waiter.

Meg grabbed the happy hour menu from the coffee table next to us. I ordered the white wine on special and Meg predictably went for the Prosecco, along with Italian meatballs and prosciutto. Those riding pants hid no sins. Someone should study Meg's metabolism to figure out how it defied calories.

"I only have time for one drink, unfortunately. I need to get back to the office to finish some research for the hearings."

Meg truly was burning the midnight oil. It was rare for her to cut happy hour short. "That's okay. One drink is my limit, too. I should really get back to Doug and Clarence. I haven't been able to spend much time with them lately."

Our drinks arrived and Meg grabbed her glass and clinked it to mine. "That's right, I almost forgot. Congratulations!"

I was confused. Had Doug told Meg something in confidence she'd misinterpreted? I felt my face flush. Was Doug planning a big surprise?

"Did Doug let you in on a secret I should know about?"

"No, silly! Not Doug. Clarence! He's on track to win the top dog title, of course."

Trevor's comment about my permanently single status had muddled my thinking. Of course Doug would never tell Meg about marriage proposal plans. He barely trusted her to water our plants when we went on vacation.

"Clarence is still winning the online competition?"

"You didn't know? I thought you might have engineered his success by promising Maeve's vote to end the shutdown!" She giggled.

I pulled out my iPhone and navigated to the Capitol Canine website. Sure enough, Clarence's cute mug appeared in the number one slot. This morning's results were no fluke. Somehow he'd managed to amass five thousand votes in the past twenty-four hours. He was adorable, but this made no sense. It certainly wasn't because everyone on the Hill knew his owners, either.

"This is terrific. I'm not sure how it happened."

"You didn't orchestrate a coordinated campaign for Clarence? That's usually how you win the top dog title."

How did Meg know those details? Even though she loved Clarence, Meg didn't own a dog, or any other living thing for that matter. She once remarked betta fish were beautiful, but she wouldn't want to ruin her nails changing the water. Meg gave new meaning to the adjectives "independent" and "self-sufficient," even by Washington standards.

"No, I've been a little busy. You know, with the murder—the one where my boss is the prime suspect."

"Right. Well, it looks like someone else decided to help out Clarence with Capitol Canine. There's no dog even close in votes. What are you going to wear to the big party tomorrow evening?"

"Party?"

"Kit, I might as well accept the award on behalf of Clarence. You're clueless." She grabbed my phone out of my hand and touched the screen. She waited a moment, and then showed me the phone. "The award ceremony is tomorrow night, as soon as the voting closes."

I rolled my eyes. Not that I wasn't glad Clarence had achieved such impressive status, but I had other matters on my mind right now.

"I'm not sure how I'm going to fit that in. I really need to focus on clearing Maeve's name."

Now it was Meg's turn to roll her eyes. Her drink was almost empty. She picked up her glass and pointed it at me. "What would you do without me?" She tilted her head back and finished it off. Meg had a flair for the dramatic she occasionally used to her advantage.

"I don't know. Drink less?"

"Clarence winning this contest is the luckiest thing that could happen to you. Just look who's heading the awards committee!" She pointed to my iPhone's screen again.

"I've never met that man before in my life."

"Precisely. That's Jordan Macintyre, Jack's widower. Didn't you want to figure out a way to talk to him?"

Meg was right. Macintyre was on my short list of suspects since he likely stood to gain financially from Jack's death.

"Do you think he'll come to the ceremony tomorrow night? He might skip it because of Jack's death."

"I don't know, but you could call Capitol Canine to find out. He's deeply involved with the contest because the dog he owned with Jack is a past winner. All the proceeds go to charity so he may feel obligated to participate."

Meg had a point. Given his dedication to the contest, there was a chance Jordan might show up at the party. I didn't have any other plan to interact with him, so this opportunity could be critical.

"Thanks for letting me know. Guess who I ran into before I texted you for drinks?"

Meg was putting on her coat as if eager to return to the office for several more hours of work. Meg had progressed professionally by leaps and bounds in her new job. I buried a pang of jealousy. As a legislative director, I'd moved up in the world, too. Unlike Meg, I was fighting to keep my position. I'd managed to land on my feet once after a Hill scandal. Twice would be pushing it.

"Who? I'm sorry, but I need to run back to the office."

"Trevor. He was coming into Cannon as I was leaving."

Meg slung her sleek Kate Spade bag over her shoulder. "Tremendous. I hope he's enjoying life on the dark side as a lobbyist."

Meg and Trevor had a rocky relationship. Actually, "rocky" was an understatement. Meg detested Trevor, and the feeling was mutual.

"He's going to introduce me to someone he knows in the Sergeant at Arms office so I can find out more about the conflict between Gareth Pressler and Jack."

Meg gave a perfunctory nod, waved goodbye, and started to walk toward the staircase. Then she turned around abruptly. "Who does Trevor know in the Sergeant at Arms office?"

I racked my brain. Names were always a challenge, which disadvantaged me in the political world. "It's hard for me to remember. He's going to email us both tomorrow morning." Then it popped into my brain. "I think his first name is Trent."

Meg broke into a wide grin. "Trent Roscoe?"

"That's it."

"You're in for a treat."

"Trevor made a weird remark to that effect. Why?"

"Trent was recently named one of the fifty most beautiful Capitol Hill staffers. He's eye candy, for sure!"

Leave it to Meg to know the hotties. She'd made several appearances on the infamous Capitol Hill list of attractive people.

"I'm not there to ogle him. I need him as a contact so I can determine if Gareth killed Jack."

As Meg walked away, she yelled over her shoulder, "Be sure to remember that tomorrow when you lay eyes on him!"

When I arrived home, Doug and Clarence were watching a television documentary on the History Channel about White House pets.

"Did you know that LBJ owned two beagles named Him and Her?" asked Doug.

"No idea."

"They were on the cover of *Time* magazine with the president."

"But they never held the title of Top Dog on Capitol Hill."

Doug laughed and scratched Clarence's ears. "Good point."

A plate with crackers, veggies, and other delectable snacks littered the coffee table, along with a half-empty bottle of pinot grigio.

"Did you and Clarence have a happy hour at home?"

"We deserved it after a hard day's work." Clarence sat up next to Doug as if to agree with this pronouncement.

I flopped down on the couch next to them and popped a carrot in my mouth.

"Stressful day?" Doug asked.

"You could say that. At least Maeve managed to escape the headlines today. That can't last forever."

Doug stayed silent, so I kept talking. "I talked to your former student Melinda today. She was helpful. Apparently Jack Drysdale had a big beef with Hill Rat. Do you read that blog?"

Doug crinkled his nose. "I try to avoid journalism written by rodents."

"I'm not a fan, either. If I want to solve this murder, I may have to figure out the Rat's identity, though."

Doug popped a sesame cracker in his mouth and answered with his mouth full. "How are you going to do that? Hasn't the entire Washington D.C. press corps been trying to expose him for months?"

"I have other leads, but there's only one way to catch a rat."

Doug looked at me expectantly. I picked up a piece of Gouda and waved it around for emphasis. "You have to set a trap with the right kind of cheese."

Chapter Ten

I WOKE THE next morning with a renewed and determined focus. Yesterday had been a mess, but the situation wasn't disastrous, at least not yet. Maeve's involvement had remained under wraps, and other legitimate suspects with motives existed. Maybe clearing her name wouldn't prove impossible. The person who discovered the body always faced tough questions, just like I had last summer. Although it had been a rocky road, the actual perpetrators had been caught in the end. Thomas Jefferson's famous quote, "Justice cannot sleep forever," fueled my optimism.

My calendar confirmed it was going to be a busy day: lunch with Judy Talent from the Majority Leader's office, a likely meeting with Trevor's contact at the Sergeant at Arms office, and then the Capitol Canine awards ceremony in the early evening.

Clarence sat obediently next to me while I checked my phone. He was trying to behave, but I could tell from the increasing rapidity of his tail wag he was losing patience. We had already been outside for our morning jog and he wanted his breakfast. Dogs are creatures of habit, and Clarence was no exception. If I didn't comply with expectations soon, he would progress to a whimper, then a staccato bark, and finally a full-throttle beagle mutt howl. Mrs. Beauregard, our neighbor two doors down, relished documenting Clarence's lapses in canine decorum. Every unleashed escape into the hallway and each early morning howl eventually made its way back to us, usually with the threat of a condo board "pet sanction." Thus far, we'd managed to avoid an actual monetary penalty because Clarence seemed to understand subconsciously he was only allowed so many mistakes in any thirty-day period. I wondered if Clarence's triumph as top dog on Capitol Hill might buy him some slack with the powers that be on the condo board. After all, he was about to become a bona fide Washington D.C. celebrity.

After I filled the dog's bowl, Doug appeared in the kitchen. He always looked disoriented when he woke up, his bushy brown hair disheveled and his glasses slightly askew. He'd slept in the t-shirt I bought him for his birthday, which sported the slogan, "TRUST ME, I'M A HISTORY PROFESSOR." He made a beeline for the espresso machine and began filling it up with fresh beans.

"Are you free this evening?" I asked.

Normally, I would have allowed him to ingest an initial caffeine infusion before interrogating him, but the clock was ticking.

"Um, I think so. What day is it again?"

"It's Wednesday, all day."

He grumbled as he removed the coffee mug with his espresso. He carefully tilted a small pitcher of heated milk and added it to his caffeinated masterpiece.

"I don't remember anything on my schedule tonight. I was planning on teaching my class and then heading home for a long afternoon of writing."

What else was new? That was Doug's schedule every day. When he had an evening event, like a Georgetown faculty wine and cheese reception, he complained bitterly about forfeiting precious research time.

"It looks as though Clarence is going to win the Capitol Canine contest, so can you bring him to the awards ceremony tonight?"

Doug took a long sip of his latte and wiped a frothy mustache from under his lip before responding. "He's winning? How did that happen?"

"It's another mystery to solve. I thought maybe you decided to get your students involved. I haven't had any time to marshal votes for him."

"Nope, it wasn't me. I didn't even look at the website to monitor the voting."

Clarence ran in between us and abruptly rolled over on his back. After his morning jaunt and breakfast, he typically requested a belly rub.

We both bent down to rub his pink stomach, and he gave a low growl of appreciation. Doug had to commit, since it would be almost impossible to get Clarence to the awards ceremony otherwise. "Can you meet me tonight for the event? One of the suspects in Jack Drysdale's murder might be there, and it's my best chance to talk with him."

"Now I get it. You need me to handle Clarence while you interrogate suspects."

I stood and put my hands on my hips. "No, I can handle our dog and my interrogations. But if he's going to win Capitol Canine, then Clarence needs to make an appearance!"

The exasperation in my voice had caught Doug's attention. He stopped rubbing Clarence's belly and glanced up. "All right, I get it. Clarence and I will be there with bells on. Just text me the time and the address. At least we'll spend some time together."

"That's the spirit. Thank you." After giving Clarence a pat on the head and Doug a kiss on the lips, I bolted for the door. As usual, I was already behind schedule.

With the shutdown still in full force, Metro traffic remained sparse. Absent of delays caused by overloaded cars, the subway zipped along to the Hill in record time. During the long escalator ride from the Capitol South station to the surface, I determined there was enough time for a brief stop at my favorite morning breakfast stop, Le Bon Café. The tiny French bistro next to the Library of Congress's Madison Building was reminiscent of the numerous eateries that populated Parisian neighborhoods. Usually stepping inside Le Bon Café was enough to transport me momentarily to my favorite European city, providing a nice respite from the persistent cloud of stress surrounding our nation's capital.

This morning, Le Bon Café lived up to expectations. It was filled with the aroma of rich coffee, egg strata, and freshly baked pastries. I inhaled deeply, thankful that smelling delicious food wasn't fattening.

Usually, the line stretched the length of the café. This morning, only one other person stood in front of me. If I was going to treat myself to a French breakfast, I typically went for scrambled eggs or a waffle with fresh fruit. But later today I had a pizza lunch scheduled with Judy. Sighing, I opted for a skim latte and a yogurt parfait. I had just grabbed my breakfast off the counter and was about to head for the door when Detective O'Halloran breezed through the entrance.

There was no way to avoid him in the tiny café. "Good morning, Detective!" The cheer in my voice sounded forced, but I didn't want O'Halloran to know I was worried about the status of Maeve's involvement in Jack's murder. Keeping up appearances was the better strategy.

"Ms. Marshall. Just the person I was hoping to speak with this morning."

Not a good sign. Maybe O'Halloran had some good information to share about the murder. Police weren't supposed to talk about investigations in progress, but O'Halloran had exhibited loose-lipped tendencies in the past.

"You want to talk to me?" I asked, feigning innocence. My words had fallen on deaf ears. Staring over my shoulder, O'Halloran eagerly eyed the pan of oat bran crisp, fresh out of the oven. The sweet smell of brown sugar floated past us. Since I stood between him and a delicious breakfast, he'd want to keep this conversation brief.

After a moment's pause for a deep inhale, O'Halloran returned his focus to me. "Ah, yes. Ms. Marshall. You saved me a phone call. Any reason why Jack Drysdale would place a Post-it with your name on it in the middle of his desk?"

So much for staying one step removed from this murder. "I have no idea, Detective. As you know, I met with Jack the day before he was killed. Representative Dixon had an appointment with the Speaker, and I spent fifteen minutes with Mr. Drysdale while our bosses chatted."

"Why am I not surprised to find you connected to yet another crime in Congress, Ms. Marshall?"

"I have no idea, sir. Did the note on Jack's desk say anything else other than my name?"

"Actually, it did. The name 'Clarence' was also on the Post-it."

I couldn't suppress a broad grin. At least one mystery was solved. "Clarence is my dog. Jack was trying to help him win the Capitol Canine contest. It was his attempt to persuade me to sell Dixon on the Speaker's proposal to end the shutdown. He'd help Clarence win the contest, and I'd make sure the congresswoman would support the Speaker when push came to shove."

O'Halloran shook his head. "Now I've heard everything. You're telling me Drysdale tried to bribe you by fixing a dog popularity contest?"

"Not exactly. He wasn't fixing it. But if he told his numerous contacts to vote for Clarence, they'd do it. As you know, Detective, Jack Drysdale was the most powerful staffer on the Hill."

O'Halloran sighed. "Yeah, I know. So powerful that even a

member of Congress might want him out of the way." He gave me a sideways glance with a half smirk.

"What are you implying?"

"Nothing, at least yet. Your boss doesn't have a fancy congressional trip abroad planned for the near future, right?"

"Not that I'm aware of. But our scheduler is on furlough due to the shutdown."

O'Halloran huffed. "Then I'll tell you instead. She shouldn't leave Washington until we solve this murder." He saluted military style with his right hand and moved past me to place his order.

His dismissal had been abrupt and the conversation disconcerting, to say the least. Maeve was still a person of interest. Even though the police had kept her name out of the press so far, that wouldn't matter if O'Halloran gathered enough circumstantial evidence to label her a formal suspect.

The morning had started out so promising with the speedy commute and stop at my favorite breakfast joint. As I shoved the yogurt parfait into my purse, I could feel my body tense up. No amount of tasty food or libations would give me relief. The only solution was to find Jack's killer so Maeve Dixon could resume her role as a marginal yet ambitious member of Congress.

In five minutes, I opened the front door to the office and retreated to the safety of my desk. The suite seemed quiet, but appearances could be deceiving. I had just enough time to turn on my computer and suck down half of the yogurt parfait before the door to Representative Dixon's private office opened. My boss emerged, wearing an athletic zebra tank top, gray spandex shorts, and a matching black headband.

"Early workout at the House gym?" I asked.

"Since I never made it yesterday due to the fiasco with Drysdale, I did the early morning CrossFit circuit."

Maeve was referring to a killer regimen several younger

representatives followed when the House was in session. They met in the gym reserved only for members of Congress and apparently knocked out a workout fit for cage fighters. My boss was a regular, mostly for the exercise, but also because it gave her an opportunity to network with colleagues she might not interact with otherwise.

"I'm impressed. Unfortunately, I have news for you that might make you wish you stayed at the gym."

She grabbed a towel and wiped the sweat still beading on her face. "What's wrong now?"

"Nothing at the moment. But I ran into Detective O'Halloran from the Capitol Hill Police, and he indicated you are still a person of interest in the murder."

I cringed, waiting for the explosion. Instead, Maeve gulped down half a bottle of water, swallowed, and nodded her head.

"I expected this. That's why I consulted with an attorney yesterday."

"What are you going to do if you're named an official suspect? Won't that hurt you politically?"

"It won't help. My attorney will handle the police, and I'll have to lie low for a while until this mess is solved."

"What about the shutdown? I thought you wanted to help broker the solution?"

Maeve smiled. "That's why I hired you, Kit. You're the consummate public servant, always looking to find the perfect public policy solution to heal our nation's woes. I'll have to retreat from the shutdown negotiations if the murder investigation focuses on me. I would be a distraction, and neither party would welcome my presence."

"Did you tell Dan about this?"

In the midst of a leg stretch, she answered my question. "I have. He understands and supports my decision. Dan may not know Washington D.C., but he has been a loyal soldier throughout my short political career."

"Maybe I can help. You know I solved the murder of my boss in the Senate last year."

Maeve gave a short, dry laugh. "I heard about it and Dan reminded me last night." Her face turned serious. "Listen to me. I don't want you investigating the murder of Jack Drysdale. You were lucky once to find a killer in the Capitol. Luck like that doesn't strike twice. Believe me, I know from firsthand experience in combat."

"I'm really concerned if we leave it to the police," I said. "They might settle on you as an easy target."

Maeve stepped right up to me and put her hand on my shoulder. "I appreciate the gesture, Kit. I was trained as a soldier, and that means I put my faith in the system. They might focus on me initially, but the police will figure this out. I don't want anyone getting hurt in the line of duty." Her smile returned. "And that's an order."

"I understand. You don't have to worry about me."

"I'm counting on it. Try to keep Dan focused. He's a worrywart." She gave me a playful wink, then continued, "I'm headed for a shower. After that, I'll be in my office."

Now I knew why the voters of North Carolina chose my boss to represent them in Congress. She was a class act. Despite her concern about my informal inquiries, I didn't give a second thought to my plan for the day. There was nothing wrong with asking a few innocent questions.

My email inbox indicated the push to find a solution to the shutdown had begun. Several legislative options had emerged, including one from the Majority Leader. I clicked on the file to open the document describing the proposal and groaned inwardly. A two-page summary preceded fifty pages of drafted bill language. Lunch with Judy was in three hours. At least part of that conversation hinged on an informed discussion about this deal. No time for procrastination.

Usually there was a dull roar in the background of a congressional office. Multiple televisions blared, with the House's floor activity broadcast from one set along with various cable television political talk shows on the others. Staffers were constantly on the phone, talking with colleagues, constituents, or reporters. "Controlled chaos" described it well. Ensuring consistency in all interactions executed in the congresswoman's name was no small task. Without the comforting din, my mind wandered as I stared at the computer monitor.

I was getting nowhere fast. It was time for a change of scenery. Where could I go? Smaller cafeterias throughout the congressional complex were good places to escape, but the shutdown had restricted food service to the main cafeteria in the Longworth Building. That wasn't an option because it was a lobbyist cruising ground. I'd never eaten a meal there without numerous interruptions from notorious K Street peddlers.

After a few minutes of concentration, an idea popped into the recesses of my overtaxed intellect. The problem wasn't just the lack of background noise; it was everything surrounding me. I needed to get out of this building entirely. Congress was one big tangled web of conflict and confusion these days. Before the winter chill set in, I'd accidentally happened upon an oasis of relative serenity. Adjacent to the Cannon Building was the Madison Building of the Library of Congress, where I'd attended a legislative process class on the intricacies of House committee procedure. After the class ended I was, as usual, hungry. The search for the elevators to the upstairs cafeteria led me to the La Follette Reading Room, a small resource facility at the Library reserved for members of Congress and staff. Members of Congress never used La Follette because they also had access to the ornate Congressional Reading Room in the Library's historic Jefferson Building. Since that day, I'd made several trips to the hidden treasure when the pressures of daily Hill life became too much.

After printing the legislative proposal and grabbing my portfolio and coat, I headed to the Library. An underground tunnel connected Cannon to Madison, so going outside wasn't required. But after I was done with my work, it would be time for lunch with Judy Talent at the pizza eatery on Pennsylvania.

I exited the elevator on the second floor, hoping La Follette remained open during the shutdown. Madison was even emptier than the House office buildings. Vaguely, I remembered a librarian telling me La Follette was open as long as Congress was in session. They certainly weren't getting anything accomplished, but technically, Congress was scheduled to convene today. Grabbing the handle of the heavy door to La Follette, I saw my hunch confirmed as it swung open.

A middle-aged woman with oversized black glasses and a tight bun nodded as I entered. Sometimes clichés proved true; this was the Library of Congress, after all. Probably every librarian in the United States wanted to work here. Apparently, the need to escape Congress was not uncommon. Several other staffers sat at tables and carrels, quietly reading or working at computer terminals.

I found an empty chair and sat down. I was about to open my portfolio and begin work when I glanced over at a book on a display shelf. It was a historical monograph on the Speaker of the House, and on the cover was a photograph of Sam Rayburn holding a gavel. The image got the gears in my brain churning, but not on the subject of the legislative proposal in front of me. I shifted back to Jack's murder. How did that gavel make its way from the floor of the House of Representatives to the crime scene?

So far, this detail hadn't made it into the press, which meant the police were keeping a tight lid on it. Murder weapons were important pieces of the puzzle, but this one was such an unusual artifact, it could potentially lead investigators to the killer. Unfortunately, my boss had presided over the House floor the evening before the murder, so the weapon was pointing Detective O'Halloran squarely in the direction of Maeve Dixon.

I snuck a peek at the librarian sitting at the desk. She was flipping through the latest edition of *National Journal* magazine. Appearances suggested she wasn't overwhelmed by work. Maybe she could provide valuable research assistance.

I sauntered over and she looked up from her reading with a broad smile. This was an auspicious start.

"How can I help you?"

Returning her smile with a grin, I said, "Do you have any research materials about the Speaker's gavel?"

Her eyes narrowed. "That's an unusual request. May I ask why you want information on the gavel?"

Lying wasn't morally defensible. A college lecture on Kant's categorical imperative flashed through my mind. Could I split the baby somehow? I doubted Kant would agree, but he'd never worked in the United States Congress for a vulnerable politician accused of murder.

"It's a project for my chief of staff." That wasn't a complete fib. Dan had ordered me to figure out who killed Jack Drysdale.

Her jaw relaxed. "We're not really supposed to research issues unrelated to the shutdown." She paused. "But no one else has asked for my help, so I guess it won't hurt."

I breathed a sigh of relief. "Thank you. I appreciate it."

She pushed her glasses up and wrinkled her nose. "No problem. Do you mind having a seat while I gather materials for you?"

"Not at all." I returned to my spot and immediately dove into the legislative proposal from the Majority Leader's office. There were several provisions in the bill my boss could support. Not surprisingly, there were also a few specific examples of language she'd oppose. As I worked through the document, I jotted down copious notes for my lunchtime discussion with Judy. I was almost at the end when the librarian walked over to my table with several sheets of paper in her hand.

"I found some information about the Speaker's gavel for you. You might also want to check with the House Historian's office."

"That's a great idea. Thanks." For good measure, I added, "My chief will be thrilled with this."

She smiled politely. "Happy to help."

I quickly rifled through the printed information. One image caught my eye. It was another photo of Speaker Sam Rayburn. He was holding an armload of gavels, handed over by the man standing next to him. According to the caption, a United States Capitol engineer was giving Rayburn a stash of gavels in anticipation of the end of the summer recess in 1943. Why multiple gavels?

After flipping through the documents, I discovered that more than one gavel existed at any given time. Many Speakers in American history had broken gavels by banging them too hard. The raucous House rarely came to order when the presiding officer asked politely; therefore, many Speakers simply pounded the gavel harder. In 1931, John Nance Garner broke three gavels in rapid succession. This led House engineers and carpenters to supply a set of gavels to the Speaker or whoever presided over the House.

Why hadn't this possibility occurred to me earlier? There wasn't a *single* gavel. There were many gavels, and therefore, a whole array of potential murder weapons. I tapped my pen to the side of my head and allowed myself a tentative smile.

Chapter Eleven

THERE WAS NO time for self-congratulation. Multiple gavels meant the one that smashed Jack's head in wasn't necessarily the same gavel Maeve had wielded the night before the murder. Though a positive development, it didn't exonerate her.

I finished reading the document before noon with only minutes to spare. After packing up my papers and donning my coat, I waved goodbye to the helpful librarian. A few minutes later, I was hustling down Pennsylvania Avenue. We The Pizza was only one and a half blocks away, but I walked as fast as I could without breaking into a jog. Something told me Judy Talent didn't tolerate the fashionably late.

The aroma of baked cheese, garlic, and pepperoni drifted as far as the intersection of Pennsylvania and Third Street. The typical We The Pizza line usually ran the length of the restaurant's ground floor, but today there were only three patrons waiting to order at the counter. I'd never met Judy before today, but I'd seen her photograph several times in various D.C. publications listing the fifty most powerful Hill staffers. She hadn't arrived yet.

I took a deep breath and shifted my attention to the pizzas behind the display glass. The restaurant boasted an eclectic assortment. Of course, the traditional cheese and pepperoni options were available. However, the signature offerings of We The Pizza were far from conventional. Slices with unusual toppings such as pulled pork, truffles, or boneless buffalo chicken wings populated the menu du jour. I'd begun to narrow down my lunchtime options when I heard a voice behind me.

"Excuse me. Are you Kit Marshall?"

I turned around to discover my lunch companion had arrived. Judy Talent was the very model of a Washington D.C. power broker. She was in her early forties, yet her figure was as trim as that of a woman a decade younger. Her brown tresses had understated auburn highlights that fell right above her shoulders in angled layers. I was no hair snob, but I could spot an expensive cut and style, likely the work of Vidal Sassoon in Tysons Galleria or even Cristophe's. If possible, her outfit was even more impressive. She sported an unbuttoned mid-length black wool coat over a chic tan designer pantsuit that screamed Saks. As she shifted her purse to shake my hand, I noticed the Burberry label on the lining of her overcoat. Hillary Clinton had nothing on Judy Talent when it came to presenting the image of a flawless female politico. Her appearance projected one unified message: *I am a professional.*

I pulled my jacket across my body to cover up my outfit, one of my standard black suits with a red blouse. Compared to Judy, I felt like a reliable Toyota next to a tricked-out Ferrari.

Judy looked at me expectantly. She'd asked me a question and was offering her hand. I took it and croaked, "Yes, that's me. I mean, I'm Kit." I followed up my awkward introduction with a nervous laugh.

Judy flashed an expensive smile. "Terrific. I didn't know what you looked like, but they aren't exactly breaking down the doors during the shutdown, are they?"

"No crowd is certainly unusual for this place. Have you eaten here before?"

Judy made a face. "I'm embarrassed to say I haven't, even though I know it's one of the best eateries on the Hill. I'm afraid my job doesn't give me many opportunities to go out for lunch."

I nodded sympathetically. At the front of the line, I placed my order for a slice of Poblano Spicy Mexican with a side salad and a premium sour cherry soda.

Judy stared at the menu on the wall behind the counter. "I really should have the farmers market salad. But it seems like a missed opportunity not to eat the pizza."

I had just taken a big sip of my custom soda. "You should definitely treat yourself." I wiped the red fizz from my upper lip. "These homemade sodas are delicious."

Judy laughed. "Sold!" She proceeded to order the two slice special, opting for the pineapple ham combo and mushroom truffle. She topped it off with a Shirley Temple soda.

While we waited for our slices to emerge from the wood-fired oven, Judy wasted no time. "Have you seen the Majority Leader's proposal to end the shutdown?" she asked.

Before I had a chance to answer, our beepers went off, indicating our pizza was ready. Judy's eyes grew wide as an employee placed her lunch on the counter for pickup. The slices at We The Pizza were huge. As we picked up our trays and headed upstairs to find a seat, Judy shook her head in dismay. "This is the biggest lunch I've had in five years. I'll be working it off at the gym all week."

I peeked at Judy's behind as I followed her to a table. It was perfect. Even while admiring her physique, I felt sorry for her. My entire life, thinness had eluded me. But I also wasn't one to deprive myself of a pizza lunch. If I could guess, I'd wager that Judy's intensity pervaded her whole existence—her work, appearance, and personal relationships.

Judy only allowed herself one bite before cutting to the chase. After taking a sip of her soda, she opened her leather portfolio, placed the legislative proposal on the table, and slid it toward me. "Here it is. I know you've seen it already, since it made the email rounds earlier today. I don't need to tell you how important it is for the entire party caucus to stick together on this vote, and I know Representative Dixon wants to get into the action. This is her chance to make a difference, both to the people of North Carolina and the Majority Leader."

At least Judy had made a good faith attempt at persuasion. That was more than I could say for the late Jack Drysdale, with his hard sell. I gave Judy a polite smile and finished my mouthful of pizza before speaking. "I appreciate you taking the time to meet. Can we go over some details? I have a few questions."

In between bites of pizza, Judy and I went back and forth on the finer points of the bill. Not all of her answers would make my boss happy, but to her credit, Judy answered each inquiry with complete and apparently honest answers. After twenty minutes, I was satisfied, at least with the political part of the conversation.

I glanced at Judy's tray. She had plowed her way through the pineapple ham slice, but her mushroom truffle was untouched. I still had my salad to eat. Judy needed to invest a few more minutes in our lunch so I could probe her about Jack's murder. Judy glanced at her watch. Two factors were working against me, namely Judy's desire to minimize the caloric damage of our meal and the fact she'd already spent more time with me at lunch than she typically devoted to anyone.

Before she started packing up, I needed to intercede. "You haven't touched your other slice of pizza."

She laughed. "I guess my eyes are bigger than my stomach. I'll get a box for this. Someone in the office will eat it as soon as I get back." She turned to gather her purse and designer overcoat. Uh-oh.

"Wait a second," I blurted out. She turned to look at me with a curious stare.

I racked my brain for a reason to keep Judy at the table. My eyes drifted to her tray. "You don't want to take that pizza to go."

Judy narrowed her eyes. "Why not?"

"It's their specialty. You don't want to give that pizza up. Trust me."

Judy stared at me for several seconds, which felt like forever. Then she burst out laughing. "I like you, Kit. You're refreshing."

The muscles in my face relaxed, and I grinned. "Thank you. I think that was a compliment."

"Yes, it was. So this pizza is really worth it?" She pointed to the slice.

"You don't want to miss it." I was telling the truth. Their mushroom truffle was divine.

"I'll take your word for it." Judy let go of her purse and coat, picked up her knife and fork, and dived in. This was my opportunity. Unlike Judy's pizza, my salad could wait.

"Can I ask you a question unrelated to the shutdown?"

"Sure. By the way, you're right. This pizza is fantastic. I'm glad I didn't give it to one of those scavengers in my office. It wouldn't have lasted two minutes."

"Are you upset by Jack Drysdale's death?"

I studied Judy's reaction. She didn't appear alarmed or taken aback. In fact, she didn't miss a bite. After swallowing, she offered, "Yes and no. I knew Jack for many years so it's upsetting. But we weren't friends." She raised her eyebrows before continuing. "Everyone knew that."

Playing innocent might help elicit more information. Besides, I couldn't exactly explain my interest in Jack's death. "I only met Jack the day before he died. I know what's appeared in the gossip columns, though."

Judy scoffed. "Don't believe everything you read. Especially from that menace, Hill Rat."

Just the opening I needed. "I heard Jack knew Hill Rat's real identity and wanted to expose him … or her."

Judy shrugged. "I'm not surprised. Jack despised Hill Rat.

He thought scandal-driven blogging made relationships even tougher to maintain within the Capitol. No one could trust anyone with Hill Rat publishing confidential missives and secrets."

Did Judy have a motive for killing Jack? According to the rumor mill, she and Jack had routinely competed for the most prestigious Capitol Hill jobs. Emerging on top with his Speaker's job, Jack had bested Judy in the end. She might have decided the only way to eliminate the competition was murder.

I leaned in closer and softened my voice. "Do you have any idea who might have killed Jack?"

Judy's face was expressionless for several seconds, which felt like five minutes. Once again, she burst into laughter. "You're just full of surprises. Why do you care who murdered Jack Drysdale? Isn't Representative Dixon giving you enough work these days?"

Luckily, my reputation preceded me and provided the perfect alibi for my nosiness. "Last year, I helped the police solve the murder of my boss in the Senate. Jack's murder is right up my alley." I tapped two fingers to the side of my head. "It's time to put the little gray cells to work." I looked at Judy expectantly. When she didn't get my reference, I said, "Hercule Poirot. He's always calling on his little gray cells to solve the crime." I tapped my temple again for emphasis.

Judy shook her finger at me playfully. "I knew I recognized your name. You're the former Senate staffer who almost became the killer's next victim. Isn't that right?"

"It was a close call. But I wouldn't let that stop me from trying to figure out who killed Jack." Prevaricating made me feel guilty but I had limited options to keep Judy from clamming up.

"Good luck on this one. I hope your detective skills are up to the task. Because there's a long list of people who wanted to see Jack dead."

I looked Judy squarely in the eye, gauging her reaction to my next question. "Are you one of them?"

I was expecting Judy to laugh me off, but she didn't. She grimaced, showing the fine wrinkles underneath her expensive makeup. Her eyes weren't angry. Instead, they softened, and for a brief moment, I thought I noticed a trace of moisture. If there were any tears for Jack, they had dried as soon as they had appeared. Judy straightened in her chair. "Absolutely not. Why would I kill Jack?"

"Weren't you in competition with him for years over the top staffing jobs on the Hill? His boss became Speaker and he claimed the most powerful position in Congress. If something happened to Jack, wouldn't the Speaker consider you as a replacement?"

Judy scoffed. "I seriously doubt it. There are enough people in the Speaker's orbit who will be standing in line for Jack's job. He doesn't want someone with loyalties to another member of Congress. More importantly, it's well known that I'm leaving the Hill soon."

That was news to me. "You have another job lined up?"

Judy started to gather her bag and coat, indicating she'd had enough pizza and enough of me. "I'm headed to K Street as a lobbyist as soon as the shutdown is over. I said I'd never do it, but I'm not getting any younger. Are you single, Kit?"

"I live with my boyfriend but we're not married." I didn't add the word "yet" to the end of the sentence. I had a feeling if I had, Judy would have lectured me about it.

She smirked. "That means you're single. So here's some advice from one unmarried D.C. gal to another." With her coat on and her bag slung over her shoulder, she touched both of my shoulders with her hands. "Don't wait too long to cash in your chits. There's an expiration date on goodwill in this town. I need to provide for my future. That's something only you can do for yourself."

Judy gave a small salute as a goodbye, and I watched her march toward the exit, already furiously typing messages on her iPhone. Without turning around, she called out, her voice echoing from the stairwell, "Don't forget. We need Maeve Dixon's support on this bill. I'm counting on you, Kit."

The faces of Dan and Maeve flashed through my mind. I took a deep breath to ease the tension. Who wasn't counting on me these days?

Chapter Twelve

As I walked back to the office, I thought about my conversation with Judy Talent, a woman who didn't suffer fools gladly. Given her success on Capitol Hill, that made perfect sense. No alibi had been offered and I hadn't prodded her for one. She'd dismissed a suggested motive by announcing her new lobbying job. Was that honesty or a clever diversion? I didn't have the luxury of eliminating anyone yet, so I'd keep my eye on Judy. The ambitious, Hill-climber side of Kit Marshall liked Judy Talent. My gumshoe alter ego still viewed her as a credible suspect.

I'd just opened my computer's email inbox when I felt someone watching me. I got a similar feeling in the early morning hours when Clarence fixated on me, hoping for a walk outside and his breakfast, in that order. This was like being ogled by a puppy dog, yet I doubted the eyes belonged to a canine.

"Dan, is that you?"

A belabored sigh broke the silence. "Yes, it's me. Do you have an update?"

I spun around in my office chair. "On the shutdown?"

He waved his hand dismissively. "I don't care about the shutdown. What about clearing Maeve's name?"

"How many times do I need to tell you it takes time to solve a murder? Especially a murder of someone I don't even know!"

"If she gets labeled a suspect, how will she ever win reelection?" Dan rubbed his forehead. "No one will hire me in D.C. after this mess. I'll be ruined."

That's nothing compared to serving thirty to life for a crime you didn't commit. Rather than issue a sarcastic retort, I held my tongue. Maeve had asked me this morning to go easy on Dan. She knew he was a fragile soul.

"Settle down. I'm making progress. But a mess like this can't be sorted out overnight."

Dan perked up, his eyes finally showing a glimmer of hope. "Progress? What have you learned?"

I didn't have the energy to explain the importance of multiple Speaker gavels. It was a nuanced clue and Dan struggled with subtleties. The gavel that killed Jack wasn't necessarily the same one Maeve had used on the House floor the night before the murder. Therefore, her prints might not turn up on the murder weapon. If that was the case, it could give Detective O'Halloran and the Capitol Hill Police pause. Reasonable doubt was all we needed.

"I can't reveal anything right now." Dan's face fell in disappointment. "Don't worry. A good detective never shows her cards." I reached out and gave Dan a pat on the shoulder.

He didn't seem comforted. "That's fine if you don't want to tell me what you've found." He paused, likely for dramatic effect. "If you've found anything. But my original instruction still stands. You need to find the real killer or look for another job."

I straightened up in my chair. "I talked to Representative Dixon this morning, and she urged me not to investigate. She thinks it's too dangerous."

Dan wavered for a moment before responding. "Of course

she'd say that. She doesn't want any liability if something happens to you. She can't live with the guilt. However, I have a clear conscience."

Dan's eyes bulged and he grimaced, reminding me eerily of Bert from *Sesame Street* when he got frustrated with Ernie. Angry Bert freaked me out. Irritated Dan had the same effect.

"I'd like some clarification. You don't give a rat's ass if I become collateral damage?" I rarely cussed in a professional environment, but Dan's boorish behavior justified an exception.

"That's crude, yet accurate."

I clenched my jaw and turned to face my computer. I glanced quickly to my right. Maeve's door was open. I didn't see a coat on the rack or her briefcase on the desk. She'd likely left for lunch. No luck that she'd overheard Dan reveal his true colors. I'd pegged him for a political lightweight, not a ruthless Hill denizen who cared about little else than his political career. I'd been dead wrong.

I had nothing further to say. My brain could barely process his callous remarks, yet I forced myself to open my email inbox. Returning to work would give the impression that his crazy remarks hadn't affected me. From behind, I heard Dan return to his office and shut the door.

The list of unread email messages wasn't quite as long as yesterday's. That meant the number of credible proposals to end the shutdown had diminished. Pretty soon, there would be three or four viable alternatives. Once Maeve endorsed one of them, there would be no turning back politically.

I spotted an email from Trevor with the subject "House Sergeant at Arms." Perfect. I clicked on the message. *Trent Roscoe has time to meet with you today at 3. Don't miss this opportunity.*

Trevor even managed to sound bossy in an email. That required real talent. I hit reply. *I'll be there.* Trevor appreciated brevity.

I glanced at my watch. It was a little after two so I had some time before the meeting with Trent. I was about to focus on a long email outlining yet another solution to the shutdown when Maeve walked into the office.

I stood up to greet her and smoothed my suit jacket. "Congresswoman, if you have a moment, I'd like to tell you about a discussion I had earlier today with the lead staffer from the Majority Leader's office."

She motioned for me to follow her. Inside her office, Maeve collapsed into her high-backed chair. Her face looked drawn, and her usually energetic aura had dimmed. Her demeanor had changed drastically since this morning.

What had caused this marked deterioration? "Excuse me for asking, but is there something wrong, ma'am?"

Maeve had been staring at the wall, temporarily zoned out. She snapped to attention when she heard my question. "I'm sorry, Kit. I just met with my attorney."

She couldn't throw a loaded comment out there without an explanation. Maybe it was rude, but didn't I have the right to know what was going on?

"What did he say?"

She sighed. "The police don't have any other suspects with the big three." She ticked them off with her fingers. "Means, motive, opportunity."

"What about the other people on the Hill who hated Jack? He had plenty of enemies."

"They'll explore those leads, but I'm clearly at the nexus of the investigation. My lawyer thinks the police might name me as a formal suspect and bring me in for questioning."

I gulped. "Today?"

She shrugged. "Who knows? I'm at their beck and call."

"Look on the bright side. The media hasn't caught wind of it yet. There's a chance we can keep this quiet, even if you're questioned."

Maeve brightened. "Perhaps my attorney could negotiate those conditions."

"Absolutely. That way, once they find the real killer, no one needs to know the police suspected you were involved with the crime."

Maeve and I chatted about the Majority Leader's policy proposal and Judy's pressure to lend support to it. The situation required delicate maneuvering. Maeve didn't want to support the proposal and then get hauled downtown as a formal suspect in Jack's murder. On the other hand, jumping onboard too late would earn her little political favor with the powers that be. One more day of delay wouldn't hurt, so we'd evaluate the situation again tomorrow afternoon. As I reminded my boss, political decisions were never made quickly. In an era of contentious politics, both parties routinely procrastinated.

Unlike my congressional colleagues, I had no time to waste after wrapping up with Maeve. The House Sergeant at Arms office was appropriately located inside the Capitol itself, so I needed to boogie to make it there by three. After clearing the security checkpoint, I hustled through the underground passage connecting the Capitol to the House of Representatives office buildings.

The Cannon Tunnel was the perfect spot for a moving walkway system, but such modern amenities had not appeared yet in Congress. The tunnel always made me think of an aging airport. Those of us who walked it on a daily basis found its gray, industrial appearance uninspiring. People moved swiftly on both sides of the passage under harsh lighting, usually engaged in blatant wheeling and dealing. Staff briefed their bosses en route to an important vote, lobbyists jogged to catch up with the House member they needed to solicit, and tourists clogged the artery while gawking at politicians they recognized from cable television. Adding to the chaos was the long line of paintings covering the tunnel's walls, all winners from an annual congressional art competition featuring the best work of high school students across the country. Most visitors stopped to admire the impressive artwork or find the canvas from their congressional district. It often required the antiquated skills of an expert "Frogger" video game master to negotiate the series of obstacles in one's path.

Luckily, the shutdown had decreased the typical pandemonium of the Cannon Tunnel to a dull roar. After crossing into the Capitol, I quickly found the door labeled "House Sergeant at Arms" and pushed it open. Preoccupied with finding the correct location, I'd neglected to strategize for my meeting. Trevor's contact was the purportedly attractive Trent Roscoe, whose boss was Gareth Pressler. Jack and Gareth had gone to war in the press over the security in the Capitol complex. With little love lost between the two of them, Pressler seemed like a man with a plausible motive to kill Jack.

After providing my name to the assistant sitting at the front desk, I grabbed a seat in the small waiting room and checked my iPhone for messages. I had just clicked on a new email when I heard footsteps in the adjacent hallway.

Meg and Trevor hadn't exaggerated about Trent Roscoe. He was in his late thirties or early forties, but the years had been kind. He had a different kind of appeal than what I usually found attractive. He was ruggedly handsome, with military-style cropped brown hair, a square jaw, and the faint remainder of a tan. Although he was dressed in a nondescript black suit, I could tell he was in terrific shape. His pale yellow button-down shirt hugged his chest, showing off a chiseled upper body and trim waist. The soft, muted colors of his tie provided the perfect accent to his outfit. A guy like Trent could wear pastels and get away with it because he simply radiated testosterone.

When I stood to greet him, I might have been dreaming, but I thought he gave me a once-over. If so, it didn't last for more than a second. He immediately extended his hand. "Kit Marshall, I presume?"

Maybe I was cold—the Capitol wasn't the warmest building in the winter—but when I touched his hand, a warm sensation entered my fingers, ran up my arm, and then traveled throughout my body. I looked into his eyes briefly and he smiled. Had he felt it, too?

Then his expression turned quizzical. He'd asked me a question, after all. "That's m-me," I stammered. *Nice move, Kit.* Always the queen of suave. *Cosmo* could use me as a case study illustrating how not to behave around the opposite sex.

Trent didn't bat an eyelash at my awkwardness. "Let's head to my office so we can chat," he said.

He led me down the hallway into a very small room with only a desk and one chair. It wasn't a broom closet, but it was darn close. I squeezed past the door and slid into the available seat. He laughed at my obvious attempt to fit into the tight space. "I apologize. I realize this isn't the Oval Office."

"No worries. I've never had a private office on the Hill, so I'm insanely jealous of your real estate."

He nodded. "I'm lucky Gareth decided I could have this space. Since I frequently conduct meetings about the security of the House, he thought I should have an office with a door."

How many people could discuss the security of the House in this office at one time? A multitude of staffers might be interested, but they'd have to schedule individual meetings.

"I appreciate that you're willing to meet with me," I said. "Trevor and I worked together in the Senate before he left to become a lobbyist."

Trent nodded. "When I read Trevor's email that his friend needed my help, it was a no-brainer. Any friend of Trevor's is a friend of mine."

Times had definitely changed. Trevor hadn't exactly been the social butterfly of the Senate. He must have undergone a drastic personal makeover to succeed at his new job. The bright lights of a movie marquee flashed before my eyes: *The Wolf of K Street.* It had a nice ring to it.

"How did you meet Trevor? I wouldn't think he'd have much dealings with House security."

"There's no immediate tie. But as a lobbyist for a big defense company, Trevor needs to know everyone on the Hill. Quite a few of our employees in the Sergeant's office are former military. That's another reason for Trevor to develop a connection with our folks."

With the killer bod and buzzed haircut, Trent looked like he'd served in the military. "Are you a veteran?"

To my surprise, Trent shook his head. "Afraid not. I was in the Secret Service for a while, but an old injury prevented me from continuing work in the field. I heard through the grapevine the Sergeant at Arms wanted to make hires with a law enforcement background. Before you know it, I'm working in the House of Representatives." Trent's smile spread from ear to ear.

Not too many people these days boasted they worked for Congress. "You must really like your job."

The grin still plastered on his face, Trent said, "I love the mission. We're here to protect the elected members, staff, and everyone who visits the Capitol complex. It's a big responsibility. Who wouldn't be excited?"

Trent's enthusiasm struck a familiar chord. "In my experience," I said, "staff work on the Hill for a variety of reasons. With all the political nonsense that goes on, sometimes we forget the bigger goal of public service."

Trent's eyes lit up. "I couldn't have said it better myself." His line of sight drifted to my left hand, which was resting on the edge of Trent's desk. He quickly averted his gaze when he realized I'd caught him checking out my ring finger.

No need for another awkward moment. It was time to get down to business. "I wanted to meet with you because my boss had mentioned there was controversy concerning the level of security in the Capitol and House buildings. We have a lot of North Carolina constituents who visit our office and she'd like to know if any changes are planned." It was a load of bunk with a grain of truth, but I needed to get Trent talking about the hullabaloo between his boss and Jack.

"Calling it a controversy is an understatement. Congress is a top terrorism target, and the Sergeant at Arms is responsible for the safety of those inside these buildings. We need to make sure we have the right protocols in place to guarantee security. Unfortunately, many of our elected members of Congress don't want to impede the flow of visitors in the chamber."

"I think I read a newspaper article about that man who was murdered, Jack Drysdale, and someone who leads your office. Didn't they disagree about this issue?" I asked innocently.

"Yes. Luckily, the papers didn't report half of it. Let's put it this way: there was no love lost between Drysdale and my boss, Gareth."

Now we were getting somewhere. "Why do you say that?"

Trent sighed. "Drysdale fought with Gareth about implementing tougher security protocols. They weren't able to arrive at a sensible compromise. Instead, their meetings usually ended up in shouting matches, with Jack storming out of Gareth's office."

"Sounds serious. How did you negotiate that land mine?"

"I didn't. Those decisions are above my pay grade. But I listened to Gareth complain after the meetings."

There was a tap at the door. Trent said loudly, "Come in."

I scooted my chair as far away from the door as I could so it could open. A middle-aged man appeared. He seemed surprised Trent had a visitor. "Don't forget we have that meeting about identification badges in a few minutes."

Trent's demeanor changed instantly. He straightened up in his chair, all business. "I will be there. Sir, this is Kit Marshall from Representative Maeve Dixon's office. She wants to learn more about House security procedures. Ma'am, may I introduce you to the Deputy Sergeant at Arms, Mr. Gareth Pressler."

Ma'am? Wasn't I at least a "miss"?

Before I had a chance to speak, Pressler said, "What does Representative Dixon want to know about security? Is there a problem I should know about?"

"No. I mean, no, sir. She's a freshman member of Congress and we want to know about any proposed changes to tourist access or visits to the Capitol."

He stared at me intently. "I'm always available—the Sergeant at Arms is as well—to answer questions from members of Congress. We find it's better to deal with the members directly on this issue. Staff don't always act in their bosses' best interests when it comes to security."

I was about to give Gareth Pressler a piece of my mind, but Trent cut me off. "Thank you, sir. We were just finishing our conversation. I'll see you in a moment."

Pressler took the hint. He nodded curtly in my direction and closed the door behind him.

"I'm sorry about Gareth. Since his disagreement with Jack, he doesn't think highly of congressional staff."

"No problem. One more question. Is the Sergeant at Arms office involved with the Drysdale murder investigation?"

"The Sergeant himself serves on the board for the Capitol Hill Police. So he's staying informed at that level. Even though we're law enforcement within the Capitol, we're leaving the detective work to the trained investigators."

"Makes sense. Thanks again for meeting with me. My boss might have more questions down the road about this security business." He hadn't seemed to notice that my ostensible reason for visiting with him had never been satisfied. I hadn't learned anything about their security procedures. I had learned some valuable information related to my real objective, however.

Trent and I both stood up, and he came around to my side of the desk. He placed his hand lightly on the small of my back to guide me toward the door, which was completely unnecessary since only three feet separated my chair from the exit.

"I'm sure we'll stay in touch," he murmured.

I felt the heat of embarrassment traveling upwards from my neck. If my face was as red as I imagined it was, Trent paid it no mind. The last thing I saw before he shut the door behind me was a sly smile accompanied by a slow, sexy wink.

I raced out of the office suite into the first-floor hallway of the Capitol. What had just happened? Sure, I wasn't the most experienced object of male admiration, but I'd been around the block a few times. Trent Roscoe had definitely put the moves on me. I took several deep breaths to clear my head.

Almost without thinking, I rummaged through my purse to find my iPhone. After swiping it on and entering the password, I touched the "Messages" green icon in the top left corner. My last texting conversation with Meg was never far from the top of the screen. I started typing furiously in the blank window. How did I explain what just happened in a text? Maybe Meg knew more about Trent Roscoe than she was letting on.

Trent was interesting. What's his deal?

The three dots flashed, indicating Meg was replying.

He's cute & single. No more to know :)

I'd need to talk to Meg later to get her reaction. I didn't have a moment to spare the rest of the day if I wanted to make it to the Top Dog party on time.

Then I noticed Meg was typing another message. It appeared a few seconds later.

Trent is least of your troubles. Hill Rat broke story about murder :o

Damn Meg and her emoticons. I wasn't sure what that last one meant. Surprise? Shock? I picked up the pace back to the office and fired off one last question to Meg.

Is it bad?

I was hitting my stride, dodging members and staff out for a leisurely walk through the Cannon Tunnel, when my phone dinged. Meg had responded.

Fraid so :(

Not a good sign.

Chapter Thirteen

I BRACED MYSELF for the inevitable chaos that would assault me in Representative Dixon's congressional office suite. I imagined Dan crying, Maeve yelling, or even the reverse. Instead, complete silence. After depositing my purse on the desk, I did a 360 to see if anyone else was around. That's when I heard soft voices from the congresswoman's private office.

I knocked on the door, and Maeve instructed me to enter. She was seated behind her desk with the phone receiver to her ear. Dan was sitting across from her, so I took the chair next to his.

He leaned closer. "She's on the phone with her lawyer."

"Is this about the Hill Rat story?"

Dan nodded.

"I haven't seen it yet. I just heard about it a few minutes ago after leaving a meeting in the Capitol."

Dan pulled his iPhone from his suit jacket pocket, swiped it on, and handed it to me. I recognized the familiar icon from his blog page—a sketch of a rat with the Capitol dome behind it. The rat wasn't cute like Chuck E. Cheese or the characters from Disney's *Ratatouille*. It was menacing, with sharp teeth and red eyes. Its ugly tail was curled tightly around the top of the Capitol dome in what looked like a stranglehold.

I scrolled down to read the story. Hill Rat's blog entries were rarely long, and this one fit the form. He or she usually got right to the point. Hill Rat explained that Representative Maeve Dixon from North Carolina had discovered the bludgeoned body of Jack Drysdale yesterday morning. Due to her recent public tiff with the victim, Dixon was a prime suspect.

I closed my eyes briefly and rubbed them. It had only taken two sentences to ruin my boss's career.

Considering Dan's insensitive comments earlier today, he was the last person I wanted to consult about this nightmare. But Maeve was still on the phone so I had no other option.

"Given this mess, shouldn't we try to put our press secretary on active status?"

"I mentioned that to Maeve. She's being told by the Speaker to keep her staff at a minimum during the shutdown. He wants Americans to understand it's not business as usual. She also didn't think her lawyer would want her or the press secretary talking to the press."

"Why aren't the phones ringing off the hook?"

Dan chuckled nervously. "After I showed Maeve the story, she told me it was time to hunker down and take cover. She must have remembered her military training. That included locking the door to the office, lowering the blinds, and disconnecting all the phones."

"That's fine for now, but I'm not sure it's a strategy we can use indefinitely."

"We most certainly can."

We both turned our attention to our boss, who had just hung up the phone. "Detective O'Halloran would like to question me tomorrow afternoon at headquarters. I will comply with the request, with my lawyer present. Until this is resolved, it is counsel's recommendation that we stay absolutely silent about my involvement in this murder investigation. Do you both understand?"

We both nodded and murmured, "Yes, ma'am."

She stood up, leaned forward, and placed her hands on the desk. "That means no talking to the press, on the record or off the record. If you are asked about my actions, you will say 'no comment.' It's as simple as that."

"Congresswoman," I said, "what about the phones? They're disconnected now, but we'll have to plug them back in soon, right?"

She rubbed her chin as she thought about my question. "I suppose we can't run a congressional office without phone lines. We will plug them back in after five o'clock, which is later than most reporters' deadlines for print editions. When the phone rings, you will answer, provide the 'no comment' response, and then hang up."

Dan's face had turned ashen again. All brightness had vanished, drained by the day's unexpected stress to a zombie-like pallor. If Dan got any whiter, he'd vanish.

When Dan didn't respond, I piped up. "Don't worry. We'll take care of the calls after five."

She gave us a curt nod. "I know I can count on both of you. The press might get wind of my trip to the police station tomorrow. You might want to make yourselves scarce. I'm sure enterprising reporters will be camped outside the door to see if they can pick up a juicy tidbit."

A day away from the office meant more time for sleuthing. Maeve must have noticed the change in my expression.

"Kit, I know exactly what you're thinking. I doubt that anything I say will keep you from investigating this murder. Please keep in mind that I did not kill Jack Drysdale. That means the person who did murder him is on the loose and might even think he or she got away with it. So be careful."

I gave her a mini-salute with two fingers. "Will do."

Maeve turned to Dan. She hesitated before giving him

instructions. "Dan, try to remain inconspicuous and out of the way, if you can."

"Don't worry, boss. I'm really good at that."

For once, I completely agreed with him.

Chapter Fourteen

UPON RETURNING TO my desk, I took a precious moment to clear my head. We couldn't have suppressed Maeve's status as a suspect indefinitely. It was pure luck her name had been kept out of the press this long. Hill Rat's exclusive also didn't surprise me. This was the Rat's typical modus operandi, namely an exclusive yet salacious tidbit that had the potential to ruin reputations, embarrass public officials, and even change political outcomes. The suspicion surrounding Maeve Dixon hurt her personally and the constituents she represented in North Carolina since she wouldn't be able to participate in the upcoming policy debates in Congress. But it also had the potential to weaken the entire party as it tried to negotiate favorable terms to the shutdown.

A quick time check confirmed I had twenty minutes before we'd allow the phones to ring again. Attending the Capitol Canine awards ceremony tonight was low on my priority list, but where else could I possibly meet Jordan Macintyre, Jack's grieving spouse? Even though D.C. social etiquette often eluded me, it was likely bad form to own the dog that won Capitol Canine and then not show up for the party.

I signed on to my computer and clicked on the contest website. Sure enough, Clarence was still in first place. Voting closed at five. Barring some last-minute flurry of voting, Clarence was headed to victory. But would Jordan Macintyre put his grief aside for the evening and attend the party? After locating the number for Capitol Canine's publicity contact, I grabbed my cellphone and placed the call.

A female voice answered on the second ring. "Christy from Capitol Canine. Are you a reporter looking for press photos of the dogs?"

Her question caught me off guard. "Um, no. My name is Kit Marshall, and I'm the owner of Clarence, who's participating in the contest."

She squealed, conceivably in delight. Was this my Andy Warhol moment, or more specifically, Clarence's fifteen minutes of fame? Visions of his adorable face on a package of Purina Dog Chow danced before me.

"Congratulations! The contest isn't over yet, but it's looking very good for Clarence."

Absent the pressure to solve a homicide in the House, I would have found Christy's enthusiasm infectious. Given the circumstances, faking it was the better option. "Great!"

To my ears, my response sounded forced, but the woman on the other end of the line didn't seem to notice. "What time will you arrive tonight with your little champion?"

"I'll try to be there by six thirty, but that's not why I called. Is Jordan Macintyre going to attend the party tonight?"

Christy's voice softened. "Isn't it terrible? We are so sad here at Capitol Canine. Jack was a big supporter of the contest. He and Jordan secured many of our sponsors and helped raise money for our charities. Did you know Capitol Canine benefits several rescue dog organizations in the D.C. area?"

I vaguely remembered reading about the worthy financial goals of the contest. As much as I supported the noble cause, I really needed to determine whether Jordan had decided to make an appearance at tonight's event. I tried again. "That's tremendous. Will Jordan be there tonight to present the charity checks?"

"Oh yes, he'll be there. Before we announce the winner, we'll pause for a moment of silent reflection to memorialize Jack. Did you know both of them?"

This was my opportunity. "I only met Jack once, but I'd like to pay my respects to Jordan. Can you introduce me?"

Christy responded instantly with gusto. "Of course. He'll want to meet Clarence." She quickly added, "You, too!"

I got the drift. I'd play second fiddle to Clarence tonight. That was fine with me, especially if the "little champion" could help me interrogate Jordan without drawing too much attention.

After telling Christy I'd track her down soon after my arrival, I hung up. My phone dinged a few seconds after the call ended. It was a message from Doug, asking for the address for the event. I reminded him he should arrive with Clarence by six thirty. Then I copied the address and pasted it into a new text to Meg. Besides the cute dogs, Capitol Canine's allure was primarily social. Meg loved attending soirees featured in the Capitol Hill newspapers, and this one would be front and center.

Ping. I glanced at her response.

I really should stay here and work on the investigation.

I checked the clock. Five minutes before we had to turn the phones back on. I thought for a moment before answering. Before Meg had a boyfriend, I could usually convince her to join me at almost any event on the Hill if I promised her I'd heard attractive men were planning to attend. That argument didn't work quite as well now that she was attached.

There's free drinks and pizza.

My iPhone remained inactive for a long moment. Then the three dots appeared.

I'll meet you there.

Meg's valuable assistance in our previous murder

investigation had been based largely on her remarkable ability to wrap the opposite sex around her pinky finger. Jordan wasn't interested in women, so Meg would have to devise another angle. Meg's resourcefulness continually exceeded expectations, so I had no doubt she had other tricks up her sleeve.

At five o'clock on the dot, Dan turned on the phones. The calls didn't stop for a solid hour. The fervor diminished as time went on because reporters undoubtedly let each other know that the Dixon office had offered "no comment" to every single inquiry. After Dan heard I needed to leave at six fifteen to interrogate a possible suspect, he shooed me out of the office with the warning, "Don't come back until you know whodunit." Not deigning to respond, I grabbed my purse and coat and headed outside to find a taxi.

I gave the cabbie the party's address and we sped off down Independence Avenue toward the adjacent Penn Quarter neighborhood. Located near Chinatown, the east end of the city remained one of my favorite haunts. Home of Ford's Theater, the Newseum, the Verizon Center, the Shakespeare Theatre, the Spy Museum, and the National Portrait Gallery, this area of the District bustled. The numerous attractions supported a wide variety of restaurants, ranging from high-end contemporary Indian fare to popular chains. Penn Quarter resembled the urban core of other major American cities. Washington D.C. had its advantages, but it was a government town. With its flashing lights and busy nighttime sidewalks, the five blocks of Penn Quarter provided a glimmer of New York. Even the most devout politico needed a break from the inspiring monuments and stately federal buildings, and this part of town helped satisfy those urbane desires.

The driver turned his head sideways to glance in my direction. "You work on the Hill?"

I'd been fiddling with my phone, looking for a text from Doug indicating he and Clarence had arrived. I muttered a barely audible "yes" in response.

"That's something about the female congressman killing the staffer. Did you know the guy who got whacked?"

He had my attention. "What did you say?"

"Didn't you hear? Some woman in Congress murdered the guy who works for the Speaker. Or something like that."

"Where did you hear that?"

"It's more like where didn't I hear it. All the talk shows have the story." He motioned toward the radio in his cab, which was set on a popular station for local news.

We were almost at the destination. After swiping my credit card and gathering my things, I piped up, "You shouldn't trust the media."

I opened the door and thrust one foot on the sidewalk. Over my shoulder, I heard his final retort. "Lady, I don't believe half the stuff I hear. All I know is if they don't end this shutdown soon, more bodies are going to pile up."

I heaved myself out of the taxi, shut the door, and watched it speed away, praying his prophecy wasn't true.

Chapter Fifteen

A FANCY CONSULTING firm had donated its office space to host Capitol Canine's festivities. After exiting the elevator, I didn't need to make sure I had the correct suite. A cacophony of excited barks traveled the length of the hallway. The entrance had been decorated with photos of the dog contestants. Clarence's cute mug was in the center of the puppy collage. Someone had pasted a crown on his head, ostensibly in anticipation of the big announcement scheduled for later this evening.

About ten dogs had already arrived with their owners. A *National Geographic* documentary I'd watched over the summer explained that domestic dogs exhibited the widest variation in size and physical characteristics of any mammal. The motley crew in attendance certainly attested to that fact. There was a Scooby-Doo look-alike Great Dane, a sizable chocolate Lab, a sturdy American bulldog, a petite Yorkie, and a slightly overweight dachshund. The remainder, I was glad to see, appeared to belong to Clarence's polyglot category, affectionately known as "mutt."

I spotted Doug and Meg in the corner of the room. Doug

had put Clarence's harness on him, and he was gripping his leash tightly. I waved from across the way and walked over to join them. Their personalities being on opposite ends of the spectrum, Doug and Meg weren't best buddies. Doug was as cautious as Meg was impetuous. Doug preferred quiet evenings at home with his history books, and Meg never met a happy hour she didn't like. Doug happily ate vanilla ice cream, and Meg tried every flavor before settling on Caramel Sutra with a twist of Bohemian Raspberry. The contrasts were endless and often presented entertaining challenges when we hung out together.

If Meg and Doug had been trading barbs, Clarence looked no worse for wear. Seeing me approach, he wiggled his butt enthusiastically. I bent down to pet Clarence on the top of his head and in return, he gave me a wet kiss on the cheek.

Out of the corner of my eye, I saw Meg recoil briefly at Clarence's lick. Meg liked dogs in theory, but not in practice. Her taste for expensive couture did not mesh well with dog hair and the occasional slobber.

After giving Clarence a few more scratches behind his floppy ears, I stood up. Doug was holding the dog close. "Why do you have a death grip on his leash?"

Doug grimaced. "Clarence is acting strangely. He seems overly excited. You don't want any problems here, right?"

I looked down at Clarence. His adorable face with big brown eyes stared back at me angelically. "There's nothing wrong with him. Why are you so nervous?"

Doug tended to exaggerate risk. "He's not used to being around so many dogs at once. I'm telling you we'd better keep an eye on him."

Meg was texting on her phone, clearly bored with our argument. Without looking up, she said, "Don't be such a stick in the mud, Doug. Let Clarence live a little. After all, it's his night."

Under his breath, Doug murmured, "Thanks for your input,

Dog Whisperer." He loosened his grasp of the leash, giving Clarence more room to wander.

Meg finally put her phone away. She smiled and gave me a hug. "How are you holding up after the Hill Rat debacle?"

Before I had a chance to respond, Doug said, "That's a tough break."

I sighed. "Yes. Hill Rat, the one and only, somehow figured out Maeve discovered Jack Drysdale's body yesterday." Then I turned to Meg. "Thanks for asking. Our office is still standing. For how long, I'm not sure."

Meg lowered her voice and inched closer. She motioned for Doug to do the same. "What are our assignments for tonight?"

Doug narrowed his eyes. "Assignments?"

Meg gently punched him in the arm. Clarence growled softly, not appreciating Meg's jostling of his owner. Meg shushed him. "Clarence, be quiet. We all have to pull together to solve this mystery before Kit's boss gets tossed in the slammer." As if paying careful attention, Clarence cocked his head and sat down in the center of the tight circle the three of us had formed.

"Thanks, Meg. I need to talk to Jordan Macintyre, the grieving widower. My instincts tell me he's going to want to meet Clarence, so Doug should stick with me." I checked out Meg's attire. She sported a fitted dark purple sweater dress with gray tights and knee-length black leather boots. The small bow tucked into the side of her blonde bob perfectly matched her outfit. She looked smart, sexy, and professional. In other words, a perfect fit for this crowd. "Is your boyfriend joining us tonight?"

Her sunny visage turned gloomy. "No, Kyle isn't coming. He has to work late due to negotiations in the Senate on the shutdown." Meg nervously fiddled with the amethyst ring on her right hand. I could tell she wasn't buying Kyle's excuse any more than I was.

"That's too bad. But it suits our purposes for solving this

murder. I think you need to turn on your famous charm tonight and see what you can find out in this room."

Meg stopped staring down at her hands and perked up. "Do you think that's dishonest since I have a boyfriend?"

Doug snickered. "Are you telling me you were honestly interested in every guy you flirted with before you met Kyle?"

Meg put her hands on her hips defiantly. "I never led anyone on, Doug. Besides, you of all people should not be offering relationship advice!"

That caught Doug's attention. "What is that supposed to mean?" His body language implied his question wasn't directed only at Meg. Sensing conflict, Clarence's ears flattened.

Time to intervene. "No harm meant, Doug." I put a hand on Doug's left shoulder and Meg's right. "Let's call a truce. Can we all just get along? Let's try to pick up a few clues at tonight's party."

Meg and Doug nodded their heads slowly. I reached down to pet Clarence and he gave me his right paw, a sign that he'd accepted the plan.

"Terrific. Meg, I think many of Jack and Jordan's friends will be here tonight. See what you can find out about motives and alibis." I briefly recounted my conversations earlier today with Judy Talent, Trent Roscoe, and Gareth Pressler.

Doug listened carefully. He was always reluctant to participate in my amateur sleuthing, but his superior intellect came in handy. "It sounds like you have no shortage of suspects with solid motives. How are you going to eliminate them?"

That was the million-dollar question. I shrugged. "Right now, I don't know."

Meg patted my shoulder lightly. "Don't worry. We've been down this road before. Something will turn up."

Clarence gave a small bark, either a gentle reminder we were there to celebrate his victory or a command to get to work. Either way, we parted ways to start the interrogations.

I scanned the crowd for Christy, whom I'd chatted with

earlier on the phone. I hadn't thought to ask her for a physical description. After surveying the people and the dogs in attendance, I spotted a woman bustling about and directing another volunteer about something. A nametag was stuck to the upper right-hand corner of her chest, but I couldn't make out the writing. I walked toward her for a closer look and confirmed she was my mark.

Timidity at a Washington D.C. party was verboten. I charged forward with my hand outstretched so Christy couldn't escape. "Hello, I'm Kit. We spoke earlier today about my dog, Clarence." I turned around and noticed Doug and Clarence hadn't followed, so I motioned for them to come over.

Clarence pulled enthusiastically. I followed his line of sight. Helpers were placing boxes of pizza on the table behind Christy, and the enticing smell had drifted across the room. One whiff spelled trouble. This was no ordinary cheese pizza—it was definitely pepperoni. Doug and I often joked that Clarence would kill for pepperoni pizza. In fact, whenever we had it delivered to our condo, Clarence routinely attempted to overtake the poor soul who delivered it. To avoid a scene, we'd put Clarence behind the closed bedroom door until we secured the pizza safely on the stovetop. Then we carefully shared one piece of pepperoni per slice with him. As long as we kept it coming at a reasonable rate, Clarence waited patiently. But if we missed his share, Clarence threw the doggie equivalent of a terrible twos tantrum. It wasn't a pretty sight.

I mouthed silently to Doug, "Pepperoni." He helplessly shook his head from side to side.

After shaking my hand, Christy smiled and bent down to pet Clarence. "This must be our champion!" She quickly clapped a hand over her mouth. "Whoops. You didn't hear that from me. It's not official until Jordan makes the announcement at seven thirty."

"Our lips are sealed. By the way, this is my boyfriend Doug, who also takes care of Clarence. Can you introduce us to Jordan before we start the program?"

"Of course. I'll take you over to meet him now. Follow me."

We fell in line behind Christy. Doug tightened his grip on Clarence's leash as we passed by the tables with the pizza. Clarence's nose wrinkled and his tongue passed over his teeth and lips in anticipation. When pepperoni was involved, Clarence meant business.

Jordan Macintyre stood between the food station and the bar. He was younger than his deceased husband by a decade, but strongly resembled Jack in handsomeness and style. Jordan looked like Washington's version of Christian Grey. Tall and lean, he wore a fitted suit jacket and pants that hinted at muscular definition. His tousled, dishwater-blond hair seemed to be the product of a professional stylist, yet, like the Beltway crowd, he wore conservative clothing. The dark rectangular frames of his Prada eyeglasses made him appear both shrewd and sensual.

Christy interrupted Jordan's conversation with another contestant and owner. The cute retriever/shepherd mix was edged out of the way in favor of the three of us. "Jordan, I know you want to meet this VID." She winked at me. "That stands for Very Important Dog." Out of the corner of my eye, I saw Doug roll his eyes.

Jordan turned in our direction and smiled confidently. "This must be Clarence and his owners, Kit and Doug. Welcome to the Capitol Canine family."

I was almost mesmerized by Jordan's sparkling blue eyes and his perfect teeth. He played for the other team, but a girl could still enjoy the view, right? I eked out a response, something like, "Nice to meet you."

Immune to Jordan's charms, Doug pushed past me and extended his hand. "We're sorry about Jack and wanted to offer our condolences."

"I appreciate it. This is a difficult time. We'd only been married for a few months…" his voice trailed off, and he reached behind his glasses with a handkerchief to blot a tear.

His grief seemed genuine, but he'd have to play the part of the grieving spouse convincingly, especially if he was the killer. "Were you at home when you found out what happened to Jack?" I asked innocently.

Jordan narrowed his eyes. "Yes, I was. Jack had left early for work. He always kept strange hours, and it was worse during a political crisis."

No alibi for Jordan. Clarence wiggled and whimpered. We'd have to move quicker. Surrounded by the pungent aroma of pepperoni, Clarence was losing patience. We needed to get over to that food table and give him a slice.

"Do you have any idea who might have killed Jack?" I reached down to pet Clarence in a feeble attempt to keep him under control.

Jordan peered down at me over his designer frames. "My husband had a lot of enemies, Ms. Marshall. It came with the territory."

I took in his stoic expression. Jordan was a man of few words.

Doug piped up, perhaps sensing I had struck out thus far. "Are you planning to stay in the D.C. area?"

"As a matter of fact, once the estate is settled, I'll be putting together investors for my latest venture. I hope to open a chain of canine restaurants."

Doug looked skeptical. "Did you say restaurants for dogs?"

Jordan smoothed his suit coat. "Yes, I did. There are eighty million dogs in the United States. That's a lot of untapped consumer potential."

As if on cue, Clarence barked. Jordan laughed. "See, I think Clarence is a future customer."

Only if pepperoni is on the menu. Clarence was clearly exasperated, but I had to keep pushing with Jordan. I might not get another chance to interrogate him about Jack's murder.

"What about Hill Rat? I heard Jack knew his identity. Did he tell you?"

Jordan pursed his lips. "You certainly ask a lot of questions.

Yes, Jack hated Hill Rat, and he said he'd figured out who he was. He never told me the name, but he did start referring to Hill Rat as 'he' and mentioned his identity was surprising."

"Did Hill Rat know Jack was going to expose him?"

"Jack hadn't confronted him in person yet. If he had, he would have told me. As I understood it, Jack floated the rumor he was getting ready to reveal his name to the congressional press corps. He said something about wanting to see if the rat took the cheese." Jordan blinked back a tear. "That was his idea of humor."

Doug broke in, "We appreciate the opportunity to talk with you. Once again, our sincerest condolences."

I whispered to Doug, "Let's grab pizza before Clarence explodes." We had just started to walk toward the food table when Jordan put his hand out to prevent me from leaving.

"Wait a second. Did I read on the Capitol Canine website that you work for Representative Maeve Dixon?"

Uh-oh. I'd hoped Jordan hadn't noticed my place of employment. Hill Rat's revelation earlier today fingered Maeve as a suspect. Now I was in Jordan's crosshairs.

He shook his finger. "I remember now. Jack mentioned you the night before he died. He said something about emailing all his contacts and telling them to vote for your dog so he could win favor with you and therefore your boss. I told him it was a ludicrous idea—that he shouldn't use Capitol Canine as a political pawn."

Doug offered, "Given the circumstances, would you like us to withdraw Clarence from the contest?"

I shot daggers at Doug. Sacrifice Clarence? Was he crazy?

"I don't really care which dog wins the contest. I do care who killed Jack," Jordan sniffed. "I haven't heard much from the police, but the media is reporting Maeve Dixon as the prime suspect."

Jordan glared at me. Just as Jack had transformed instantaneously in his office when annoyed, his husband stopped pouring on the charm. When I didn't respond immediately, he maintained the angry glower coupled with an uneasy silence.

Jordan wasn't going to let me end this conversation without an answer. A cardinal House of Representatives rule repeated itself in my head: when in doubt, always toe the party line. I took a deep breath and spoke in my calmest voice. "Representative Dixon sincerely hopes this murder is solved quickly. She has no further comment at this time."

Jordan's eyes bulged behind his fashionable glasses, and his cheeks flushed. "Typical Washington bullshit." He squared up and shook a defiant fist in the air. More of a lover than a fighter, Clarence immediately stood up from his reclining posture with an anxious look on his face. We'd denied him a pepperoni feast and now a random stranger had threatened violence.

Jordan turned to walk away, but not before a parting shot. "Mark my words. Whoever did this to Jack is going to pay." Again, he pumped his fist aggressively, presumably indicating he planned to deliver a mammoth knuckle sandwich to Jack's murderer. His last maneuver must have been the last straw for poor Clarence.

My dog sprang into action. With the grace of a hippo lunging at its prey in the Amazon, our normally mild-mannered puppy leapt into the air and lunged at Jordan's arm. His canine teeth weren't even visible. Maybe Clarence thought Jordan's fake punches in the air were a game. His substantial beagle snout hit Jordan in the side, which caused him to stain Clarence's white fur with the entire contents of the red wine he'd been nursing. In the midst of the confusion, Doug dropped Clarence's leash. As soon as Clarence realized he was free, he lunged toward the food table. All I saw was his chunky behind.

At the top of my lungs, I yelled, "Stop! He's going for the pepperoni!"

But it was too late. In one smooth move, Clarence put his front paws on the edge of the table, grabbed a pizza box with his teeth, and dragged it to the floor. In a matter of seconds, at least ten other dogs had joined him in the pepperoni feast.

Doug and I stared at each other, truly mortified at the mess Clarence had made. But the whole scene was so outlandish, I couldn't contain myself. The stress of the last several days must have done a number on my mental health. No one said a word, but I doubled over in unstoppable peals of laughter. Doug smiled nervously and whispered, "Kit, can you please stop? Everyone is staring at us."

I wiped the tears from my eyes, drew myself up, and gradually regained my dignity. Doug had recovered Clarence and secured his leash. Exceedingly pleased with himself, Clarence bounded over to me with his tail wagging triple time. I couldn't resist my own version of a parting shot. I reached down to pet my dog, who licked my hand appreciatively. While rubbing his ears, I remarked loudly, "We'll take that pizza to go."

Chapter Sixteen

"I'll have a glass of the Chardonnay."

The bartender asked dully, "Which one?"

"Cakebread, please. I need something buttery and oaky that fills up my mouth."

"You got it, sister."

Doug tossed me a disapproving glance. After the Capitol Canine debacle, we persuaded Meg to join us for a quick dinner and drink in Arlington. A District dweller, Meg rarely crossed the Potomac willingly. The three jurisdictions comprising the greater Washington D.C. metropolitan area each had their own flavor and culture. The denizens of each locale swore by their respective dominions and predictably attempted to persuade friends from the other two, usually in a futile effort, to visit them instead of venturing outside the motherland. The District/Arlington divide wasn't unbridgeable since the Orange line of the Metro connected them. Thank goodness Meg didn't live in a Maryland suburb. Due to the inconvenient lack of a subway transfer, I'd never see her outside Capitol Hill.

Within five minutes of Clarence's meltdown, the governing authority of Capitol Canine, led by Jordan Macintyre and the irrepressible Christy, decided our pepperoni-loving pooch wasn't worthy of the big prize. Citing a bylaw giving them power to override the popular vote and name the winner if a contestant "displayed behavior unworthy of the title," Jordan announced a golden retriever named Wonk as the "Top Dog" on Capitol Hill. Clarence did receive honorable mention. Given the circumstances, we concurred the consolation prize was generous.

The three of us piled into the Prius and headed for the hills. The hills of Arlington, that is. After depositing Clarence in our condo, we walked to the ever-popular Green Pig Bistro. No tables were available, which was par for the course since *Washingtonian* magazine named the French-inspired restaurant one of the top local eateries. Luckily, we claimed three open seats at the bar.

After ordering drinks and several appetizers, it was time to get down to business. With Meg on one side and Doug on the other, I summoned the gods of deduction. Turning toward my best friend, I asked, "Were you able to find out anything at the party?"

Meg stopped typing on her iPhone and shoved it into her purse. "Sorry. I had to text Kyle. I wanted to give him a heads up if my name ends up in a gossip column tomorrow related to Clarence's fiasco."

On my right flank, Doug rolled his eyes. He thought Meg's obsession with D.C. culture bordered on pathological. His assessment wasn't far off the mark, but without that influence from Meg, I'd have no idea what happened on the Hill after hours. Much to Doug's chagrin, intelligence wasn't everything on the Hill. More often than not, the political became personal, and vice versa.

After a moment of silence, she said, "Right, I almost forgot. Solving the murder. You asked me what I found out?"

Did Kay Scarpetta have to deal with such a lack of focus amongst her band of faithful crime-solving helpers? I doubted it. Since I was no Scarpetta, I waited patiently for my comrade to elaborate.

Meg took a sip of her bubbly. I needed to get the information out of her before she had any more drinks, particularly on an empty stomach. Meg's recollection abilities were inversely related to the amount of the alcohol she consumed.

"I would have extracted additional tidbits if Clarence hadn't imploded. That said, I was able to talk to a longtime buddy of Jack and Jordan's. He knows them from their fundraising efforts at the Human Rights Campaign." HRC was the leading gay and lesbian national advocacy group in Washington D.C.

Our food arrived, distracting Meg. The eatery's signature dishes looked almost too good to eat, except that all three of us were starving. Clarence had been the only one in our party to consume a pizza dinner. The lineup of buffalo pork ribs, kung pao sweetbreads, and pig tostadas made up for what we'd missed earlier.

After we filled our plates and enjoyed our first bites, Meg continued, "I can't remember the guy's name, but he was more than happy to chat with me about Jordan and Jack's relationship."

Doug interrupted her. "Why was he so forthcoming?"

Meg smiled. "He was wearing a Gucci suit from the winter line. The gray wool checks gave it away. As soon as I asked him about it, he was putty in my hands."

Many times I had borne witness to the fact that Meg's allure with the opposite sex transcended age and race. After this interaction, I could add sexual orientation to the growing list.

"After we commiserated about the federal government shutdown for a bit, I inquired about Jack and Jordan."

"What, specifically?" I asked.

Meg finished her drink and motioned for the bartender to pour her another. Her food-to-booze ratio was too low; thus her mental focus had officially lost its edge. Ironically, "Danger Zone" from *Top Gun* played softly in the background.

Meg popped the remaining tostada in her mouth and then took a long swig from her refill. "I couldn't be too obvious. I expressed my condolences about Jack and asked how Jordan was handling it."

Doug prodded, "And? What did he say?"

"Impatient, aren't we?" Her willingness to chide Doug indicated she was getting tipsy. "He said Jordan was holding up well. Then I asked why that might be the case."

The bartender cleared our plates and asked us if we wanted anything else. I was about to ask for the check when Meg pointed to the menu. "Yes, I'd like the banana bread pudding, please."

The look of astonishment on his face said it all. I knew what he was thinking. He didn't need to say it out loud. Where the hell did this woman put all those calories?

With an amused expression, he asked, "With ice cream and caramel?"

"Of course! No need to ask," Meg stated emphatically.

I giggled. Meg was truly one of a kind.

With an incredulous look, she said, "Why are you laughing? I read online this dessert was not to be missed!"

"I'm laughing because even though you're not a dog lover, you and Clarence have more in common than you think."

Meg tapped her chin with her finger, lost in thought. She said slowly, "You might be right. We both enjoy a delicious meal."

Doug listened without comment. He had a limited tolerance for inconsequential banter. He rarely intruded on my alone time with Meg, especially when drinks were involved.

Doug's growing impatience required an inquiring prod. "Meg, what were you going to say about Jordan holding up well under the difficult circumstances?"

"Right. The well-dressed friend said it was because he planned to use his inheritance from Jack for a new business venture."

"Do you mean the dog restaurant?" asked Doug.

As we chatted, waiting for dessert, Doug listened without comment.

Meg's banana bread pudding arrived. It smelled like a Yankee candle had just been shoved under my nose. Without a second's hesitation, Meg grabbed her spoon and dove in. After a few bites, she came up for air. I could barely make out what she was saying due to the considerable amount of caramel impeding her speech. "Delicious," she mumbled.

I cleared my throat. Meg gave me a sidelong glance and then asked sheepishly, "Would you like to try it?"

"Thank you." After stuffing a sizable helping into my mouth, I understood why Meg had been reluctant to share. The combination of banana, vanilla, walnuts, and caramel could only be described as a dessert lover's nirvana.

I pointed to the few remaining bites. "You need to try it, Doug. It's amazing."

Wrinkling his nose, Doug answered, "Smells a little too strong for my taste." Then he added, "Maybe Jordan can serve it in his new restaurant."

Meg nodded enthusiastically. "One of us should tell him!"

I licked the remnants of caramel from the corner of my mouth. "I doubt he'll be taking my calls after tonight. Meg, back to what you found out about the financing for the project… that sounds like motive to me."

Meg took the final bite and pushed the empty dish toward the edge of the bar. "You got it. That's exactly what I thought. According to my source at the party, Jordan had pitched the idea to several venture capitalists but none of them had bitten yet." She grinned. "His pun, not mine."

Doug generously placed his credit card on top of the bill. Meg tried to offer him cash, but he refused. Never mind that Doug never had to worry about finances, thanks to his old-money family and trust fund. Chivalry wasn't dead, at least at the Green Pig Bistro. After our bartender took his credit card,

Doug remarked, "If Jack hadn't died, Jordan's restaurant might never have come to fruition."

We gathered our coats to prepare for the frigid weather. Meg donned her vintage floppy cloche hat, leather gloves, and matching silk blend scarf. Only Meg managed to coordinate her winter accessories in addition to her outfit. My gloves were mismatched and my scarf had a tear, mostly likely because Clarence had mistaken it for a pull toy. I'd lost my hat a few months earlier when winter first reared its ugly head. Meg and I qualified as the contemporary female version of *The Odd Couple*.

After arranging her cute bob underneath the designer hat, Meg answered, "That's the general consensus. It would explain why Jordan isn't too broken up over Jack's death."

We walked Meg to the subway stop and said our farewells. She gave me a quick hug and motioned with her right hand to call her. When she saw my blank stare, she mouthed the name, "Trent Roscoe."

I placed a hand over my mouth so Doug wouldn't ask what was funny. In response to my reaction, Meg pointed a finger at me with a knowing look. "I want the scoop tomorrow," she whispered.

I jogged to catch up with Doug, who was speed-walking determinedly toward our condo building. The cold weather was one of his few motivations to move quickly. I knew better than to begin a conversation when he was fixed on seeking warmth so I waited until we were inside the refuge of our condo.

Due to the craziness of the afternoon, there had been no time to update Doug on the murder investigation. Before we settled on the couch, he poured us each a small glass of tawny port. A rare indulgence, a twenty-year-old dessert wine remained one of the most reliable ways to warm up on a cold winter's night. This particular selection, opaque and richly dark, had a full-bodied chocolaty velvet taste, a perfect ending to a day filled with trials and tribulations.

As Doug sipped his drink and sighed in contentment, I updated him on the case. With one notable exception, I spared no details, recounting the impromptu breakfast chat with Detective O'Halloran, my research mission at the Library of Congress, lunch with Judy Talent, the unfortunate conversation with Dan, the meeting at the Sergeant at Arms office, and then Hill Rat's breaking news.

Naturally I glossed over the meeting with Trent Roscoe, underplaying his looks and sexy vibe.

Doug mostly listened, offering brief congratulations when I mentioned what the librarian had found for me about the gavels. He rubbed his chin thoughtfully. "You're not going to like what I have to say about this."

Now it was my turn to take a generous sip of port. "Go ahead. I'd like to hear your reaction."

"I know there are clues pointing to a setup of your boss. Something tells me we're missing the obvious. Have you ever heard of Occam's razor?"

Bic and Gillette constituted the extent of my knowledge on razors. Rather than profess total ignorance, I shook my head.

"It's a principle from a fourteenth-century English philosopher. There's a lot of math behind it, but the general idea is the hypothesis with the fewest assumptions is often correct. Unnecessary complications should be shaved away because the simplest explanation is often the right one. Get it?"

Living with a professor had its ups and down. Lectures about the relationship between philosophy and razors counted as a negative. Nonetheless, I responded affably, "Keep going. What's your point?"

There was that eye roll again. This time, it was exasperation, not pure annoyance. "I was trying to break it gently to you. Maeve Dixon had the motive, means, and opportunity to kill Jack Drysdale. It's the simplest explanation of the crime."

Anger and despair welled up inside me. I didn't know if I wanted to scream or cry. Trying to keep my voice calm, I asked, "How could you say that my boss is a murderer?"

He tried to put his arm around me, but I moved toward the edge of the couch, out of reach. He seemed surprised at the rejection of his affection. "Kit, what's wrong? You asked me what I thought of the situation and I told you."

"I'm glad you weren't the head of the United States Capitol Hill Police last summer when Senator Langsford was murdered. Don't you remember? I was the prime suspect in that investigation because it was the easiest explanation."

Doug pursed his lips. "No, this situation is different. You were the obvious suspect because you discovered Langsford. You had no motive. That's not the same as what you're dealing with now."

He had a point, yet it still irked me that he thought Maeve was a murderer. "What am I supposed to do? Dan may be insane, but he's right on one account. If she's convicted, our careers are finished." I took another sip of port. "Besides that, I'll be emotionally scarred if it turns out I worked for a murderer."

"You should take the approach I've counseled all along. Don't get involved. Dan can't fire you, and if Maeve is found guilty, it won't matter because you'll be unemployed. Just stay out of it and be careful around her."

I realized I was gaping and shut my mouth. "You think Maeve could try to kill me?"

"Listen, I don't know. I'm trying to bring some logic to the table. All these other explanations seem convoluted to me. If you really don't think she did it, there is one way to prove she's innocent."

"Okay, Mr. Razor, or whatever you called it. How do I prove that she's not the murderer?"

Doug placed his drink on the coffee table and leaned toward me. "It's quite easy. Come up with an explanation with fewer assumptions than the scenario I offered. Once you're able to come up with that version of events, you've got your killer."

Another negative to living with a professor: his reasoning is always dead on. No pun intended, of course.

Chapter Seventeen

Repeated blares of the Sherwood Forest trumpet interrupted my peaceful sleep. I really needed to change my text message alert, which often elicited a Pavlovian response that involved throwing my phone across the room.

This time, I resisted the conditioned response and forced open an eye to identify the early-bird texter. Our bedroom was still pitch black. The glare from the smartphone forced me to squint until I could adjust to the unwelcome intrusion of concentrated light. One minute after six a.m. The last time pre-dawn text messages started flying, my boss discovered a dead body and became a prime murder suspect. This couldn't be good. Was it Maeve, in trouble again? Or Dan, perhaps sending me a threatening message about the fragility of my job if I didn't solve Jack's murder in the next fifteen minutes?

It was neither. It was Trevor.

Breakfast at seven at Pete's?

Was he insane? Pete's Diner, a Capitol Hill favorite, was situated one block from the Metro station and two blocks from my office in Cannon. No one appreciated a calorie-laden meal more than I (well, maybe Meg) but even the tasty coziness of

Pete's couldn't lure me out before daybreak in the middle of winter.

Too early. How about 8?

The three dots flashed as Trevor typed his response.

Late for me. OK.

The Pentagon crowd started their days notoriously early. Trevor must have adjusted to those hours after becoming a defense lobbyist last summer. I mentally scratched off that option as a future career move.

Both Clarence and Doug snored softly. As much as I wanted to drift back to sleep, the likelihood of that happening was the same as the government shutdown ending today. Roughly nil. Sighing, I threw off the covers and quietly closed the door behind me.

At least getting up before my alarm meant there was ample time for a custom-made coffee drink. I opened the refrigerator and scanned the contents. A bag of Italian espresso beans hid behind a box of takeout Thai. I'd bought these a week ago and never had the chance to try them. After tearing open the bag and inhaling the heady aroma, I emptied a cup of beans into our grinder and chose the appropriate setting. The aroma grew stronger as the espresso brewed. Maybe Clarence's obsession with pizza was understandable. The smell of pepperoni had the same effect on him as coffee did on me in the morning. I poured two dark shots into the steamed milk, added a spoonful of sugar, and headed to the couch to enjoy my java masterpiece.

I still had a few minutes before I had to get ready for the day. Under normal circumstances, catching up on the news about the shutdown would make sense. My current situation was anything but normal. Although Dan, with his hostile approach to his chief of staff duties the past few days, had exhibited all the charm of Jabba the Hutt, he was correct about one thing. Coming up with a workable deal on the shutdown meant squat if the police charged Maeve with Jack's homicide. While I hated to admit it, Dan had a point. Finding the real killer, or at least identifying a plausible suspect, was the task at hand.

To that end, I grabbed an old notebook and jotted down the facts thus far. Writing down what I knew about the case helped organize my thoughts. Doug's reasoning from last night was hard to ignore. Reluctantly, I listed Maeve as a suspect, along with Judy Talent, Gareth Pressler, and Jordan Macintyre. Upon reviewing my conversations with each of them, I confirmed Doug's rational conclusions. Each person had a good motive, but the hard evidence against Maeve was more substantial than the other three. Of course, there was another person to consider, but his/her status as a suspect posed even greater complications. Hill Rat had a terrific motive for wanting Jack dead. If Jack had gone through with his plan to reveal Hill Rat's true identity, the blog would be finished. No doubt Hill Rat was a great suspect. But without knowing his (assuming Jack was right) true identity, I was just Don Quixote, tilting at windmills.

What was my next step? I had a legislative directors' meeting at ten this morning. Despite the urgency to solve Jack's murder, I couldn't completely neglect my official duties. Besides attending that convo, nothing else warranted my immediate attention. What else could I do proactively? I turned back a few pages in my notebook.

The murder weapon remained the one piece of physical evidence that warranted further investigation. Maeve's status as the prime suspect wouldn't change as long as Detective O'Halloran believed her access to the gavel placed her in the most advantageous circumstances to commit the crime. My trip to the Library of Congress had raised the possibility that multiple gavels existed, but I needed to know more. Instinct told me another trip to visit the helpful librarian would arouse unwanted suspicion about my obsession with the Speaker's gavel. I'd have to figure out another way to dig up more information on the murder weapon. Since that tidbit about the crime hadn't made its way into the press yet, hopefully my sleuthing could fly under the radar.

A cursory check of the iPhone confirmed it was time to proceed with my morning duties. I showered and dressed, escorted Clarence outside for an abbreviated walk in the cold February air, greeted Doug as he awoke from his slumber, and shuttled out the door to face the lonely commute.

Pete's Diner was an anachronism on Capitol Hill, a surviving tribute to an earlier era when trendy restaurants operated by celebrity chefs didn't dominate the culinary scene. The luncheon menu offered a few unusual Asian selections and novel vegetarian options. Otherwise, Pete's was a greasy spoon frequently patronized by old-school pols who gladly eschewed the yuppie eateries of Pennsylvania Avenue.

I pulled open the door and scanned the two rows of seating. Trevor was seated at the booth farthest from the door. Ensconced in his newspaper, he raised a hand to indicate his presence without looking up to actually acknowledge my arrival. I hurried inside, sat down opposite him, and shrugged out of my winter coat.

"What are you reading?"

Trevor raised a finger to silence me.

"Please wait a moment, Kit. I'm nearly finished with a fascinating article about the threat of asteroids traveling near Earth."

I pressed my lips together to suppress the snarky retort that almost burst from my mouth. Trevor had summoned me to breakfast, after all. I didn't haul myself here to watch him read science fiction.

Clearing my throat, I motioned to the waitress for hot coffee. She obliged immediately. Although a no-frills establishment, Pete's prided itself on prompt service. Many of its Hill patrons only had a few minutes to enjoy their meal.

"Know what you want?" she asked.

I didn't need to study the menu. "Chocolate chip pancakes, thank you."

The waitress turned her attention to Trevor, who was still reading. "What about you?"

Trevor glanced up. He must have seen the irritated expression on her face because he promptly folded up the newspaper and placed it on top of his coat. "I'll have an egg white omelet with peppers and mushrooms and two slices of rye toast. No butter or hash browns, please." He handed her the plastic-covered menu and smiled.

To my surprise, she returned the grin. "Sure, Mr. Trevor. Coming right up."

My eyes widened. "How does the waitress know you?"

Trevor arranged his paper napkin neatly on his lap. "I often come here before spending a long day on the Hill." He adjusted his glasses, smoothed his suit jacket, and tilted his head toward the grill area. "I find it comforting."

"You never fail to surprise me, Trevor."

"No doubt. What else might be in store?"

"I'll just have to wait to find out. I like Pete's, too, but why did you ask me here for breakfast?"

Our meals arrived, along with a refill of hot coffee. I grabbed the bottle of Log Cabin syrup on the table and drenched my three pancakes.

Trevor cast a disapproving glance at my meal. "How will you enjoy the pancakes underneath that mountain of syrup?"

I deserved the comment but that still didn't make it less insulting. Leave it to Trevor to aggravate me in less than ten minutes. "If possible, I'd like to eat my pancakes without judgment. Now can you tell me why you asked me to join you this morning? I hope it wasn't to criticize my choice in breakfast foods."

"Certainly not. That's simply an added benefit. I wanted to learn the status of your informal investigation concerning the murder of Jack Drysdale."

I dipped my pancake in a pool of syrup. I would have liked a few more squirts, but I couldn't bear another smart remark from Trevor. "I wish I had more to report, like the name of the actual killer. Jack had a lot of enemies, and I can't seem to narrow down the list of suspects." I briefly recounted yesterday's interactions and the relevant details.

Trevor took a bite of his dry toast and chewed slowly. He wiped his mouth neatly before speaking. "You need more opportunities to question the suspects. You've only scratched the surface, I'm afraid."

"I agree, Trevor, but I'm running out of time. Detective O'Halloran is under pressure to solve this murder as soon as possible, and my boss fits the bill."

"What is your plan for today?"

"I thought I might try to learn more about the murder weapon."

Trevor perked up. "Which is?"

I forgot the gavel hadn't been included in the media accounts of the murder. I told him about my trip to the Library of Congress and the discovery about multiple gavels.

I could never finish an entire serving of chocolate chip pancakes at Pete's. The pancakes weren't huge but the syrupy sweetness mixed with the chocolate got me every time. At least the sugar and caffeine overload guaranteed I wouldn't fall asleep anytime soon. I pushed my plate away to indicate I couldn't ingest another bite.

Trevor listened intently. "Why not track the gavels to their point of origin? Then you can find out if they still make more than just one or two for a Speaker."

"Good idea, but for all I know, those gavels are made halfway across the country."

Trevor wrinkled his nose. "Doubtful. The Architect of the Capitol is responsible for the maintenance and construction of all congressional buildings. That includes the tradecrafts necessary for daily operations. This doesn't seem like something the Speaker of the House would outsource."

"How do you know all this stuff?"

Trevor waved his hand dismissively. "I acquire information using two different methods." He signaled with one finger, and then two fingers for emphasis as he spoke. "First, I read voraciously. Second, I ask good questions." He peered over his glasses. "If you continue to engage in these investigations, you may want to engage in both activities."

"I'll keep that in mind, Trevor. I'd still need to figure out where those gavels are made, even if it's within the Capitol complex."

The bill came, and we both threw down money for our meals plus a generous tip. Fortunately, stinginess was not one of Trevor's many off-putting personality traits. While I gathered my coat to prepare for the ten-minute walk to my office in the frigid weather, he surprised me by saying, "Don't go yet. Let me try to find an answer to your question."

He grabbed his phone, and after studying it for a few minutes, he put it to his ear. "Hey, Trent, this is Trevor. How goes it, man?"

My eyebrows arched. Did I just hear Trevor use the phrase, "How goes it, man?" He hadn't been joking when he said he'd been working on his people skills.

"Thanks for meeting with her yesterday. Hey, I have a quick question for you. I know this isn't in the Sergeant at Arms office, but is there a woodworking shop in the Capitol?"

Trevor listened to Trent's response with a fixed expression of concentration. "Got it, man. Thanks again."

How many other people did Trevor call "man"? He was almost like a different person. Kevin Spacey's infamous portrayal of Keyser Söze in *The Usual Suspects* came to mind. Which version of Trevor was real? After this performance, I wasn't quite sure. Forever his nemesis, Meg would be interested in this tidbit.

Trent must have added something before Trevor got off the phone. "Interesting. Good luck with that. See you around." He punched a button on his phone to end the call.

I placed my purse on my shoulder and edged toward the end of the booth. "Trent Roscoe, I presume?"

"You are correct."

Back to "normal" Trevor, whoever that was these days. "Does he know where the gavels are made?"

Trevor answered in a scolding tone. "You heard the conversation. I never asked him such a thing. Isn't his boss Gareth Pressler still a suspect? You don't want to reveal too much, Kit." He shook his head. "I can't watch over you like I did during the last investigation. You've got to be more careful in covering your tracks."

"You're right. I'll try to be more cautious. What did he say about a woodworking shop?"

Trevor stood up and I followed. "My instincts were correct. There is a carpentry facility in the Capitol. I'm sure you can locate it using HouseNet." Trevor was referring to the internal House of Representatives website that provided employees with directories and useful administrative information about the Capitol complex.

"I'll do that. Thanks for your help, Trevor."

I was just about to cross Second Street to head toward the Cannon Building when he caught my arm. "I almost forgot something important, Kit."

I turned around to face him. "What is it? It's almost nine, and I need to report for work."

"Trent told me he's going to ask you out for drinks tonight."

I gulped. Despite the cold, my face flushed. "As in a date?"

Trevor shrugged and responded with a question. "Isn't everything in life what you make of it?"

Chapter Eighteen

I didn't linger to discuss the details of Trent's romantic intentions. After muttering an awkward goodbye, I fled to my office and thought about Trevor's revelation. Yes, Trent had sent signals during our meeting yesterday. For a variety of reasons, I'd chosen to play them down, but now they had confronted me directly, like a car's glaring "check engine" light. Once the alert flashed on the dashboard, ignoring it was impossible. Trent's advances presented a similar call to action.

I couldn't deal with this conundrum alone. Immediately after clearing my building's security, I punched a text message to Meg.

Need to chat 911.

Our version of the Batman signal, the emergency designation was saved for crises requiring urgent consult.

Meg replied in less than thirty seconds.

Break in case?

Given the distress call, that would have made sense. This was a different type of predicament, but Meg would undoubtedly agree as to the gravity of the situation.

Not quite. Trent Roscoe.

Although Meg's office was located in another House building, I could practically hear her squeal of delight.

Lunch at Longworth?

I readily agreed to meet at the main House cafeteria. Meg would know exactly how to handle this problem. She received both wanted and unwanted male attention on a daily basis. It was foreign territory for me. Her help secured, I felt one hundred percent better about my dilemma. Although figuring out if Trent's interest fell in the "wanted" or "unwanted" category might require some soul-searching.

My high spirits plummeted the moment I rounded the corner of the main hallway leading to my office. I'd completely forgotten the journalists we'd dodged yesterday. They had returned today with a vengeance. Like a pack of hungry wolves, reporters had surrounded the area immediately outside the entrance to Maeve Dixon's congressional suite. A quick pivot reversed my course and I darted inside the nearest women's restroom to strategize and regroup.

Maeve's interview with the police was scheduled for later in the day. Given the press attention, she wouldn't be likely to venture into the office this morning. Instead she'd go directly to the station from her apartment building, hopefully with her lawyer in tow. That left only Dan.

Reluctantly, I texted him. He might not answer a phone call but hopefully he'd glance at an incoming message.

Are you inside the office now?

Standing inside a stall, I stared at my device, waiting for a response. Had it really come to this? When I first landed a job in Congress, I hadn't imagined it might necessitate hiding inside a public bathroom.

The three dots flashed. Dan had received my message and was composing a reply.

Yes. Help me. I'm stuck inside.

Before answering, I considered my options. It was almost nine thirty, and I had a legislative directors' meeting at ten in the Capitol Visitors Center. Why should I force my way past the reporters when I would have to force my way out in fifteen minutes to leave again? I fished around in my purse. I had a notebook so I could jot down any important information at the meeting. The only downside was lugging around my winter coat. I'd gladly make that tradeoff if it meant I could successfully dodge the bevy of reporters for now.

Dan needed to hunker down, and he wasn't going to appreciate it. A short, sweet reply would suffice.

Have meeting then lunch.

After sending the message, I added one more detail.

Important leads on case.

That wasn't a lie and maybe it would make him feel better about the abandonment.

I shoved my phone back in my purse and hightailed it out of the restroom. With many competing priorities, the weekly Democratic meeting for all legislative directors often had spotty attendance. Due to the shutdown, today's gathering would be an exception. Everyone wanted to know if the party's leadership had decided on a proposal to end the standoff. If I arrived a few minutes early, maybe I could chat with Judy Talent. Yesterday's pizza lunch seemed like an eternity ago. When we last spoke, she'd wanted Maeve Dixon's support for the Majority Leader's proposal. However, that was before Hill Rat's revelation about Maeve's involvement in the murder.

The Cannon Tunnel was nearly empty this early in the morning. Congress didn't espouse the "early to bed, early to rise" culture. The only fellow travelers in the tunnel were other legislative directors en route to the Capitol Visitors Center and caffeine-dependent staffers returning to their offices with steaming cups of coffee in hand. Before this morning, I'd never noticed the pipes delivering heat on the left flank of the corridor, slithering like two monstrous concrete snakes alongside the tunnel's travelers. The huge volume of people routinely masked the bleakness of the passageway. This morning, lacking the usual hordes, its industrial décor was laid bare. Crowds made it difficult to navigate, but the disguise provided by the masses was preferable to the unvarnished, naked version.

Instead of heading into the Capitol, I took a hard right at the end of the tunnel and entered the Capitol Visitors Center. The CVC, as it was popularly called, was built to accommodate the throngs of tourists who regularly descended upon Capitol Hill. Patriotic Americans and sightseers eager to visit the nation's legislature streamed in throughout the calendar year, especially in the summer months. Before the CVC's construction, navigating within the Capitol complex during June and July was nearly impossible. Demonstrating that it can act reasonably, Congress decided to build a massive 580,000 square-foot visitor center underneath the east side of the Capitol. The new facility provided a comprehensive educational experience for those who wanted to learn about Congress and its history, complete with films and exhibits. At least that was the "official" justification for the $621 million spent on its construction. Privately, everyone who worked in the Capitol complex celebrated the intentional displacement of the summer tourist onslaught.

Congress hadn't forgotten its own needs when it shelled out the small fortune of taxpayer money to build the CVC. It had included a congressional auditorium and a sizable number of meeting rooms. Since we had such a large group of legislative directors in the party (after all, we were in the majority), today's meeting had been scheduled for the auditorium. Normally, members of Congress organized important events in this space. Due to the shutdown, all official business other than solving the current crisis had been canceled. That freed up the auditorium for our staff meeting. Attendance ebbed and flowed, depending on the perceived importance of legislative business in any given week. Given that congressional inaction had caused the government to stop functioning, I predicted a heavy turnout.

After zipping past the CVC gift shop, I rode the escalator to the lower level and strolled through Emancipation Hall, the centerpiece of the CVC. Congress named the 20,000 square-foot central gathering space after the slave laborers who built the Capitol.

I'd walked through the CVC countless times, but normally I kept my eyes fixed on my iPhone rather than paying attention to the impressive feat of construction surrounding me.

Those in charge of designing the CVC had mimicked the architecture of the original Capitol Building. The sandstone pillars resembled the massive Capitol columns built over 150 years ago by enslaved craftsmen, and the marble for the floors was obtained from the same quarries that had produced the marble for the Capitol in the 1800s.

The twenty-foot plaster model used to cast the Capitol Dome's famous bronze Statue of Freedom welcomed visitors to Emancipation Hall. Other famous sculptures formed a border around the massive open space. I gave a silent salute to Montana's Jeannette Rankin, the first woman elected to Congress. Chief Washakie, a Shoshone Native American warrior from Wyoming, was unusual because portions of his statue were painted in color. And everyone loved King Kamehameha, who had unified the Hawaiian Islands. The gold and bronze of his regal attire drew a regular crowd of admirers who snapped photo after photo of the colossal figure.

I headed toward the corridor that led directly to the auditorium, breezing past several House meeting rooms and the appointments desk. I took a hard left and pulled open the big double door. At three minutes to ten, plenty of seats were already filled. This was no regular legislative director meeting. People were showing up en masse to find out what in the hell was going on. It's a myth that congressional staff know every detail about ongoing negotiations. In reality, Capitol Hill forms a hierarchy in which a select few understand exactly what is transpiring at any given time. The rest of us rely on our precious contacts to try to piece together the puzzle for our bosses. This meeting would provide direction for those staffers whose bosses hadn't been approached earlier by leadership for their input on the critical legislative proposals.

No aisle seats were available. *Damn*. Everyone always wanted an aisle seat at briefings like this. Boredom or a demanding boss often required a quick exit. Much like on an overseas flight in coach, aisle seats were a valuable commodity and therefore scarce. I squeezed past several colleagues who were too busy surfing their phones to make room for my passage. I finally wedged into an open seat and shoved my bulky coat under my chair.

As I fished through my purse to find my notebook, I felt the not-so-casual stare of the woman sitting next to me. She looked vaguely familiar, but with 230 other legislative directors in the party, I didn't know everyone by name. Her blonde hair had been straightened yet didn't quite behave perfectly, sort of like my brown mane. She wore boxy black frames conveying the message that she preferred to be viewed as intelligent rather than fashionable.

I'd finally located my notebook and a pen that worked when she cleared her throat. I turned to her and introduced myself, offering my hand. "I'm Kit Marshall and I work for Representative Maeve Dixon from North Carolina. I've seen you around but I don't know your name."

Smart-Not-Sexy smiled, but not too broadly. "I thought you worked for Dixon. Have you seen Hill Rat's latest posting?"

If she didn't realize I already knew what Hill Rat had posted yesterday, she wasn't fooling anyone with those smart glasses. But it wasn't good politics to alienate a friendly colleague. "Yes, we aren't commenting to the press about Representative Dixon's discovery of Jack's body."

I turned my attention to the front of the room. Judy Talent was milling around, smiling at familiar faces and shaking hands with others. The meeting was about to begin so this meaningless conversation needed to be wrapped up.

My next-door neighbor shook her head. "Not yesterday's post. This morning's."

I whipped my head around. Smart-Not-Sexy had captured my full attention. "This morning?"

She swiped open her smartphone and skillfully used two fingers to scroll down the litany of emails. She selected one and waited for it to bring up a web page in the phone's browser. Then she handed me her device. "I get notifications when Hill Rat posts a new blog," she explained. She kept talking as I enlarged the writing on the screen. "This one went up about ten minutes ago."

The meeting had come to order. Judy began her spiel summarizing the Majority Leader's proposal to fund the federal government. I'd focused on most of this information yesterday with her, although the bill might have changed since our lunch. Unfortunately, Hill Rat was the more pressing problem.

The title of the post was in big capital letters: HOMICIDE IN THE HOUSE. Underneath the headline, Hill Rat had kept it brief:

> The murder weapon in the Jack Drysdale killing has been kept under wraps … until now. Drysdale was bludgeoned to death with nothing less than the symbol of the House of Representatives itself, the Speaker's gavel. Who had access to the gavel prior to the crime?

Underneath the three-sentence post, there was a video link. I didn't want to interrupt the meeting but I needed to see what Hill Rat had posted. Flipping the phone to "mute" would have to suffice. No words were needed. The video was a five-second clip of Maeve Dixon, banging the gavel on the House floor the night before Jack's murder. Damn those C-SPAN archives!

Chapter Nineteen

FEELING A SUDDEN need to scream, I managed to remain silent as I handed the phone back to the staffer. She shot me a questioning glance. I mouthed the word "Thanks."

Maeve needed to know about this latest development, especially if she still planned to visit police headquarters today for questioning. Dan also needed to know, since the reporters camped outside the office were likely to increase both their numbers and volume. He'd have to handle that situation on his own. No way was I going back there. Images of rabid Capitol Hill reporters waving pitchforks and torches came to mind. It was better if we didn't provide them with someone they could try to interrogate.

Maeve replied quickly to my text informing her about Hill Rat's latest revelation. She agreed that returning to the office didn't make any sense and urged Dan to "stay put" as long as possible. Each of us was on our own.

Half-listening to Judy's information about the plan to end the shutdown, I scanned the auditorium. Most people were staring at their phones while ostensibly heeding the message from congressional leadership about the way forward. No doubt about it; Hill Rat's posting would go viral. Maeve Dixon's tenure as an influential legislator in Congress was about to be cut short. The only way to stop the inevitable progression leading to total career destruction was to find the real killer. Hill Rat had given me a shove in the rear. I had to find the killer *now*.

I was tempted to bust out of the meeting and resume my investigation. Under normal circumstances, listening to rapid-fire questions about the shutdown would have been enjoyable. More than anything, I loved figuring out the nitty-gritty policy details. Today's summit offered a veritable smorgasbord of wonkiness. But none of this mattered if Maeve couldn't prove her innocence. Despite the urge to split, I forced myself to remain seated; getting up in the middle of the meeting would draw even more attention. Besides, Judy Talent had a good motive to kill Jack Drysdale. She'd hated him, and her line about leaving the Hill didn't mean anything. She could turn down the K Street job in a second if the Speaker asked her to serve as Jack's replacement. Given how busy she was, I might not get another chance to talk with her. After the meeting concluded, I would have the perfect chance to pounce, especially if I waited patiently for the opportunity to present itself.

The questions concerning the finer points of the proposal kept coming. It was a quarter past eleven before the attendees collectively decided they'd heard enough. Judy surveyed the crowd. With her fingers counting off the numbers, she bellowed, "Going once, going twice." She paused. When no one interrupted her, she concluded, "Sold! Congratulations, team. We have an offer to end the government shutdown." Judy flashed a radiant smile and turned to chat with one of her dutiful acolytes.

Along with the masses, I filed out of the row of seats. Judy was yakking up a storm, and a receiving line had formed. Some people might have legitimate questions about the legislation, but the bulk of the posse surrounding her just wanted a moment of face time. Judy was the Capitol equivalent of a high school prom queen.

I took a seat a few rows away from the confab and buried my face in my iPhone. If Smart-Not-Sexy knew about Hill Rat, it was a safe bet most of those in the room did, too. In ten minutes, the crowd had dwindled. After Judy took care of the remaining devotees, I could ambush her without drawing too much attention. I was about to make my move when a legislative director from another House office appeared next to me.

"Kit, is that you?"

I looked up. His name was Stuart and he worked for another Southern member in the Democratic caucus. There weren't too many of us from the region so we'd become acquainted. I groaned inwardly. Stuart was a nice enough guy, a well-meaning nerd of sorts. This was not the time for small talk.

"Hello. I'm sorry, I can't talk right now. I'm reading an important email from my chief of staff." Mentally I crossed my fingers. I didn't typically resort to lying. I'd say an extra Hail Mary before bedtime. Although I wasn't a churchgoer, old habits die hard.

Stuart ignored my excuse. He placed his hand gently on my shoulder. "Don't worry. I'm sure another House member will hire you after the dust settles."

What did he say? I stood so he'd have to remove his hand. Keeping my voice even, I said slowly, "I'm not looking for another job, Stuart."

Stuart nodded. "I agree with your strategy. Loyalty is crucial around here. You shouldn't jump ship until the very last minute." He laughed nervously. "Of course on the *Titanic*, that meant getting sucked under."

The image of Leonardo DiCaprio hanging onto an iceberg jumped into my head. Before the *Titanic* theme song could form an earworm, I answered Stuart, a little louder this time. "Maeve Dixon didn't kill Jack Drysdale. So while I appreciate hearing your views on loyalty, it's not necessary."

I shoved my iPhone in my purse and stormed past Stuart, who appeared stunned at my response. As I hurried to the front of the room to catch up with Judy, he yelled after me, "Don't worry! I'll let you know if we decide to hire in our office!"

Stuart's riposte was loud enough to alert Judy. As I marched toward her, one of her twentysomething lieutenants whispered in her ear. Her eyes widened. Stuart had ruined my surprise attack.

Judy smoothed her hair and extended her hand. "Hello, Kit. What can I do for you?"

After politely accepting her gesture, I gave her some good news that would hopefully put her at ease. "I spoke with Representative Dixon and she's willing to support the Majority Leader's proposal. She may have a few minor issues she'll mention to him on the floor, but in the end, she'll vote for it." I flashed my highest-wattage smile.

Judy's reaction wasn't exactly what I'd anticipated. Her face scrunched up into something between a forced smile and a grimace. She almost looked constipated. "I appreciate your willingness to follow up after our meeting." She fixated on me for a long moment. Then she tugged at my sleeve, pulling me several feet away from where her young minions were drifting about.

Judy squared up to face me directly. "I'm going to be honest with you. A day ago, I would have been fighting for Maeve Dixon's support on this bill. I might have even gone to my boss with your requests to change a few of the funding numbers." Judy shook her iPhone with the Hill Rat blog displayed on the screen. "But today, thanks to her purported involvement with Jack's murder, her political future is dicey. For Pete's sake, she had the murder weapon in her hands a few hours before the police found her hovering over the body!"

I could feel the heat of acute embarrassment in my face. Stuart had alerted Judy to my approach, but his obtuseness didn't matter one bit. She'd already labeled Maeve Dixon a political liability. Considering the volatile politics surrounding the government shutdown, adding fuel to the fire made absolutely no strategic sense. My goose was cooked.

The lady doth protest too much. I knew my *Hamlet.* Still, I couldn't help myself. No matter what Doug, Judy Talent, Hill Rat, or the rest of the world thought, Representative Maeve Dixon did not kill Jack Drysdale.

"You've got it wrong. It's all circumstantial evidence. If you give me a few days, I'm sure the real killer will surface and Maeve will be exonerated."

She scoffed at my outburst. "Now you seem desperate. Your boss has enlisted your services as a detective?"

I realized I had said "give *me* a few days." I'd meant to say "give *it* a few days." Judy's comment stung. Sure, I wasn't Adrian Monk. That didn't mean I couldn't solve a murder. I'd done it six months ago and there was no reason I couldn't do it again. Her snide remark made me reckless.

"As a matter of fact, I *am* conducting an informal investigation concerning the death of Jack Drysdale. Where were you the morning of his death? Do you have an alibi?" I stood with my arms akimbo in an attempt to deliver the message that I meant business. Just because Judy had seniority and rank didn't mean she had license to bully me … although in actuality, seniority and rank *did* imply the privilege to bully someone on Capitol Hill. I shoved that dismal thought aside.

Judy smiled, a less than friendly grin. She wrinkled her nose. "Why should I tell you my whereabouts the morning Jack was killed?"

Was she trying to avoid my question? Leaning in, I lowered my voice for dramatic effect. "If you don't have anything to hide, then what's the harm, Judy?"

She pursed her lips in obvious distaste. I'd cornered her. Either she'd 'fess up or give me good reason to think she'd murdered Jack.

"If you must know, I was at Results Gym that morning for Gary's famous Boot Camp class. Check with him or any of the other women who wake up before dawn to stay in shape." She gave me a once-over. "I can tell that's not your crowd, but believe me, I can come up with numerous alibis."

Ouch. Judy was revealing her true colors, and they were dark—not the kind that come shining through, as in Cyndi Lauper's song. She hadn't climbed her way to the top of the Capitol Hill hierarchy without the benefit of a sharp tongue. At least I'd found out she claimed to have a strong alibi for Jack's murder.

"I'm sure the police will check to make sure your story holds up. If you change your mind about needing my boss's support, let me know." I began to walk away.

"Wait a second." She jogged to catch up to me. "Sorry for being so rude. I'm not usually like that."

While I had my doubts, there was no reason to push the issue. "Apology accepted."

"When Maeve Dixon is cleared of all suspicion, then the Majority Leader will welcome her help to end the shutdown."

It wasn't ideal, but given the circumstances, Judy's proposition seemed fair. I nodded and presented my hand as a peace offering. She accepted it with a firm shake.

I retraced my steps back through Emancipation Hall, up the Capitol Visitor Center escalator, and toward the Cannon Tunnel. It wasn't quite time for lunch with Meg so I took my time walking in the tunnel, admiring the high school art competition entries that populated the drab corridor. My phone buzzed. It was a text from Doug. *Are you OK?*

Obviously, Doug had seen Hill Rat's latest dispatch and wanted to check in. I clicked the "return call" button on my phone. I didn't have the energy to exchange a chain of texts with him on the topic.

Doug picked up immediately. "How are you doing? I read the blog about your boss."

"It's getting ugly around here. The Democratic leadership is starting to distance themselves from Maeve."

Doug's voice was filled with concern. "Maybe you should follow their lead."

"I can't abandon my boss at a time like this. Besides, I know she didn't do it."

There was a brief silence on the line. "Kit, I'm concerned about your safety. Working in Congress shouldn't be life threatening."

His point was valid. "Doug, I'm always careful. I'm having lunch with Meg so I have to run. Talk to you tonight." Doug's circumspection sometimes annoyed me, but it was obvious his caution arose out of a desire to keep me out of harm's way. That realization buoyed my spirits and warmed my heart. Yes, Trent Roscoe was easy on the eyes. Was that a fair trade for Doug's genuine concern for my well-being? Doubtful.

When I reached the Cannon basement rotunda, I stopped to look for one of my favorite Capitol Hill employees who had operated the shoeshine stand for the past twenty years. As I peeked around the corridor, watching for my buddy, I heard a familiar voice behind me.

"Ms. Marshall, are you lost?"

I turned to face Detective O'Halloran. "No, sir. I thought I'd chat with Martha. She also operates the key cutter." With a sheepish grin, I explained, "I lose the key to my condo on a regular basis. I help keep her in business with all the requests for duplicates."

"Why am I not surprised to hear this? Perhaps if you spent less time trying to solve murders in the United States Capitol, you'd have better luck locating your keys."

"Thanks for the advice, Detective. But I don't think the two activities are connected."

After a chuckle or two, he turned serious. "I'm afraid we've asked your boss to speak with us today about the murder of Jack Drysdale."

"I'm aware, Detective. Is she an official suspect?"

O'Halloran sighed. "At this time, she's voluntarily answering questions, which we appreciate. She's not under arrest."

I released the breath I'd been holding. O'Halloran heard my audible exhale and added, "Yet."

"Detective, I'm sure that once you examine the facts of this case, you'll arrive at the same conclusion as I did. Clearly, my boss was set up to take the fall for Drysdale's murder."

"I'm listening. What evidence substantiates that theory?" O'Halloran had given me a shot to exculpate Maeve. I had to take it.

"First, the supposed phone call from Jack the morning of the murder to our chief of staff doesn't make sense. The call was made from a random phone in the Capitol Visitor's Center. Anyone could have made that call. If Jack had done it, why not use his cell?"

O'Halloran waved his hand dismissively. "He might have left his phone back in his office. Or maybe he didn't want anyone to know he wanted to speak with Maeve Dixon to patch things up after the fracas the day before."

"But why would Jack call Dan instead of me? Maeve had instructed Drysdale I was in charge of the shutdown negotiations. I even went with her to the Speaker's meeting the day before."

"I see your point, but that's easily explained. He might have forgotten your name so he simply defaulted to calling the chief of staff who runs the office."

I shifted my bulky coat to my other hand so I could emphasize my words to O'Halloran with an emphatic gesture. "That doesn't make sense, Detective. Remember, you found my name on Jack's desk. He certainly knew who I was. He'd recently emailed all his friends to make sure my dog Clarence would win the Capitol Canine contest. There's no way he would forget I was Maeve's point person on the shutdown."

O'Halloran's eyes met mine for several seconds. "Your logic does call into question some of the circumstantial evidence against Representative Dixon." I grinned triumphantly. He quickly continued, "But it doesn't get her off the hook. Remember, we found her standing over the body. If that isn't enough, she had access to the murder weapon the night before. We all know she served as the presiding officer on the House floor less than ten hours earlier."

"Lots of people had access to the gavel, Detective."

He shook his head. "That's where were disagree, Ms. Marshall. It's the exact opposite. It's not an object that's left lying around."

I pursed my lips. *That damn gavel again.* "I've done some research, and there are several gavels, not just one."

"That is correct. Your boss contends she didn't touch anything after she discovered Drysdale's body. So if another gavel was used to kill him, we won't find her fingerprints on the murder weapon, correct?"

O'Halloran's reasoning seemed sound. Nonetheless, I didn't want to concede any point that could implicate Maeve's involvement in the crime, so I maintained a poker face as best I could. Time to go back on the offensive. "Speaking of the gavel, I'd appreciate it if the police didn't leak information about the case."

O'Halloran appeared surprised at my accusation. "We have an ironclad policy about speaking to the press informally. We take it seriously because so many of our cases involve sensitive subjects." He added pointedly, "And sensitive people."

"You might want to reexamine the policy and how it's working. This morning, Hill Rat published a blog in which he revealed the gavel as the murder weapon and linked it to my boss." I whipped out my iPhone and showed O'Halloran the online post.

He shook his head slowly. "I'm sorry about this, Kit. I will double-check, but I'm confident no one in the police gave this information to the press, especially Hill Rat. No one even knows who Hill Rat is."

"Precisely, Detective. So it's entirely possible that Hill Rat might have overheard one of your officers talking about the case. His anonymity gives him or her a lot of power around here."

"I can't disagree with you there, Ms. Marshall."

It was almost time to meet Meg at the cafeteria. "Thanks for the chat. I hope you'll think about the evidence you've collected against my boss. It's circumstantial and it doesn't add up."

"You may have a point. But she's our best suspect, and you know what they say."

"What do they say, Detective?"

"The simplest explanation is usually the best one."

Damn. Occam's razor strikes again.

Chapter Twenty

DURING THE SHUTDOWN, discontented souls, or excepted staff, wandered the hallways in search of any news about a viable solution. Bathrooms were shuttered, wastebaskets overflowed, and abandoned committee rooms added an extra creep factor.

The Longworth cafeteria was an exception. The only available lunchtime eatery inside the House, it had the gravitational pull of the Death Star. Everyone, no matter who they were, migrated to Longworth from their desolate, depressing office suites to find sustenance and solace.

On a typical workday, Longworth was swamped with diners. Those who built the Capitol Visitor Center had included a cafeteria to accommodate tourists. But the fancy bill of fare at the CVC had prices to match. The cost of the visitor center food mirrored Washington's economy of scale, yet most sightseers had much more modest lifestyles. Aunt Dottie and Cousin Fred took one look at the sophisticated menu in the CVC cafeteria and immediately complained to their congressman they couldn't afford the trip. In an attempt to help out cash-strapped constituents, every House office promptly directed visitors to the Longworth employee cafeteria, where the food was cheaper. Even though the visitor center planners had meant to keep the vacationer crowd at bay by attracting them to the fancy CVC cafeteria, the unintentional result had been to increase traffic in the cramped Longworth cafeteria.

I scanned the upper section of the seating area, looking for my dining companion. Not spotting her, I moved to the main section of the cafeteria, which included tables and several food service lines. A familiar hand shot up in the corner. Meg had scored the perfect seat. Given the high volume of staff, lobbyists, and journalists who frequented Longworth, even during the shutdown, nothing was private within its confines. At least Meg had found us a table on the perimeter.

"Happy fourth day of the shutdown!"

"Thanks, but the way things are going, who's counting?"

"Every news organization and interest group in town is counting, Kit."

She was right. Meg's prediction at Tortilla Coast before the murder seemed like years ago. She'd said this would be no short-lived crisis, and apparently she was right.

"Should we get some lunch before we chat?"

"Absolutely."

I followed Meg into the food court-style cafeteria. Today's outfit was tan riding pants, a black sweater sheath, and a blazer, paired with stylish boots and a silver barrette in her blonde bob. She looked ready to go fox hunting with the Queen. I, on the other hand, awkwardly toted a cumbersome winter jacket and a monstrosity of a purse. Did we make for an endearing pair, like Alvy Singer and Annie Hall? I hoped so.

Five minutes later, we were seated and ready to dish. Meg wrinkled her nose.

"Is there something wrong?" I asked.

"It's nothing. We all have to make sacrifices during the shutdown."

"What do you mean?"

"They've had to cut back on the number of cafeteria workers, and there's no supreme pizza today. Just cheese." Meg pouted and stared at her two plain slices.

Compared to my turkey on wheat sandwich, Meg's lunch looked positively delightful. It wasn't worth an argument. Better to commiserate so we could move on to the matter at hand, namely Trent Roscoe. Chewing on a big mouthful of sandwich, I barely managed an audible reply. "Yes, it's really tough these days."

Meg nodded solemnly. Her food diatribe over with, we could proceed to meatier topics, no pun intended. "You texted me a 911 message about Trent Roscoe? It must be important. You used the distress call."

We tried not to overuse the emergency code so that when we did resort to it, we both understood the severity of the situation. Once she heard what I had to say, she would fully understand my decision to employ 911.

I took a long sip of my Coke Zero, cleared my throat, and said, "Trent Roscoe is going to ask me out on a date."

The look on Meg's face resembled my free-spirited parents' when I'd told them I had a job working in Congress. For once, Meg was speechless.

"Go ahead, say something. What should I do?"

Slack-jawed shock was swiftly replaced with a wide grin. "Kit Marshall, I'm shocked you would even consider going on a date with Trent."

"The situation isn't what it seems. How am I going to solve Jack Drysdale's murder if I don't meet with suspects? Or the people who know them?"

"You can't tell me the only reason you'd accept is to solve the mystery." She waggled her index finger. "Don't lie to me. You don't find Trent at all attractive?"

I fiddled with the crust of my sandwich. "I didn't say that. But the only reason for me to go on the date would be to extract more information about his boss, Gareth Pressler."

Meg leaned back in her seat. "Fine. I see how you want to play this. I won't argue with you. But at least remain open to the possibility Trent might be a good catch."

"Am I supposed to leave Doug in the dust and run off into the sunset with Trent?"

Meg rubbed her chin thoughtfully, as if seriously considering my question. Given Meg's oil-and-water relationship with Doug, she probably was. "Of course not. At least not yet. But keeping your options open is always a good thing, *n'est-ce pas*?" She gave me a devilish smirk.

"Unless Doug finds out. Then it would be *très mal*." Meg didn't have the market cornered on basic French.

Meg stuffed the remainder of her pizza into her mouth. "I guess so. But he hasn't proposed. It's something to consider, Kit."

Meg's words were true, but they still hurt. She must have seen the pained look on my face because she retreated with lightning speed. "I didn't mean anything by that. It was a stupid comment."

If I was honest with myself, Meg's remark had validity. After all, Doug and I had lived together for almost three years. Still, I couldn't imagine life without him. "Apology accepted. I know what you were trying to say."

Her face brightened. "Let's move on. If you're going out with Trent tonight, what's the plan?"

I grabbed my iPhone and scanned my email. A ton of messages waited for my attention. Sure enough, Trent Roscoe had contacted me an hour ago. I opened his email and read it aloud to Meg.

Want to grab drinks tonight? Swing by my office at 5?

Normally, that would have been way too early to knock off work, but considering that Maeve Dixon had no political input on the negotiations taking place, it didn't make sense to burn the midnight oil. Meg gave the matter some thought before offering her opinion. "This could be the perfect plan. He invited you to his office."

I ate the last piece of my pathetic yet healthy turkey sandwich. "So what?"

Meg narrowed her eyes in disbelief. "Of all people, I shouldn't have to spell it out for you."

"I've got a lot on my mind these days. Enlighten me."

"Kit, Gareth Pressler is a suspect. His office is near Trent's, right?"

"Yes, it's around the corner."

She rolled her eyes. "This is a perfect opportunity to snoop!"

I shook my head. "No way. Last time we distracted someone to spy, you kept him occupied while I rummaged around. And that only worked because he was already in love with you." I was referring to Meg's current boyfriend Kyle. I still felt guilty that their relationship had begun with my deception, although it didn't bother Meg one bit.

Meg tapped the side of her iPhone while she mulled over the predicament. Suddenly her face lit up. "I got it! What if you had a better reason to excuse yourself from the conversation? Like an important phone call?"

"You've got my attention. Tell me more."

"It would only work if I kept the conversation going while you were gone. Didn't you say Trent loves to talk about security in the Capitol?"

"Sure. It's his job. He's enthusiastic about it."

"Perfect. You can bring me along. Write him back and tell him one of your friends wants to ask a few questions about security. After we start chatting, your phone will ring and you'll have to take the call. You can excuse yourself from the conversation for at least ten minutes. Of course, it will only work if Gareth isn't in his office. We'll have to take that chance."

"One problem, Meg. If you're along for the ride, who is going to call me on my phone? As usual, Doug is acting weird about my investigation. I don't think it's a good idea to involve him. He doesn't want me to get hurt. You know the drill."

"Yes, Doug is about as adventurous as my eighty-five-year-old grandmother. In fact, she might have him beat."

"No need to get personal, Meg."

"Sorry." She waved her hand in an apparent attempt to dismiss her impolite remark. "It doesn't matter. I have a solution."

"I'm listening."

"Have you heard about the FAC app?"

"Come again?"

She spelled out the acronym: "F-A-C. It stands for fake a call."

"I must have missed that one. Tell me about it."

"After installing the app on your smartphone, you can program it to make pretend phone calls. Let me show you."

Meg whipped out her iPhone and opened the app. In a few seconds, she had programmed her phone to ring. A few moments later, it buzzed, complete with a fake screen showing the fictitious name of the person who had supposedly called her. She swiped her phone open and answered. To my complete amazement, I could hear a voice conversing with her!

I grabbed Meg's hand. "Give me the phone. Who are you talking to?"

I put the device next to my ear and heard a guy asking me when my report would be finished. A few seconds later, he barked, "It better be on my desk in an hour!"

I must have looked utterly perplexed because Meg burst into laughter. "This is the deluxe call. It's supposed to be from your boss. It gives you the extra cover of having a real voice on the other end of the line when you answer the phone."

"I get it. So I can program my phone to ring during our conversation with Trent. I'll answer the call and excuse myself. After that, I can sneak into Gareth's office."

Meg sat back in her chair with a satisfied look. "Precisely."

"What should I look for in Pressler's office?"

"Beats me. Anything that might give him the means or motive for the crime, right?"

I gathered up my coat, purse, and trash. "Sure. I'll keep my eyes peeled. Part of the problem is there are really two related mysteries I'm trying to solve." I raised one finger then two to tick them off. "First, there's Jack's murder. Second, who is Hill Rat?"

Meg nodded vigorously. "This mystery is pretty complex. Don't worry. You'll figure it out and clear Representative Dixon's name."

I stood up and gathered my coat and purse. "Thanks, Meg. I feel like I'm chasing a ghost."

"Ghosts aren't real, Kit."

"That's the scary part. This one is very real."

Meg put her arms around me and gave me a quick hug. Then she peeled off in the direction of her office. I walked up the steps and entered the outer seating area of the cafeteria. As usual, my head was buried in my iPhone, trying to triage the mountain of emails that had arrived while we were enjoying lunch.

This section of the cafeteria was less populated than the lower portion. Even though I was focused on reading my messages, I couldn't miss a deep voice saying my name. "Ms. Marshall, how are you this afternoon?" My eyes darted upward, right into the steely gaze of Gareth Pressler.

Chapter Twenty-One

I FROZE. AFTER several moments of awkward silence, I finally stammered a pathetic excuse for a greeting. I croaked, "Nice to see you again, Mr. Pressler."

Meg and I had finished our lunches only moments ago in a completely different section of the cafeteria, all the while plotting an illegal search of his office. With the persistent din of fellow patrons, there was no way he could have overheard our conversation. I breathed a sigh of relief and mustered my friendliest smile.

"Did Representative Dixon find the information Trent gave you about Capitol security helpful?"

His question caught me off guard. I'd momentarily forgotten using Maeve as an excuse to set up the meeting with Trent. Recovering swiftly, I nodded my head vigorously. "Yes, sir. She understands now why extra security protocols might be necessary."

Pressler ran his fingers through his short hair. Everything about him was immaculate. His pressed suit, straight tie, and freshly shaved face conveyed one message: *I mean business and*

I don't suffer fools gladly. He glanced at my coat. "Haven't made it into the office yet today?"

Damn. This guy was observant. This time, I couldn't come up with a plausible lie. "I've been running around all morning with meetings. No rest for the weary."

"Especially when you work for Representative Dixon these days, as I understand."

I frowned in frustration. Pressler had turned the tables. He was interrogating me, not the other way around. "What are you implying?"

Pressler didn't blink an eyelash. Staring me down, he said evenly, "She's the prime suspect for the murder of Jack Drysdale. At least that's the story being reported."

His matter-of-fact proclamation of my boss's probable guilt galled me. *Calm down*. He's fishing for information. A deep breath steadied my voice. "She discovered Jack's body. That's it. She didn't kill him and we're confident the police will find the person who actually committed the crime."

Pressler laughed softly. "You have a lot of faith in the police."

He appeared surprised when I took a step closer. The cafeteria was full of eavesdroppers, but Pressler needed to know I meant business. "You bet I do. Justice will be served."

Pressler maintained the impassive demeanor of an expert poker player. Several seconds of silence passed. Finally he picked up his lunch tray. "I'm glad we agree that the safety of the United States Capitol complex is critical. If your boss is cleared of any wrongdoing, I would be happy to answer additional questions about our security operations." He nodded politely and strode toward the nearby exit.

What an odd duck. He reminded me of Wilford Brimley shilling for Quaker Oats. His cool, calm, and collected demeanor might mean he had nothing to hide. On the other hand, weren't psychopaths eerily hard to read?

Instead of following Pressler out the door, I sat down at his table to plot my next move. Unexpectedly running into him had thrown me off my game, and I needed to refocus.

I had several hours at my disposal before meeting Trent at his office. But first, I needed to accept his offer of drinks. My reply to Trent's email was short and sweet.

Free for drinks after work tonight. Can I bring a friend to your office first who wants to ask questions about Capitol security?

That settled my evening plans. Right now, I was running out of leads. Then I remembered Trevor's suggestion about the gavel. If I could figure out where it was constructed, then I might be able to determine if multiple gavels existed. That would at least pave the way for the possibility that someone else could have had access to the murder weapon.

I couldn't wander the bowels of the Capitol looking for the carpentry shop. I needed to use my desktop computer to find the location. Sighing deeply, I texted Dan.

Reporters still outside?

Dan replied: *Gone. Are you coming back?*

Yes I was, but not to see him.

Be there in 10.

Luckily, I didn't run into anyone else in the short walk to the Cannon Building. Dan had told the truth. No reporters were camped outside the main door. When it became clear Maeve Dixon wasn't showing up for work today, the press contingent must have decided it was a waste of time to stake out her office. I pulled the door, but it didn't budge. Locked up as tight as Fort Knox. As I scrambled to find my key, I heard a familiar voice from the other side. "Who is it?"

"What do you want, Dan? A clever knock-knock joke? It's Kit, of course. I told you I'd be here in a few minutes."

The door cracked open and one eye peered through.

I waved my hand. "See, it's me. I'm alone. No worries."

He opened the door and whispered hastily, "Get in! I don't want anyone to know there's someone in the office."

After I stepped across the threshold, he hurriedly shut the door behind me. The gravity of the situation notwithstanding,

I couldn't resist an attempt at humor. "Are you running Fight Club again? You know that's not allowed on federal government property. Don't make me turn you in."

He grimaced. "I'm glad you find this whole situation amusing. Do you know what it was like to be trapped inside the office all day with bloodthirsty reporters outside?"

I approached my desk, hung up the coat I'd lugged around all day, and turned on my computer. A clever retort was on the tip of my tongue, but I resisted. Dan was clearly upset and fueling the fire would only make the situation worse, if that was at all possible. Instead, it was better to commiserate and find out if he knew anything about Maeve's status.

"That sounds like a terrible way to spend the morning. I'm glad you survived." It took every ounce of concentration to remove all semblance of sarcasm from my voice. Before he had a chance to chime in, I added, "Do you have an update on our boss and her meeting with the police?"

Dan buried his face in his hands. Not a good sign. I grabbed his arm and tugged it. "What's wrong? Dan, you have to tell me."

He took several deep breaths, as if to keep from hyperventilating. "She called a few minutes before you texted. The interrogation isn't going well."

Odd that she called Dan, not me. Then I remembered her saying that she didn't want me to investigate the murder because she thought it was too dangerous. Bad news provided an excuse to kick into high gear.

"Are the police going to arrest her?" I held my breath as I waited for his answer.

He shook his head. "Not today. Unless she blows a gasket and confesses."

Maybe Dan was losing faith in Maeve's innocence. "Wait a second. If they don't have enough to arrest her, then why is the news so terrible?"

Dan raised his right hand and wiggled his fingers. "The evidence is mounting."

"Is that a secret signal? I'm not following."

Dan sighed impatiently. "I can see it was ridiculous to put my faith in you to solve the crime. What kind of detective are you? Fingerprints, of course!"

"Whose prints? Maeve's?"

"Yes! What else would matter? If they belonged to the Queen of England?"

"Calm down. I'm not the Mentalist. Her fingerprints were found at the crime scene?"

"Now you're getting warmer." Dan's voice dripped with sarcasm.

Oh, no. This *was* bad news. I almost whispered the question, "The murder weapon?"

"Bingo! Give this woman a prize! Guess what you've just won? A one-way ticket to the unemployment line." In a fit of uncontrolled anger, Dan picked up the first object in his path and threw it against the wall. Unfortunately, it was Maeve's North Carolina Woman of the Year Award. It shattered into several pieces.

Dan stared at me for a long moment. Finally, I broke the silence. It was unfortunate information, but all was not lost. "Her fingerprints were on the gavel that killed Jack. Is that correct?"

Dan nodded.

"It looks grim, but I think there's more than one gavel. If that's the case, Maeve might have been set up."

"Or she pocketed the gavel after presiding, replaced it with a new one, and then killed Jack with it."

"That doesn't sound like Maeve Dixon. The woman who survived Iraq and Afghanistan uses a world-famous symbol to kill a well-known political adversary? Then she leaves the weapon alongside the body with her fingerprints on it? Come on, Dan. It doesn't smell right."

"I'm not sure what I should think anymore. But I'm certain about one thing: if she's arrested and I'm still her chief of staff, I'll never work in politics again."

Dan's reasoning was accurate, yet his obsession with self-preservation bugged the heck out of me. Didn't he care that an innocent woman could go to prison for a crime she didn't commit?

It was time to bring this conversation to an end. "If you'll excuse me, I have work to finish." I turned toward my computer, which was booting up.

Before returning to his office, he issued a final jab: "Do yourself a favor. Add polishing your resume to the to-do list for today."

Oh, ye of little faith. There were hundreds of emails to read, but that work could be avoided until Maeve Dixon had been cleared. The government shutdown would have to wait. Unless I figured out what happened to Jack Drysdale, the country would lose a dedicated public servant—permanently. In that light, wouldn't Uncle Sam agree I was faithfully discharging my duties, as I'd promised when taking the federal oath of office on my first day as a congressional staffer?

This morning's breakfast conversation with Trevor rattled around in my brain. He'd called Trent about the carpentry shop in the Capitol. If I could locate it, then perhaps someone who worked there might be able to tell me more about the supply of gavels for the House floor. How many were made? Would one missing gavel attract attention? If Maeve's fingerprints were on the gavel and she didn't kill Jack, then a switch had somehow occurred between the time she presided over the House of Representatives and the next morning when Jack had been killed. Any details about the plausibility of such a switch would help Maeve Dixon establish reasonable doubt.

It took a little digging online, but I finally found the location of the Capitol carpentry shop. A quick check of the clock indicated there was plenty of time to squeeze in a call to Doug before heading out on my latest quest.

My so-called "date" later on made me uneasy. Meg clearly thought I should play the field and see what developed with Trent. There was no denying he was eye-catching, yet his appeal was the complete opposite of Doug's. The man of action versus the man of intellect. How could I find total opposites sexy? I shoved thoughts of Trent aside. No matter what Meg thought, my motivation for having a drink with Trent tonight was purely the desire to find out more about Jack Drysdale's dispute with the House Sergeant at Arms office.

I punched in Doug's cell number and waited for him to pick up. After a few rings, I heard a sleepy "Hello?"

"It's me. Did I wake you up?"

"No, but you got up early this morning and it interrupted my sleep."

"Sorry. There's a lot going on here. You know, such as a federal government shutdown and my boss being accused of murder. That kind of stuff."

"Are there new developments in the case?"

I caught him up concerning Dan's information about the unfortunate placement of Maeve's fingerprints on the murder weapon.

After a few minutes of silence, Doug said, "Kit, this doesn't look good for your boss. Like I said earlier today, it might make sense for you to disengage."

"If she's guilty, there's nothing I can do about it. But what about the possibility she's innocent? I might be her only hope."

"Even if you're right, the real killer thinks he or she got away with it since so much suspicion has been focused on your boss. If you keep asking questions, you'll become a liability to him or her."

"I'm always careful. The reason I'm calling is that tonight I need to have drinks with a guy who knows one of the suspects."

"Who's that?"

"His name is Trent Roscoe. Trevor knows him and put me in touch." The less said, the better. Doug didn't need to know the gory details.

"Are you going by yourself?"

Doug never asked questions about my social obligations on the Hill. He realized evening happy hours and receptions were part of working for Congress. Did he really know me so well that he guessed something was amiss?

"I think so, but Meg is coming with me to his office to help with the interrogation."

He hesitated before replying, "Perhaps she can join you for drinks. Meg never turns down cocktails."

"That's true, but she's got this investigation she's working on for her committee. She took off early last night to join us for Capitol Canine, remember?"

"How could I forget? Clarence's pizza escapade will be seared in my memory forever."

I giggled at the image of Clarence devouring the pepperoni. At least he'd enjoyed himself.

"I'll text you when I'm headed home. Talk to you later."

He said goodbye, and I hung up, thinking that I wished I could spend more time with Doug. When all of this nonsense was over, I'd have to focus on him. There was only so long a relationship could survive on autopilot.

I gathered my belongings and headed to Dan's office to tell him I was leaving. Then I reversed course and bolted. What was the point of informing Dan? I'd always considered him a lightweight, but he'd shown his true colors the past several days. Even if the police cleared Maeve of any wrongdoing, I knew one thing for certain: there was no way in hell I could continue to work for Dan. Any ounce of respect I'd had for him disappeared when he threw our boss under the bus.

In less than five minutes, I was chugging through the Cannon Tunnel once again. This time, instead of veering to the right to enter the Capitol Visitors Center, I tacked left. This was the hinterland of the Capitol Building, known as the basement or "terrace" level. The ever-popular flag office was located around the corner, where members could obtain United States flags flown on the Capitol grounds for worthy constituents. Dan had asked me once to retrieve a flag on short notice so Maeve could provide it to a fellow veteran visiting Washington D.C.

The dimly lit corridor resembled the abandoned basement of a dilapidated high school. There were no offices down here, just uninviting steel doors with room numbers etched above them. I was definitely in the right place for the various craftsman shops. The only other people occupying this part of the building were workmen sporting blue jumpsuits with the Architect of the Capitol insignia emblazoned on them.

After traversing the corridor several times to no avail, I concluded the room number for the carpentry shop I'd unearthed on the Internet had ceased to exist. It was time for Plan B. Several Architect employees had come and gone through a particular double-door entryway. With any luck, it was the main point of access for one of the trade shops.

I stood next to the door and waited. Sure enough, a man in a blue jumpsuit rounded the corner and reached for the handle. Before he could enter, I blocked the entrance.

"Excuse me, sir. Can you help me with something?" I flashed the toothiest smile I could muster.

My innocent victim was caught off guard. Not too many congressional staffers ambushed AOC craftsmen. Once he saw the staff identification badge around my neck, he relaxed. "What's wrong, honey? Are you lost? The flag office is closed during the shutdown."

"Actually, I'm looking for the carpentry shop. Can you tell me where it is?"

"Did something break in your office? If that's the case, there's a form you need to fill out online."

"No, that's not it. I'm looking for the place where they make the Speaker's gavels."

My friend narrowed his eyes suspiciously. "That's a new one. Why do you need to know that?"

Somehow I didn't think telling him the unvarnished truth

would get me far. "My boss has this guy she owes a favor. His kid is writing a research paper on the Speaker of the House and he wants to know more about the gavels. Since there's nothing going on these days, she sent me down here to find the place where they're made so I can take a photo for the little scholar." I waved my iPhone at him.

"Huh. Now congressmen are writing research papers for voters. They do everything but passing the bills to pay our salaries."

"You're not telling me anything I don't already know."

He shrugged. "Tell you what. Wait outside here and I'll see if my supervisor can come talk to you about the carpentry shop."

"Thank you so much."

I blew out a long breath. Lying had never been my strong suit, but lately, the deceptions rolled off my tongue smooth as butter.

A few minutes later, the door opened and a heavyset, middle-aged guy in a blue uniform emerged. GENO was written in big block letters on the upper right corner of his shirt. He had bushy hair that stuck out from all sides, scrunched under a well-worn Architect of the Capitol baseball hat.

He gave me a quick once-over. "Are you the lady who wants to know about the gavels?"

"That's me. My name is Kit and I appreciate your time."

"You're in luck. We're not supposed to be doing any work around here except what's absolutely necessary to keep the Capitol operating. Due to the shutdown and all that political business."

"Thanks, Geno. Can you show me where you folks make the gavels?"

Geno removed a stick of gum from his pocket, carefully unwrapped it, placed it in his mouth, and started chewing. "This is my replacement for cigarettes. Somehow, it's not the same."

Like a true D.C. politico, Geno had avoided my question by

changing the topic. But there was no way I'd give up that easily.

"I bet it's not nearly as satisfying. Are the gavels made inside this workshop?" I pointed toward the double door behind us.

"Nah. It's not here. But it doesn't matter. I can't show you inside our workshops for a million reasons. A nice lady like you might get hurt in a dangerous place. One misstep and bam!" He smacked his hands together. "You've lost a finger."

His ominous tone vaguely reminded me of my high school shop teacher and my subsequent fear of band saws. Maybe I didn't need to see where the gavels were actually constructed.

"I understand, Geno. But do your colleagues make the gavels somewhere in this building?"

He blew a small bubble. "Sure, we do. Done it since the 1930s. At least we have photographs going back that far showing Architect craftsmen with the Speaker's gavel."

Now I was getting somewhere. "I just have a few more questions. How many gavels do you make each year?"

"No idea."

"Is it more than one at a time?"

He laughed. "Of course. The Speaker needs more than one gavel. After all, sometimes they break, even though they're made from lacquered maple these days."

Bingo. "Where do they go once you've completed your work?"

"We hand them over to the parliamentarian's office. They take possession so they can be used on the House floor. Where they get stored after that, I have no idea."

"Geno, you've been a real lifesaver." I stuck my hand out for a friendly shake.

He plopped another piece of gum in his mouth and chomped away. "No problem. All this interest in the Speaker's gavel is pretty strange, though."

I whipped my head around. "What do you mean?"

He leaned up against the dingy wall next to the door leading to the shop. "I've worked here for a little over twenty years and no one has ever asked me about the Speaker's gavel. Today, you're the second person with questions about it."

"Someone else asked about the gavel today?"

"Yeah, that's the funny thing. This morning, I had almost the same conversation with some guy."

"Do you remember his name?"

"I don't think he offered it. Said he was doing research on the Speaker's gavel and wanted to know where it was made and where it was stored. That type of stuff."

Who could have been asking about the gavel? Was the murderer trying to cover his tracks? Gareth Pressler came to mind. "Geno, would you recognize the guy if you saw him again?"

He rubbed his chin thoughtfully. "I think so. Today hasn't been too busy, so his face is pretty clear in my mind."

"Give me a second." I grabbed my iPhone from my purse and searched for a photo of Gareth Pressler online. Google Images didn't fail me. There was a recent photograph of him on LinkedIn. I pulled it up on the screen and enlarged it for Geno.

"Is this the guy you spoke with?"

Geno took my phone and held it close to his eyes. He quickly replied, "Nope" and handed it back to me.

Darn. Nothing was ever easy. "Are you sure? His name is Gareth and he works in the Capitol."

"I've seen this guy around. He's some high yuckety-muck with the Sergeant's office. He wasn't asking about the gavel."

Geno seemed sure of himself. No point in pressing. "It's been a pleasure talking with you. If you ever need anything, I'd be happy to help."

"Sure, you can do something for me."

"What's that?"

"Get those politicians to agree on a budget so me and my guys can get paid."

Not an unreasonable request. I waved goodbye to Geno and retraced my steps back through the long, bleak underground Capitol corridor.

Chapter Twenty-Two

I HAD TIME to kill before meeting Meg at Trent's office for our evening escapade. Under normal conditions, returning to the office would have been an option. But I didn't need another dose of Dan and his meltdown mentality. Instead, I found a seat in the basement of Cannon near the array of vending machines. Luckily, the machines were still fully operational. Junk food was typically verboten, but I'd had a rough day. After finding a few stray dollar bills in my purse, I settled in with a bottle of Diet Coke, a Hershey's bar, and my iPhone. Sleuthing required sustenance, after all.

Cyberspace engulfed me with a myriad of emails, e-alerts, and notices. A breakthrough wouldn't happen tomorrow, yet the early signs of a favorable deal were emerging. If Maeve was going to have a chance to play a notable role in solving this crisis, her name would have to be cleared soon. Trains were starting to leave the station, and they wouldn't return for wayward passengers. Time flew by and five o'clock quickly approached.

I grabbed my iPhone and searched for a message from Trent. He'd confirmed our drinks and said it was fine to bring a friend to "talk shop first." Now I had to program the Fake A Call app so it would ring during our conversation. Fifteen minutes would give us enough time to begin the chatter about security. At 5:20, my iPhone would buzz, I'd excuse myself, and commence my mission. A fast text to Meg confirmed she was still on board.

After gathering my belongings, I navigated the Cannon Tunnel once again to reach the Capitol Building. The *Mission Impossible* theme might have been playing in the background—or at least I imagined it was.

I pushed open the door at the Sergeant at Arms office and was greeted by no one. Not totally shocking, given the shutdown situation and the evening hour. The silence didn't last long. Before I could whip out my phone to message Meg, Trent Roscoe appeared with a wide grin.

"Kit, I'm so glad to see you again!"

Trent rushed toward me with his arms outstretched. A handshake seemed perfectly acceptable, but Trent was not going to settle for a professional gesture. Instead, he gave me a quick hug and let his hand linger on the small of my back. He wore a dark gray suit with a deep violet buttoned shirt that hugged his broad chest. Light crinkles emerged when he smiled, yet the fine lines of age only enhanced his physical attractiveness. There was no denying it. Trent had classic good looks with a buff body to match. Pretending otherwise would be the equivalent of denying Meg's fashion acumen or Clarence's craving for pepperoni. Some things in life resembled mathematical certainties, and Trent Roscoe's hotness qualified as such.

Before I had a chance to reply, the door swung open and Meg entered the fray. Her arrival allowed me to move several steps away from Trent so I could escape the touch of his hand on my back. It wasn't exactly unwanted. If I tolerated his touchy-feely gestures, where would the night lead us? The objective was to solve the murder, not cheat on Doug.

Meg flashed a killer smile and offered her hand. "Trent Roscoe, I presume? I've heard a lot about you."

He shook her hand politely. "Hope all of it's good, ma'am."

"Of course! Don't be silly. My name is Meg, and Kit told me about your security conversation the other day. You don't mind if we can spend a few minutes chatting in your office about it?"

Trent led us through the hallway. "We can chat all you'd like, if both of you can fit into my office."

We wedged ourselves into the tiny space across from Trent's desk. I shoved Meg in first so an easy, graceful escape would be possible when my pretend phone call came in.

Meg turned on her famous charm as we talked. She giggled at Trevor's witticisms, touched his arm lightly, complimented him on his attire, and batted her long eyelashes. This was classic Meg flirtation behavior. Usually it didn't bother me one bit. Even though I intended to avoid an awkward situation with Trent, her amorous overtures irked me. She knew he'd asked *me* out. Didn't she respect any boundaries, even if my ulterior motive for accepting his invitation was investigatory rather than romantic?

Amazingly enough, Trent reacted in an unusual fashion. More precisely, he didn't react. I couldn't remember the last time a man had been so impervious to Meg's wiles. Instead, he glanced at me several times during the conversation, sending cute smiles my way.

Mesmerized by his attentions, I bounced several inches out of my seat when my iPhone rang. Sure enough, the screen displayed "Dan" as my supposed caller.

"Sorry, I need to answer this." I held the phone slightly away from my ear so Trent and Meg could hear the conversation.

"Where are you?" barked the voice on the line.

"Um, visiting a friend."

"You didn't even tell me you left the office."

Strange. How did Fake A Call know I'd left the office several hours ago?

I kept up appearances and excused myself from the office. The voice on the line kept talking. "Are you abandoning me?"

Something was wrong. I looked at my phone. The number looked familiar. Shoot. This wasn't the fake phone call. It was actually my chief of staff.

"Sorry, Dan. I didn't realize it was you. I'm sort of busy right now."

"Busy? I find that hard to believe. I got off the phone with our boss. She wasn't arrested today, but her lawyer thinks they could issue a warrant tomorrow or the next day."

I was standing at the entrance of Gareth's office. It was now or never if I wanted to inspect it. That required getting rid of Dan. "Hmm. Bad news. Listen, I have to run. I'm on the case. Don't worry!"

As I swiped the phone to end the call, I heard Dan's voice. "Wait! Don't hang up. I need to tell you something!"

Too late. Right now, I needed to focus on snooping. I had five minutes max if I wanted to avoid getting caught.

Pressler's office was immaculate. Not even a paper clip was out of place. His desk was completely unadorned, except for a huge three-ring binder. Carefully, I cracked it open. The table of contents indicated the three-hundred-page document was nothing less than a sweeping plan to revamp security for the House of Representatives. A quick glance indicated that Pressler's overhaul included changes to entrance and exit protocol, tourist access, computer security, surveillance, Capitol Hill police presence, and identification. There was no time to digest the details of the plan, but I saw enough to know that if these procedures were implemented, public access to Congress would drastically diminish. To add fuel to the fire, member and congressional staff's freedom to roam the Capitol complex was headed for the chopping block. Access to certain locations would be determined on an "as needed" basis, whatever that meant.

I'd seen enough. I closed the book and scanned the rest of

his office. A computer rested on his desk, predictably locked. There was no way a guy like Gareth Pressler would leave his office with his email or files exposed. But in the far corner of the office, another monitor emitted flashes of light. I hustled over to it. It took me several seconds before I could figure out what I was looking at. It was a wide screen divided into four quadrants. People walked through the shots, ostensibly in real time. One video displayed the Cannon Tunnel. Others showed the rotunda and the cafeteria in Longworth. After several seconds, the screen changed. Entirely different segments of the House of Representatives buildings presented themselves. Gareth Pressler had a security monitor in his office that gave him a bird's-eye view of at least three Capitol Hill buildings.

Mesmerized by the changing visual display, I heard a faint rustle from the direction of the open door. Just as I turned to make my grand escape, a loud "ruff" came from my purse. I fumbled to reach inside to locate my phone. *Damn.* I'd forgotten about the fake call I'd arranged to ring at 5:20. I'd set the ringer to mimic a dog's bark so Trent would remember I'd taken a call and excused myself. After finally retrieving the device, I swiped it to answer the call and then quickly hung up. My fingers were nowhere near fast enough to avert disaster. The sound of footsteps grew louder from the hallway as I braced myself to meet my unfortunate fate.

Chapter Twenty-Three

THE PATRON SAINT of sleuths must have been looking down from heaven with sympathy. To my surprise, Meg rounded the corner and grabbed my arm.

"Ouch! What are you doing?" I whispered.

"What am I doing?" she hissed. She pulled me closer before continuing her verbal assault. "What are you doing? You've been gone for fifteen minutes already. I can't keep Trent occupied forever."

I reclaimed my appendage. "That's never been a problem before. You couldn't hold Trent's interest for a little extra time?"

Meg's face contorted with frustration. "He's not biting. I don't know why. Maybe he really is in love with you."

My best friend's glare bored into me like a phaser set to stun on the Starship Enterprise. "Never mind. Let's get back to it. I can make up some story about Dan calling me. Actually, Dan did call me. That wasn't a fake."

"I heard your phone all the way down the hall. That's why I excused myself to come find you. If someone else had heard it, you would have been toast."

I motioned for Meg to lean in closer so I could whisper

softly, "It was worth it. I found an extensive plan to overhaul House security on Pressler's desk. Plus, he has a monitor in his office tracking the cameras in the office buildings. He would have known Jack's location, even early in the morning."

Meg's eyes widened. "Do you think he's your guy?"

We walked toward Trent's office. "I think so. I might have to check a few things out tomorrow to confirm it."

"Are you keeping your date with Trent tonight?" Meg made air quotes around the word "date."

"I don't think it will hurt. Maybe I can find out more valuable information about his boss." I elbowed Meg. "Especially if I'm really charming."

Meg gave me a suspicious look. "I wouldn't overplay your hand, Kit. Leave the art of seductive interrogation to the professionals. If you're not interested in Trent romantically, just have a drink and go home."

I resented Meg's remark. Yes, she was pretty and men adored her. But occasionally, a good-looking guy might be interested in yours truly. Doug wasn't the beefy, bulging muscles type, but he was tall, fit, and attractive in a refined sort of way.

"I'll try to control myself."

We walked back inside Trent's tiny office and returned to our seats. Trent seemed to buy my explanation about Dan's phone call and my apology. After politely thanking him for his time, Meg excused herself. Outside the doorway, she mouthed "Call me tonight" and waved goodbye.

I returned my attention to Trent. His grin was the type I'd have plastered on my face if I heard my boss had given everyone the afternoon off. Best to keep it casual. "Ready to go?" I suggested.

"Absolutely. I know she's your friend, but I thought she'd never leave." He grabbed his coat and escorted me out of the office suite. As we left the Capitol Building, I realized we hadn't discussed where we were going. We were headed in the direction of Pennsylvania Avenue, home to a number of bars and dining establishments.

"Trent, where are we having drinks tonight?" I tried to keep my voice steady. I was shooting for friendly yet not overly encouraging.

"I thought we'd go to my favorite place on the Hill." He winked playfully.

He wasn't making this easy. "Which is?"

"I don't go out after work too often, but when I do, I go to this place called the Tune Inn. Do you know it?"

My heart sank. "Sure," I said. "Isn't it on Pennsylvania and Fourth?"

"Yep. It's right on the corner. It's not the fanciest establishment in the world, but I like the homey feel."

"Not the fanciest" was an understatement. Most thought of the Tune Inn as Capitol Hill's neighborhood dive bar. I hid my disappointment, even though there was no need to take offense. After all, it wasn't a real date, right? If Trent thought we were on a date, he must not have cared about spending a lot to impress me.

In ten minutes, we'd reached the entrance. Trent politely opened the door, and I walked inside. Dark and dingy, the décor wasn't conducive to romance. Stuffed deer, bears, boar, and swordfish adorned the wood-paneled walls. Obviously, the Tune Inn singlehandedly kept several taxidermists in business. In the spaces without mounted animals, a variety of guns and swords enhanced the atmosphere.

This wasn't a place with a hostess so we sailed past the bar underneath the antler chandelier and wood rafters lined with Christmas lights to find an empty booth. Trent was almost giddy with delight. "Isn't this place great?"

"It's certainly unique. It's the only place in D.C. where I can eat dinner across from a stuffed deer's butt." I pointed at the specimen on the opposite wall.

Trent nodded approvingly. "Don't forget the big bear with a beer in his hand at the entrance."

He handed me a menu. I took it politely. "I'll probably just have a drink. I'm not terribly hungry."

He frowned. "That's not possible. The food here is legendary. Guy Fieri even said so!" Trent offered the last comment as legitimate proof.

I stifled a sarcastic retort. If I sounded too snide with Trent, he'd wonder why I agreed to go out with him in the first place. It was in my best interest to keep him motivated … and talking.

Instead I asked in all seriousness, "What was his recommendation?"

Trent grinned. "He loved the beer-battered burger."

How many calories would that have, I wondered. A thousand? I'd have to work out from now until Doomsday. "Is that what it sounds like?"

"Yep. A beef burger dipped in batter and then fried to perfection."

"Did the Food Network have any other suggestions?" It was a shot in the dark. Guy rarely sampled veggie burgers or salads.

"He also liked Joe's West Virginia roast beef sandwich with the special sauce."

That didn't give me too much to work with. "What are you having?"

"I always want to try something new, but I usually get the fried burger."

Despite my earlier pronouncement, my stomach rumbled with hunger. If I was going to drink, I could use a little something. I scanned the menu, searching for a snack that wouldn't bust my calorie count for the next week. Trent looked at me expectantly. Sometimes it was just easier to play along. "I'll go with Joe's West Virginia special."

Trent's face lit up. "Excellent choice, Kit! Is Pabst Blue Ribbon on tap okay for you?"

"Sure." At least the PBR would cut the richness of the beef, cheese, and special sauce.

We made small talk while we waited for the waitress to take

our order. It seemed like an eternity, but Trent appeared to be at ease. When I remarked that the service seemed a little slow, he called it "part of the ambiance" and kept chattering.

Finally we placed our orders. It was time to get down to business. If I was going to binge on fried food, my sacrifice had better pay off.

"So," I said, "tell me more about your job. What's it like working in the Sergeant at Arms office?" The pitcher of beer arrived, and Trent poured us frothy glasses.

"It's a great job. The best part is keeping everyone safe who visits the House of Representatives. It's rewarding, and I take it very seriously."

"So does your boss. His name is Gareth, right?"

"Yep. We're in lockstep on our priorities."

I took a long sip of the PBR. Its hipster cool status aside, it was remarkably refreshing. Maybe Trent had a point about the Tune Inn.

I needed Trent to divulge details about Pressler that might help finger him for Jack's murder. Commiseration often pushed the right buttons. "These days, my chief of staff is acting paranoid." I paused for a moment to increase the dramatic effect. "Now that I think of it, he's a pretty weird guy. What's it like working for Gareth?"

Trent took a swig of his beer and wiped his mouth. "He's intense. Definitely wants to make his mark at the Sergeant's office. Former military. You know the type." He gave me a knowing glance.

"What branch of the service?" I asked casually.

"Special Forces. Army Green Beret."

Something stuck in my head from one of the meetings I'd conducted with military officers from Fort Bragg. "Aren't Green Berets proficient at direct combat?"

Trent appeared surprised at my grasp of military knowledge. "That's right. They're organized into elite commando units and often engage in ambushes or other stealthy operations." He took a sip of PBR. "Or so Gareth tells me."

If the details Trent told me were true, Gareth would have had no trouble overpowering Jack Drysdale and killing him with the gavel. Time to try another line of attack, figuratively speaking.

"Given your jobs, do you have to arrive at work early in the morning?"

Trent shrugged. "We're largely concerned with the time of day when House members, staff, and the public are inside the buildings. But we have all-access identification badges, so that means we can be at work at any time, if necessary."

Gareth had the physical ability to commit the crime and access to the building during the early hours. That made him a promising suspect, but what about motive? Just as I was about to ask, our food arrived. The waitress plunked down my specialty sandwich. The roast beef and cheese oozed out the sides of the buttered rye bread. Alongside this delectable delight sat a formidable mound of crispy french fries. I popped one in my mouth. Absolute heaven.

"Why are these fries so good?" I hoovered in a few more before Trent had a chance to answer.

"I forgot to tell you. The fries are battered, too. So they're particularly scrumptious." He grinned mischievously.

I grabbed Joe's West Virginia special and took a bite. Fattening food tasted fantastic. No wonder Meg was so darn happy all the time.

Trent refilled my glass as I polished off the first half of my sandwich. After a long swig of brew, I resumed my interrogation. "When we met, you told me your boss wanted to tighten security, but Jack Drysdale from the Speaker's office didn't agree. Now that he's dead, do you think Gareth's plans will move forward?" The huge binder in Pressler's office proved that he meant business. That plan hadn't been put together overnight.

Trent raised an eyebrow. "You seem really interested in this topic. Do you feel unsafe at work?"

His question seemed innocent enough. "No, I have faith in your office and the Capitol Hill Police. I wondered if Jack's murder changed the situation." I gave Trent my most angelic smile. Then, I added, "I'm just trying to ask polite questions about your job. It's really impressive."

Stroking egos wasn't my forte. But this time, I seemed to be doing an okay job. "It's too early to tell, but I think there will be increased security in the House. As the Speaker's top aide, Jack threw up roadblocks to maintain open access for everyone and his brother to traipse through Congress."

Trent's altered tone caught me off guard. I couldn't resist a quick comeback. "Isn't it the people's House?"

Trent snorted. "The people have their say when they go to the voting booth. That's my opinion."

To keep our meal congenial, I bit my tongue. Trent had a lot to learn about Congress. Politicians cared about what their constituents thought, and they wanted to meet with them on a regular basis—both in Washington D.C. and in the home district. To prevent myself from spouting off, I took a big bite of the second half of my sandwich.

Trent eyeballed me. "What about you? How did you get a job with Maeve Dixon?"

I'd wanted to keep the conversation as much about him as possible, but I had to play along a bit or he might get suspicious. "I accepted a position with Dixon after the senator I worked for passed away."

"Was that the guy who was murdered last summer in his office?"

With my mouth full of roast beef and french fries, I could only nod. Trent kept talking. "I knew you looked familiar. Weren't you involved in solving that case?"

I sipped my beer. "You could say that," I answered vaguely.

"Is that why you're so interested in Jack Drysdale's murder?

Trying to reprise your role as Sherlock Holmes?" Trent laughed.

"I'm no Sherlock, for sure. I don't look for crimes to solve in my spare time. I'm concerned because Representative Dixon is a prime suspect. But she didn't do it." Time to change the subject. I glanced at his plate, which was nearly clean. "Did you like your burger?"

Trent didn't seem focused on his food anymore. He was an intensely attractive guy so it was doubly uncomfortable to feel his crystal-blue eyes fixed on me. He ignored my question. "Why do you think she's innocent?"

"She claims that she didn't do it, and I know my boss fairly well. I'd prefer to give her the benefit of the doubt unless evidence proves otherwise."

Trent seemed to accept my explanation. "Makes sense, I guess. Otherwise, you'll have to find a new job."

I smiled wryly. "Yes, exactly. I'd rather not have to go through that again."

Our food and drink almost entirely consumed, it was time to wrap up this pseudo-date. I fished around in my purse for my wallet. Trent saw what I was doing. "This is my treat, Kit. Remember, I asked you out."

Despite his comment, I kept rummaging until I found cash. I threw down a twenty. "I insist. I'm glad you introduced me to the Tune Inn."

Trent grabbed the money and tossed it back to me. "You're my guest for dinner." Reluctantly, I put the money back inside my purse. Splitting the bill would have kept it platonic, but since I wanted to keep this so-called date under the radar, avoiding a scene made sense.

After putting on my coat, I stood to leave. Trent asked, "Can I walk you to the Metro?"

I'd been trying to avoid it. I wanted to call Meg and give her a report on the evening. "Don't worry about it. I'll be fine. Thanks for dinner. I enjoyed it." I gave him a little wave. Trent sat back down in his seat with an odd expression on his face.

I couldn't tell if he was hurt, disappointed, annoyed, angry—or all of the above. None of the possibilities were positive, so sticking around to find out wasn't a good idea. I turned on my heels and weaved through the mob scene at the bar. Once outside, I took a deep breath of the cold evening air. Thank goodness it was over.

Walking toward the Metro, I pulled out my phone and called Meg. She didn't even bother to say hello. "How was it? Where did you go? Are you going out with him again?"

She would have kept going if I didn't interrupt. "If you'd shut up for a second, I could tell you what happened."

With a pouty voice, she said, "Fine. Go ahead."

I gave her a quick recap of the evening's events. Meg listened without interrupting until I finished. I could sense her disappointment through the phone. "I guess there's no love connection, then." She sighed.

"That wasn't the point of the evening, Meg. I'm trying to solve Jack's murder, remember?"

"You don't need to remind me. I just thought Trent might be your perfect match."

I was halfway to the Metro. Debating the current status of my love life with my best friend would have to wait. "I'm still glad I agreed to go out with him. He gave me a lot of good tidbits that might help solve the murder."

"Like what?" Meg asked.

"Gareth Pressler had access to all House buildings early in the morning. Those security monitors in his office would have made it easy to track Jack's whereabouts. Furthermore, he's former Special Forces, so killing Jack wouldn't have been difficult for him." I paused to take a breath before continuing, "And if that's not enough, he had a motive to want Jack dead."

"It sounds plausible, but your boss had access to the murder weapon only hours before she found Jack's body."

I was at the top of the escalator leading to the Capitol South subway station. "That's the last missing piece of the puzzle."

"It's not inconsequential. What are you going to do about it?"

"I'm not sure. I'll deal with it tomorrow."

"I don't want to put more pressure on you, but I heard through the grapevine today at work that the police might arrest Dixon soon. Your window of opportunity for finding the killer is closing quickly."

At this time of the evening, the long, descending moving staircase appeared to have no end, disappearing into a dark abyss, not unlike the trajectory of Maeve Dixon's political future and my Capitol Hill career unless someone exposed the real killer soon.

Chapter Twenty-Four

THAT NIGHT, I tossed and turned as fleeting, bizarre images of a bloody gavel, the menacing Hill Rat logo, Gareth's face, the stuffed deer's butt at the Tune Inn, and Clarence wolfing down an entire pizza invaded my dreams. The craziness and stress of the past several days had caught up with me. At six, I gave up and threw back the bedcovers. The fried food and beer hadn't helped, not to mention my guilt: I'd gone on a pretend date with a hot guy and neglected to tell my live-in boyfriend.

But there was no time for wallowing. Clarence's internal alarm was more precise than an atomic clock, and six o'clock was too early for him to give up his cozy position in bed for a romp outside. That meant I had uninterrupted time to think about the murder. After pouring myself a frothy latte, I settled into an overstuffed chair to ruminate. The caffeine slowly energized my gray cells, and they led me to one answer: Gareth Pressler.

Other than Maeve Dixon, he was the only suspect who could have done it. He'd monitored Jack's whereabouts that morning, stalked him, and committed the crime. But there was one big problem. How did he get his hands on the Speaker's gavel? My investigation wasn't over yet. If I hurried, I could get to work early and corroborate my theory. With a little luck and some sympathy from Detective O'Halloran, maybe I could prevent Maeve's supposedly imminent arrest.

After a quick shower, I threw on my last clean pantsuit and poked my head inside the bedroom. Doug and Clarence were waking up.

Rubbing his eyes, Doug asked, "What time is it? Are you leaving for work early?"

"I don't have time to explain. I might have an idea who really killed Jack Drysdale. If I'm right, there's a chance I can convince Detective O'Halloran to hold off charging my boss for the murder."

After sitting up in bed, Clarence ambled over to Doug and plopped himself down on his lap. He licked Doug's hand, indicating that he was ready for his morning massage. Then he yawned loudly. Clarence was apparently less than impressed by my pronouncement.

Rubbing Clarence's ears, Doug put on his glasses and focused on me. "Who do you think did it?"

"Gareth Pressler. He works in the Sergeant at Arms office in the House. That's why I went out for drinks last night with that guy, Trent. I wanted to pump him for information about his boss."

Doug wrinkled his nose. Was he reading something into my words? I hadn't said the word "date." Doug didn't know I'd allowed Trent to think it was more than a casual happy hour affair. "Are you sure about this, Kit? It sounds circumstantial."

I didn't have the time to convince Doug. "I know Maeve Dixon didn't kill Jack Drysdale. That means someone else is responsible for his death. Pressler is the best alternative. I need to leave now so I can wrap this up."

Doug looked disappointed. "Clarence has a grooming appointment today. I thought we'd drive in together." Clarence's groomer was located in the Capitol Hill neighborhood. If the appointment was early enough, I usually dropped him off and then brought him to the office for part of the day. Dogs were welcome in Capitol Hill buildings during working hours. Members of Congress believed they brought happy relief to the partisan battles of Congress. At least Democrats and Republicans could agree on something.

As for Clarence, he appeared to relish spending the occasional working day on the Hill. The constant attention, pats on the head, and belly rubs were appropriate compensation. He seemed to know when he looked his best. He liked to show off, particularly if the groomer gave him a doggie scarf to wear. Unfortunately, this wasn't a good time for a Clarence visit to the Maeve Dixon office.

"I forgot about that. Thanks for taking him. It's been absolutely crazy the past several days. Between the shutdown and trying to solve this murder, I can't remember if I'm coming or going."

"I noticed," Doug murmured.

"What did you say?"

"Nothing. Don't worry about it. I'll make sure Clarence gets to the groomer."

I gave Doug a quick peck on the cheek and bent down to pet Clarence. He responded with a wet puppy kiss.

"By tonight, life should start to return to normal, especially if Detective O'Halloran listens to reason."

Doug looked skeptical. "Be careful. If you're right, this guy isn't going to appreciate being fingered for the murder. He probably thinks he got away with it."

While heading out of the condo, I called over my shoulder, "Don't worry! Once I get what's needed, I'm turning everything over to the police. I'm not going to confront Pressler."

Less than thirty minutes later, I walked with purpose toward the entrance of the Cannon Building. The first-floor corridor was completely empty. After several days into the crisis, most "essential" congressional employees had given up on early bird arrivals in the hopes of discovering a miraculous solution. Meg had been right all along. We were in for a long haul.

I headed to my office and then reversed course. Stopping there would be an enormous waste of time. Dan had called last night when I was in the process of snooping around Gareth's office and I'd never called him back. Most likely he wanted to engage in another rant about the futility of our situation and the dismal, downward direction of Maeve Dixon's political career. He'd only delay the last part of my investigation, and it made little sense to explain my theory to him. After the police realized Pressler was a viable suspect and eased off Maeve, I could circle back to Dan, walk him through the details, and make him eat crow. After all, even though he'd asked me to investigate Jack's murder, he'd never actually thought I'd solve it.

Instead, I headed downstairs, breezed through the Capitol Hill Police metal detectors, and marched toward the dismal Cannon Tunnel. Over the course of the past week, I'd traveled the connector between my office building and the Capitol more times than I could count. The collage of paintings decorating the walls was becoming increasingly familiar. All in all, the collective talent of the high school artists was impressive. Their colorful canvases were the only sign of life in the monotone hallway. After weaving through the basement corridors and boarding the elevators tucked away in an inauspicious corner, I entered the House press gallery on the Capitol's third floor.

It would have been prudent to email Melinda on the walk over to the gallery. It seemed like ages since I'd met her to learn more about Jack Drysdale and potential suspects. With any luck, she'd remember me as her professor's generous girlfriend who liked ice cream breaks.

I provided my name at the front desk and asked for Melinda Gomez. Thus far, there hadn't been many lucky breaks in this case. This morning I was looking for the final nail to pound into Gareth Pressler's coffin.

To my relief, Melinda appeared in under a minute. Shaking her hand vigorously, I bellowed, "Thanks for seeing me on absolutely zero notice."

She adjusted her glasses with a shy smile. "No problem. You're Professor Hollingsworth's girlfriend. We met for ice cream."

I groaned inwardly. No time to educate Melinda about identifying women by their male romantic partners. "Yes, that's me. It's Kit. I'm glad you didn't forget."

Melinda shifted her weight nervously. "Oh, I'd never forget Professor Hollingsworth."

Her affinity was definitely with Doug, not me. But her willingness to talk worked in my favor. There was no point beating around the bush.

"I think you might be able to help me with my murder investigation."

Her eyes widened. "That's right. You're trying to figure out who killed Jack Drysdale. Isn't your boss the prime suspect?"

I gritted my teeth. "Yes, but she didn't do it. There's a credible suspect out there the police haven't focused on. But I need your help with the final clue."

Her face brightened, then she looked nervously at her watch. "This sounds exciting but we need to be quick about it. The House floor opens in thirty minutes. When we're live, I have to make myself available for questions from reporters, especially due to the shutdown."

I nodded. "This won't take long. Here's a question for you. Who is allowed on the dais when the House is debating a bill?" In the front of the House chamber, a tiered platform served as the stage for legislative action. Only certain people who were involved in House floor operations were allowed on it. The presiding officer—the substitute for the Speaker of the House—stands or sits at the very top of the raised platform. Maeve Dixon had served in this role on the night in question.

After giving the matter some thought, Melinda said, "Several

House staffers work on the dais. The enrolling clerk, the bill clerk, the journal clerk, the tally clerk …" her voice trailed off.

I shook my head. "Not on the lower levels of the platform. What about the top level? Where the Speaker or whoever is presiding over the House of Representatives at the time sits or stands."

She adjusted her glasses again. "That's a smaller number. You have the presiding House member in the Speaker's chair, the parliamentarian, the timekeeper, and the Sergeant at Arms. Sometimes the Clerk of the House is also on the top tier. I think that's everyone who's supposed to be up there."

Bingo. "So the Sergeant at Arms always has a place on the top level?" From my many hours of watching endless debate in the House, I'd thought that was the case. But I needed to make sure.

"I'm not certain there's always a staffer from the Sergeant's office at that table, but there's definitely a space reserved for the Sergeant or his deputy."

Now we were getting warmer. "Have you ever seen Gareth Pressler sitting on the top level of the dais?"

Melinda wrinkled her nose. "I haven't worked here too long. I'm not sure what he looks like."

That was easy to remedy. I whipped out my iPhone and searched for an image of Pressler. I found his official congressional employee photograph and showed it to Melinda.

She nodded. "Yep. I've seen that guy around. He's definitely sat on the platform before. The Sergeant at Arms is in charge of the mace, so that's why a representative is entitled to a spot on the top tier."

The mace is the symbol of legislative authority for the House of Representatives. It resembles an ancient fighting weapon, consisting of a long stick with an ornate eagle at the tip. It remains on the House platform during debate, and depending on its position, it indicates the type of legislative session the House is engaged in. Since it looks rather menacing, the

Sergeant at Arms supposedly uses it as a way to regain order if a member of Congress becomes unruly. Personally, I didn't think the Sergeant at Arms capitalized on the intimidation afforded by the mace nearly enough during heated debates. If the Sergeant waved the mace more regularly at House members who caused problems, then maybe we wouldn't find ourselves in the current political mess.

"Thanks, Melinda. You've been very helpful. I have one more question for you. I know there are extra gavels in case one breaks during House proceedings. Do you know where the extra gavels are kept and who has access to them?"

She shook her head. "Sorry. You got me there. I have no idea."

This was literally the last kernel of information I needed before contacting Detective O'Halloran. Hopefully Maeve hadn't been arrested yet.

Grasping at straws, I asked, "Maybe your boss would know?"

"I doubt it. We never actually go on the dais during debate. And I don't think a reporter would ask about a detail like that."

We were both lost in thought for several minutes. Then Melinda snapped her fingers. "I've got it. If we hurry, we might be able to catch my friend who works as one of the reading clerks. He might know. Follow me!" She took off and headed down the stairs toward the entrance to the House gallery.

A minute later, we were hurrying down a side aisle in the House chamber. We approached the Speaker's rostrum and Melinda scoured the room. Finally, she flagged down a guy scurrying around to ensure all the necessary papers were in place for the day's legislative proceedings.

She cleared her throat. "Excuse me. Is Charlie working today?"

The staffer ignored her question. "Who wants to know?"

She drew herself up, apparently not intimated by the snotty tone. "I work in the press gallery. Can you tell him that Melinda Gomez needs to speak with him?"

The guy sighed. "The floor opens in fifteen minutes." He motioned with his hand. "Members are already arriving for their opportunity to stick it to the other side about the shutdown."

Melinda didn't cede an inch. "Please. I need to speak with him." She lowered her voice. "It's a matter of life or death."

I wouldn't have been quite as dramatic as Melinda, but her approach caught Mr. Snotty's attention. "What isn't a matter of life or death these days?" he asked rhetorically. But then he said, "I'll see if I can find him. Just wait here."

Facing Melinda, I exclaimed, "You were terrific! Don't take no for an answer."

Melinda pushed up her glasses, which tended to fall down her nose. "Thanks. I'm learning to act more assertively on the job. I can't let reporters and staffers push me around."

"I doubt anyone ever pushed you around, Melinda."

A moment later, a tall, thin middle-aged man wearing a gray suit emerged from one of the side anterooms. Melinda waved so he'd see us.

"I'm sorry we asked to see you on such short notice, Charlie. This is Kit Marshall, and she has a question to ask you. We can't tell you right now why it matters, but trust me, it might be very important."

Charlie seemed to have a better attitude than his colleague. He laughed. "I'd rather not know the reason. I have too many secrets up here." He pointed to his head. "I can't keep them straight."

At Melinda's nod, I asked my question. Charlie answered immediately. "It's not a state secret about the extra gavel." He raised his eyebrows. "As long as you promise you're not going to steal it."

I crossed my heart.

"You came to the right person," he said. "The extra gavel is kept in the drawer of the reading clerk's desk. If the Speaker or presiding officer breaks a gavel, we replace it immediately with our spare."

"Charlie, does everyone have access to that drawer?"

"Certainly not! The desk belongs to the Clerk of the House and her employees."

"Is the drawer locked? You know, the one with the gavel," I added.

Charlie hesitated. "I can't say that it's always locked. We keep other items in that drawer and sometimes people forget to secure it."

"Do members of Congress know where you keep the extra gavel?"

"No, because otherwise they might try to pocket an extra one. As a souvenir for some lucky constituent or donor."

"I have a few more quick questions for you. Were you working the evening when Representative Maeve Dixon was in the chair? It was a few nights ago. She's my boss."

His face softened. "I heard she's a suspect in the Drysdale murder. I don't believe it for a second. Maeve Dixon always goes out of her way to act friendly when she's presiding over the House floor. It doesn't seem consistent with her personality. And yes, I worked that night. She liked my tie, as a matter of fact."

Charlie was a snappy dresser. He'd likely not forget it if a member of Congress complimented him. "Do you remember if you had to go to your drawer for the spare gavel that night?"

"It's such a rare occurrence, I would remember that. No, we haven't had to replace a gavel in a while."

Melinda broke in, "So that means the spare gavel should be in the drawer now, right?"

"Absolutely. There would be no reason for it not to be."

Unless Gareth Pressler had nabbed the gavel Maeve used and then replaced it with the spare gavel. If he did it swiftly enough after she exited the dais, no one would have noticed. He could have pocketed the gavel with her prints on it and then used it a few hours later to kill Jack Drysdale.

"Charlie, do you mind checking on the extra gavel?"

He glanced at his watch. “Okay, but then I have to skedaddle. If my boss thinks I’m not ready for the opening of the House, she’s going to kill me.”

Little did Charlie know that in our little world, bosses did kill. Only not mine. He hustled to the dais and sat down at the reading clerk’s desk. The look of surprise on his face told us the result. The spare gavel was missing.

He opened a few more drawers, but came up empty-handed. He walked back over to where we were standing. “I don’t know how you knew the spare gavel was missing, but it is. I’ll have to tell my boss about it.”

There was no time to waste. Every last detail had fallen into place. It was definitely enough to persuade Detective O’Halloran he needed to take a hard look at Pressler. Hopefully that meant he’d hold off charging Maeve later today.

“Charlie, you’ve been a lifesaver. You too, Melinda. If I’m going to prevent a disaster, I need to run now.” As I turned to leave, I said over my shoulder, “Drinks are on me once the shutdown is over!”

Melinda yelled after me. “Wait a second!”

I turned around. “What’s wrong? I don’t have a lot of time before my boss is arrested for a crime she didn’t commit.” Normally, I tried to avoid acting like a drama queen, but extraordinary circumstances called for desperate measures.

With a tentative look, Melinda offered, “Come upstairs for a few minutes so we can check on a detail about the night in question.”

“No can do. It’s almost nine thirty and the Capitol is open for business. I need to make sure the police don’t file charges against Maeve Dixon.” The sands of time had almost run out. I hurried toward the chamber’s exit just as the House was called to order for the day and the House chaplain began the daily prayer.

Behind me, I heard, “Dear Father, grant us the fortitude and perseverance to help us do your will today.”

Well said! Perhaps the Almighty had heard the chaplain's prayer. A little divine intervention never hurt.

Chapter Twenty-Five

MEMBERS FLOODED THE House floor entrance. Normally, the opening of a legislative session was sparsely attended. The shutdown attracted a bigger crowd of politicians who wanted to speak on the House floor, even for one minute, about the funding fiasco. I waded through the masses until I reached the periphery of the Capitol Rotunda.

At this time of day, throngs of schoolchildren, international tourists, and patriotic Americans typically swarmed the Rotunda. This stately room was located in the absolute center of the Capitol, immediately underneath the dome. "Majestic" was an understatement. Perhaps at no other time in my life would I find myself almost completely alone inside its walls. Other than me, a single Capitol Hill Police officer remained on patrol. I was drawn to the splendor of it all—the beautiful assortment of neoclassic friezes and statues. This was America's pantheon, plain and simple.

My favorite Rotunda artwork was the group statue of leading women's suffragists. I felt the eyes of Elizabeth Cady Stanton, Susan B. Anthony, and Lucretia Mott fixed upon me. This monument had been relegated to the basement of the

Capitol after its completion decades ago, but in 1997, it was relocated to its now prominent location inside the Rotunda, where thousands of visitors could appreciate it. What would the suffragists say if they knew a female congressional staffer was trying to save the career of her boss, a woman who had served proudly in two wars before winning election to Congress? There was no question. They'd be proud. That's why they fought to give women the right to vote and participate in politics in the first place. I was quite certain the foremothers would agree it was time for action.

I grabbed my phone and fired off an email to Detective O'Halloran, asking to meet him as soon as possible due to information I had come across concerning the murder of Jack Drysdale. I could provide the details later. Before sending the message, I added, *Maeve Dixon didn't do it.* He needed to know my scoop would cast doubt on Maeve's status as the prime suspect.

I'd wait for O'Halloran to contact me back at the office. With my head buried in my iPhone, I took off for the homestead in Cannon. There might be a chance he'd read the message and ask to meet inside the Capitol or somewhere else on the Hill. Wherever it was, I'd arrange to rendezvous with him immediately. Since my eyes were focused on my device and certainly not on the path ahead, it was no surprise that I almost suffered a direct collision with another staffer headed in the opposite direction.

A familiar voice said, "Hey, watch where you're going!"

My head jerked up. Dan gazed at me with pursed lips, his countenance scrunched in exasperation.

At precisely the same moment, I exclaimed, "Dan!" and he bellowed, "Kit!" We both chuckled.

"You never called me back last night." Dan sounded hurt, almost like a lovelorn teenager whose crush had dissed him.

"I'm sorry. I was busy tracking down a lead in the murder investigation."

Dan waved his hand dismissively. "You shouldn't waste your time. Maeve Dixon did it. The police are convinced, and there are no other suspects. You should be using these precious hours to find another job."

I shook my head. "You're wrong, Dan. Someone else had means, motive, and opportunity. In fact, I just emailed the police detective in charge of the case so I can meet with him and explain my theory. I don't think they'll charge Maeve once he hears it."

The color drained from Dan's face. He stammered, "Are you s-sure?"

"I might not have enough for a conviction, but it will cast doubt on Maeve's status as the prime suspect."

Dan gulped for air and rubbed his forehead nervously. "I wish you'd called me back last night."

"Why? What did you do?"

"I talked to several chiefs of staff and they said I should resign immediately. It's critical to get off Dixon's payroll before the bottom falls out. So I called Maeve earlier this morning and quit."

Dan's words hit hard. "How could you do that? It's going to make her look even more suspicious if her senior staff start to jump ship."

"I know, I know. But I left everything in North Carolina to move here. I can't go crawling back. I need to figure out a way to find another job in D.C." Dan looked like a puppy that had just made a mistake on the carpet.

"You can't call her back and retract?"

"I don't think so. She accused me of abandoning her."

"She's not off the mark."

Dan frowned. "None of this would have happened if you'd kept me in the loop about the investigation. I never thought you'd actually succeed in finding a credible suspect."

Again, Dan's words stung. "I appreciate your vote of confidence. What's your plan now?" I glanced at my phone. No reply yet.

Dan's demeanor brightened. "I'm on my way for an interview as chief of staff for another member of Congress."

Astonishing. Dan was a political and policy lightweight. He didn't know the difference between a conference committee and a concurrent resolution. How could he already have another plum job lined up? There had to be a catch. "With who?"

Dan's outlook went dark again. "Jerry Bowser."

I suppressed a snicker. Representative Bowser, although a reliable vote for the left-wing establishment, had a reputation that preceded him. Specifically, a reputation for berating staff, throwing small items in fits of anger, and demanding curb-to-curb car service. Bowser went through staff like Kleenex.

"Good luck with that." My iPhone email icon showed I had an unread message. Time for Dan had dried up. I gave him a quick salute and concentrated on my device. Sure enough, I'd piqued Detective O'Halloran's interest. He asked to meet at Representative Dixon's office in twenty minutes. That was perfect timing. After replying, I shoved the phone back inside my purse.

I descended into the bowels of the Capitol basement yet again. A few minutes later, I reached to open the door leading to the Cannon Tunnel. A muscular arm reached over my right shoulder and grabbed the handle instead. Startled, I turned around to confront Trent Roscoe's handsome grin.

"Good morning, Kit. I saw you were headed for the tunnel and ran to catch up with you."

I breathed a sigh of relief. "You scared me. It's pretty deserted around here this early."

He opened the door and ushered me through. "Sorry about that. You left so abruptly last night, I figured this was my opportunity to chat with you again. Where are you headed in such a hurry?"

"Back to my office. I'm meeting a Capitol Hill Police detective shortly."

Trent fell into stride alongside me. "About what?" he asked innocently.

"Jack Drysdale's murder." I preferred a solitary walk to my office rather than answering nosy questions from Trent. It was bad luck running into him in the tunnel. Even if Doug wasn't in the picture, I couldn't imagine dating someone who worked on the Hill. Its insularity made it worse than high school. Meg continually struggled to maintain a wall between her dating and professional life. As she plowed through more guys on the Hill, successful compartmentalization was becoming statistically less possible. Besides, I'd decided Trent wasn't really my type. Sure, he was good-looking but the macho persona had worn thin.

Conspicuously avoiding Trent's stare, I trotted along at a good clip. He asked, "Did you figure out who did it?"

We were right next to the vending machines tucked inside a corner off the main basement intersection in Cannon. My stomach rumbled. There had been no time for breakfast this morning. I needed a caloric infusion, preferably sugar, to keep my mind from wandering into a fog when I met with Detective O'Halloran. I slowed down and grabbed my wallet, ignoring Trent's question.

In a noticeably impatient voice, Trent inquired again, "Well, did you?"

This man had become exasperating. Meg's fanciful notions about him as a potential romantic interest seemed like crazy talk right now. Hotness did not make up for an annoying personality, and Trent Roscoe had gotten on my last nerve.

I hit the button for a large bag of frosted animal crackers—the sweetest and most substantial option available in the quasi-healthy vending machines the House had installed in a futile attempt to impose federal nutritional standards on lowly congressional staffers. He touched my arm, ostensibly to get my attention. I whirled around to face him directly and looked into cold, implacable eyes. Something told me to stay silent.

I reached down to retrieve my breakfast. Once again, Trent leaned closer. At this point I hoped he was trying to hit on me. The alternative was too horrible.

His hand suddenly gripped my forearm. I said, "Trent, I'm really not in the mood for your overtures." I'd aimed for neutral but heard the fear in my own voice.

"Too bad. You're not a stupid girl, so I'm guessing you've figured it out." His voice had turned to ice and his grip tightened. At that precise instant, I felt a sharp object press into my right hip. As I tried to jerk away, Trent pulled me close. I could feel his breath on my neck. "You're going to do what I say or I'll kill you right here."

My eyes darted to the pressure. I saw the glint of a box cutter sandwiched against my body. Instinctively, I wriggled against Trent's powerful grasp. True to his promise, he pressed the weapon deeper. Razor sharp, it ripped through my suit jacket and blouse and into my flesh. With one swift move, he stifled my scream with his left hand. From his efficiency, I knew that Trent had done this before.

"No funny business, Kit. You do what I say or I won't hesitate to hurt you more." I believed him.

We were hidden in the vending machine alcove without another person remotely near us. I nodded to let him know I understood. He shoved me in the direction of a desolate hallway leading deeper into the recesses of the Cannon basement. One of these hallways led to committee staff offices and the Library of Congress. But he was forcing me down a separate, deserted corridor. After we'd taken a few steps, he opened the door to the now-closed Cannon Carryout, a small cafeteria designed for quick food service. The Carryout had been shuttered for several months. Since its closure, I doubted anyone had ventured down this hallway, except the random maintenance worker. He reached into his pocket and produced a key, which he inserted into the lock. The door opened and he shoved me inside, bolting it behind us.

Even without a knife threatening to rip me to shreds, the abandoned Carryout would have sent shivers up my spine. The small window on the door had been papered over so that no one could see in or out. The open area that formerly displayed hot soup, cookies, and fruit was completely bare. The refrigerated shelves sat empty. A long metal counter had separated hungry lunchtime staffers from the made-to-order grill and food preparation area. A stale odor of french fries, onion rings, and chicken tenders lingered in the air.

Trent prodded me to keep walking. "Get behind the counter." The gravelly voice seemed to come from a different man than the one I'd dined with the night before at the Tune Inn. The box cutter's razor-sharp point restricted my options, so I followed his instructions. My back was up against the grill in the corner of the exposed kitchen area. Since he had me cornered, Trent let go of his tight grip. He stood squarely in front of me, his weapon brandished in his right hand.

There were two explanations. Either Trent knew his boss had killed Jack and he wanted to silence me, or Trent was the murderer. Unfortunately, both scenarios were equally deadly. I couldn't physically overpower him and no one would hear my screams. The only alternative would be reasoning with him.

I raised my hands to signal surrender. "Why are you doing this, Trent? Talk to me."

He sniggered. "*Now* you want to talk. That's typical female behavior. As soon as you got the information you wanted last night, you made a beeline for the door."

I tried to ignore his sexist comment but couldn't resist a retort. "From my perspective right now, it was the worst first date in history."

"Don't get snarky." He waved the knife back and forth.

"Okay, okay. But this is crazy. Last night, we were on a date. At least, I think it was a date. And now you're poking me with that." I pointed toward the box cutter in his hand.

Trent seemed to consider my argument. His face softened.

"I actually liked you. But it was trouble when you came to see me about security in the House. Something seemed familiar. I remembered the news stories about a staffer who'd figured out the identity of her boss's murderer in the Senate. A quick Google search verified my concerns. Even worse, you started poking around. It wasn't hard to discover your real motivation for asking all those questions."

Just above a whisper, I softly stated what I now knew was true, "You killed Jack Drysdale."

Immediately, Trent's face became agitated. "You don't understand. Gareth is all talk and no action. He'd complain day after day about Jack." He changed the intonation of his voice to indicate he was mimicking Gareth. "We'll never tighten up security in the Capitol because JACK is standing in the way. JACK won't let the Speaker restrict access. JACK is a thorn in our side. JACK is the most powerful staffer in Congress."

Every time he said Jack's name, the volume of Trent's voice increased by several decibels. If I could keep him talking about Jack, he might speak loudly enough to alert a random passerby in the hallway.

I stated the obvious. "You killed Jack because Gareth wouldn't do it."

He snorted. "I didn't even bring it up with Gareth. He's the worst type of boss. He complains incessantly without offering any solutions. I did what had to be done."

"So it was a personal hatred of Jack that pushed you over the edge?"

Trent shook his head. "You've got it wrong. It was never personal. This was patriotic."

I'd read somewhere it was smart to empathize with a psychotic perpetrator. "You wanted to protect Congress. Jack was standing in the way."

Trent's eyes lit up. "Exactly. Jack didn't understand how his decisions put the lives of elected politicians and even staff at risk. He had to be—"

"Eliminated?" I offered.

"I prefer to think of it as 'set aside,' actually."

"Set aside" seemed too mild a phrase for the occasion, but I wasn't in a position to argue semantics with a menacing hulk of a guy brandishing a box cutter. My side ached and I could sense a sticky wetness in the vicinity of where he had dug the box cutter into my flesh. I didn't dare look to see the damage that had already been done. I'd lose my edge. Keeping Trent chatting was my only hope.

"Jack's murder was premeditated, wasn't it?"

"The original plan was to kill Jack and pin it on Jordan Macintyre. Your friend Trevor gave me a tip that he was in dire financial straits. A good motive, you know?" He glanced at me for approval of his pre-murder plans.

This was all about acting calm. I forced myself to muster a smile. "Makes sense."

"Then your boss got into a public fight with Jack. She was a war hero and I started thinking …." He tapped his forehead in case I wasn't appreciating his criminal mastermind. "Why not pin it on Maeve Dixon?"

"So much for honoring those who served," I muttered.

Trent appeared to consider my sarcastic comment. "I didn't like that part, but everyone knows she's a gym rat, always lifting weights and staying in shape. She'd have the strength to kill, even a guy like Drysdale."

The combination of skipping breakfast and being stabbed and held at knifepoint was doing a number on my flip-flopping, gurgling stomach. Still, the longer I could keep Trent blabbering, the more likely Detective O'Halloran was to look into why I was missing our appointment.

"Even if Congresswoman Dixon had a motive for killing Jack, it didn't mean she had the opportunity. How did you arrange that?"

He grinned broadly. By all objective standards, Trent was a ruggedly handsome guy. But now all I saw was a cold-blooded killer. Good looks and a wicked soul made for a terrifying combination.

"That was a lucky break. I'd already planned to lure her to the scene in the morning hours. Her discovery of the body along with the public fight with Jack would give the police plenty to work with."

The rest was obvious, but I said it anyway. "But then you saw she was going to preside over the House debate that night on the floor."

"Exactly. You figured everything out already, right?"

"Almost. I'd fingered your boss Gareth as the killer. So obviously I missed something."

Trent moved closer. Backed into a tight corner with the Carryout's grill at my back, I had nowhere to go.

"That's what I surmised from our conversation last night," he said. "The gavel was the last piece of evidence. Sure enough, you ran to the press gallery this morning to track it down."

His revelation caught me off guard. But then it made sense. There was no way he'd simply run into me by chance this morning. The move had been deliberate, just like his plan to kill Jack and incriminate Maeve.

"How did you know where I was this morning? Did you place a tracker on me at the Tune Inn?" It wasn't too far-fetched for a former Secret Service agent.

"Didn't need to go to that expense. I have access to every person's movements inside this complex. Twenty-four hours a day, seven days a week."

Did Trent have some sort of magic map charting the comings and goings of all House employees? Images of a super-sized Marauder's Map flashed through my brain. But the dark eyes staring at me were more like Voldemort's, not Harry Potter's. Trent was no benevolent wizard; he was pure evil.

Then it clicked. "The security monitors in Gareth's office."

"There are cameras everywhere in this complex. I came in early this morning and scanned the screens for you. You were easy to find since not many people had reported for work yet." Trent's voice was steady. He might have been recounting the details of his latest fishing trip instead of his plans to stalk and kidnap me.

"I bet you also know where the blind spots are."

"Also correct. That knowledge came in handy when it was time to kill Jack. There are a few alcoves and corners, especially in the ornate parts, where the cameras don't reach. We disabled the cameras in this hallway when the Carryout closed down." He flashed his teeth in a menacing leer that sent shivers throughout my body. "Very convenient for today's unfortunate events."

Instinctively, I took another step backward. Trent pulled out a large roll of duct tape from his pocket. "Sit down on the floor," he commanded.

There was no way to hide the panic in my voice. "What are you going to do?"

He wrapped the tape around my wrists in front of my body and then my legs. He made numerous loops on each of the binds, effectively creating shackles. For good measure, he wound the tape around my hands and fingers.

"Not sure yet. I can't do anything now because too many people have already shown up for work. There's no way to move you out of here without being noticed. I'll have to wait until later tonight to figure something out."

The more I could keep him talking, the greater the chance someone would find us, slim as it was. He tore off another long piece of duct tape. I knew that section would cover my mouth.

"Wait a second. What about the gavel?"

Trent stopped before putting the tape in place. "That was my last stroke of genius. Once I knew Maeve Dixon was going to preside over the House, I had my weapon. I made sure I was on the dais when she was in the chair, presiding over the floor debate. During a vote, when the clerks were busy with recording the 'yeas' and 'nays,' I swiped the extra gavel from the desk drawer. That drawer hasn't been locked for as long as I've worked in the House. I pocketed the gavel and waited."

Trent paused, adding more drama to his storytelling. The

look of excitement on his face told me he was more than pleased with himself. He'd planned an airtight murder and pinned the crime on a known enemy of the victim.

"When my boss's duty as presiding officer was over, then what did you do?"

"That was easy. She left the gavel on the desk. I switched it with the duplicate. It took me less than five seconds." Trent beamed with malevolent pride.

"Maeve's prints were on the gavel used to kill Jack. If you grabbed it from the dais and bludgeoned Drysdale, why didn't your prints turn up when the police analyzed it?"

Trent shook his finger at me. "I was one step ahead. I needed Dixon's prints to be on the weapon, but not mine. That was the whole point of switching the gavel in the first place. That, and making sure no one noticed it was missing before Dixon was gone. So I wore a clear latex glove." His expression pensive, Trent added, "I knew the cops wouldn't focus on the switch. Their murderer's boxed up with a bow on her head and her fingerprints on the weapon. That's all they care about. People in Washington D.C. are so self-absorbed, they only see what they want to see. No one pays attention to details they think don't matter."

I was about to comment on Trent's explanation, but he cut me off. "Sorry, Kit. It's time for me to go. Can't have people at the Sergeant's office missing me."

Then he spied the package of animal cracker cookies I'd bought from the vending machine sticking out of my suit pocket. He grabbed them and put them into his own pocket. "You won't be needing these."

He stood up. "Sit tight. I wish I could say this will end better for you, but I won't lie. It's not looking good."

I strained against the duct tape. My struggles were futile, with the duct tape fastened securely around my limbs and mouth. Trent opened the door and closed it behind him. The sound of the lock clicking into place seemed to seal my fate.

Chapter Twenty-Six

Forcing myself to remain composed, I took deep breaths through my nose and counted slowly to thirty. I shouldn't have been so dismissive of Dan's meditation ritual. I could use a calming mantra right about now.

After my count, I knew Trent wasn't coming back immediately. Time to spring into action. I had one card up my sleeve, and with any luck, it was an ace.

My plan required standing up. I pushed my butt along the floor so my back was resting against the flat surface of a concrete wall. My hands and legs were tightly bound, but if I could leverage myself and summon the collective power of my thigh muscles, I might manage standing. Slowly, I inched my way vertically up the wall. My legs were killing me, but after an excruciating minute, my knees were bent. Luckily, I was the master of wall sits due to my sadistic boot camp instructor who liked to finish our sixty-minute workout torture sessions with a long stationary pose. After pausing for a few seconds, I used my last bit of strength to catapult myself into a fully upright position.

Good job, Kit. That was the first task. Now for the hard part.

Several months ago, I'd watched a news program about an abducted woman whose hands had been bound with duct tape. She'd freed herself by raising her arms over her head and thrusting downward with as must force as possible. The television show stressed that the trick worked even if the duct tape was tight. No time like the present to perform my own test.

With my legs bound closely together, it was hard to balance. I leaned against the wall for support and lifted both my arms as far back as possible. I took a deep breath, closed my eyes, and focused. I visualized Doug, Meg, and Clarence's faces. No way was I ready to say goodbye to them. Fueled by that resolve, I slammed my arms toward my midsection with every ounce of power I could muster.

I opened my eyes and looked at my hands. To my astonishment, the duct tape had a small rip. *Progress!* If one attempt had gotten me this far, another might do the trick. I repeated the process two more times until a sizable tear appeared down the middle of the binding. With all my strength, I pulled my hands in opposite directions and the tape tore apart.

Trent couldn't have gone far. Not wasting one second, I bent down and freed my legs. Now came the hard part. This was going to hurt. Bracing myself, I grabbed an edge of the duct tape binding my mouth and slowly ripped it off. The relief of breathing air through my mouth quickly replaced the searing pain of the tape's glue separating from my lips and face. I exhaled a grateful sigh.

Time to get moving. I bolted from behind the counter and unlocked the door. Trent had said he needed to make an appearance at his office. That meant he'd head toward the Capitol. I veered right down the deserted hallway and came upon the vending machines where he'd apprehended me.

The pain on my side intensified so I rubbed it with my hand. Immediately I felt a warm and sticky liquid. Blood oozed through my blouse. *That bastard!* He'd actually stuck me with that damn box cutter. Although it felt like a rodent had been gnawing on my side, the wound wasn't life threatening. I had to find Trent and make sure the police apprehended him.

He was likely headed to the Cannon Tunnel. The metal detectors operated by the Capitol Hill Police stood between us. By the time I stopped and tried to explain my predicament, Trent might manage to flee—but only if he knew I had escaped. Confusion in the vicinity of the metal detectors might be enough to alert him of funny business. No, it was better to catch up with him and cause a fuss once I had eyes on him.

Pursuing Trent down the tunnel meant blowing through the metal detectors. The red ooze of blood on my blouse wasn't too obvious, but it would attract attention if I tried to move through security the conventional way.

I took a second to summon my last reserves of energy. Then I did what thousands of congressional staff only dream of doing one day: I ran through the security area with abandon, sprinting down the tunnel. It took the officers behind me several seconds to react. It wasn't every day a staffer blew right through security without a hello and a flash of a badge. As I raced down the hallway as fast as my legs would take me, I heard an officer yell, "Hey, why are you running away?" I hoped the guy wasn't going to shoot me, but I guess I was counting on the police not to use deadly force on a woman staffer. However, I did want him there when I caught up with Trent.

And there he was—just ahead of me. Two-thirds of the way down the tunnel, sauntering along like he was taking a leisurely Sunday stroll beside the Tidal Basin. To add insult to injury, the jerk looked like he was eating something. Yes, he was helping himself to the blasted cookies he'd pilfered from my pocket when he left me bound and gagged in the Carryout.

Just as Trent was about to reach the exit leading to the Capitol's underground labyrinth, the door opened. I couldn't believe my eyes. It was Doug, Meg, and Melinda. For good measure, Clarence ambled along, with Doug holding his leash. Somehow, one of them had figured out there was trouble brewing.

I slowed down to a trot. Trent was trapped. I screamed ahead to my posse. "Don't let him leave the tunnel! Trent Roscoe killed Jack!"

The Capitol Hill Police had caught up with me and tried to secure my hands. Shrugging them off, I insisted, "You don't want to arrest me. It's that guy. He's a murderer!"

Twenty feet away, Doug appeared perplexed. He didn't know what Trent looked like. But Meg, who would have recognized him from the fifty most beautiful people on Capitol Hill list even if she hadn't met and flirted with the man, pointed and yelled, "It's the hot guy!"

Trent heard the ruckus and looked up. Still grasping a cookie in his hand, he made a break for it, dashing in the direction of the door leading to the Capitol basement. If he escaped into the maze of underground tunnels, it might take a while to find him. Meg, Doug, and Melinda looked as if they'd seen a ghost. Immobilized, they seemed unlikely to prevent his escape.

Then, an unlikely hero sprung into action. Clarence spied the animal cracker in Trent's hand. He immediately charged and leapt. Forty pounds of beagle mutt hurtled through the air in Trent's direction to claim the prize. Clarence meant no harm—he simply saw a chance to score a delectable treat—but the diversion gave Meg the opening she needed. When Trent turned to shake Clarence off, Meg administered a swift kick with her stiletto-heeled winter boots directly at Trent's crotch. Wailing, he doubled over in pain, and the cookie dropped from his hand. As if nothing out of the ordinary had happened, Clarence scarfed down the remaining snack, licked his lips, and barked for joy.

Chapter Twenty-Seven

"Can you pass the chicken wings?"

One week later, we were celebrating at the popular Capitol Hill eatery, the Hawk 'n' Dove. Hearty appetizers filled the table and drinks were flowing. There was ample reason to party. Jack's killer had been apprehended and the resolution of the case had restored Representative Maeve Dixon's reputation. Furthermore, the government shutdown had ended hours earlier when Congress and the president agreed on a compromise to fund the federal government for another year. Life was good in the nation's capital.

My other partners in sleuthing had joined Doug, Meg, and me at the historic bar. The past several days had been a whirlwind of activity as the police sorted out the details of Trent's twisted plot. Concurrent with the endless law enforcement interrogations and legal inquiries surrounding the murder investigation, Congress edged toward a grand bargain with the White House. My exonerated boss emerged as a key player in the negotiations. When I wasn't answering questions about my brief yet brutal abduction, I was wheeling and dealing with Beltway kingmakers. It had been an exhilarating series of events, but now it was time to unwind with good friends, both old and new.

Rising to my feet, I cleared my throat and said, "Thank you to everyone who joined us this evening in celebration. Each one of you played a critical role in figuring out who killed Jack Drysdale. Solving the crime cleared my boss, the distinguished member of Congress from North Carolina." I paused to tip my glass in Maeve's direction. "And also brought the real killer to justice."

Detective O'Halloran, who was being an awfully good sport under the circumstances, raised his glass of sparkling water and chimed in, "Hear, hear!"

Melinda couldn't resist a tribute of her own. "Let's toast to no more murders or shutdowns on Capitol Hill."

Judy Talent added, "For at least a year."

Each of them raised a glass, clinked with a neighbor, and took a long sip. After chatter around the table had died down, I addressed the convivial crew once again. "There is one more matter I'd like to address."

Seven pairs of eyes immediately shifted to me. Taking a deep breath, I spoke, my voice shaking a bit with excitement. "Another mystery was solved last week, in addition to Jack's murder. I've discovered the identity of the infamous blogger Hill Rat."

My pronouncement was met with audible gasps. I glanced briefly in the direction of the table's corner, where the culprit sat. He nodded in assent.

"Perhaps Hill Rat would like to reveal his identity now."

After several seconds of silence, which seemed like an eternity, Trevor spoke. "Kit speaks the truth. I am Hill Rat."

Another round of surprised exclamations prevented further discussion for almost a full minute. I grabbed my knife and hit my wine glass several times to silence the boisterous crowd. "I know you're shocked by this news. But let's give Trevor a chance to speak."

A hush fell over the table. Although not as high a priority as solving Jack's murder, unmasking Hill Rat was a Capitol Hill obsession. I saw several of my guests, namely Meg and Judy, furiously tapping away at their iPhones. Trevor knew his secret wouldn't remain at the table for long, so he was fully prepared for the inevitable press tsunami awaiting him once he left our company.

Trevor stood. The expression on his face was serious yet calm. Upon confirming my hunch about Hill Rat's true identity, I'd confronted Trevor privately. He agreed it was time to end Hill Rat's tenure. We decided this evening would be a good time to share the information with colleagues and friends. Trevor had planned a farewell post for his website that would self-publish at precisely the same time he revealed himself to our table at the Hawk 'n' Dove.

"Chaucer commented that all good things must come to an end. He was right. Writing my unpredictable dispatches as Hill Rat has given me much pleasure and satisfaction. Many people will ask why I did it. Although there are many good people who work on Capitol Hill," he motioned to those seated at the table, "there is also an underbelly. It's rarely mentioned publicly. Penning an anonymous blog was a way to keep the Hill elite on their toes."

Trevor took a sip of his drink then continued, "I knew the day would come when my anonymity would be compromised. In fact, Kit was not the first person to guess my secret, although she was the only person to live long enough to do something about it."

Trevor motioned for me to join him, so I reluctantly stood and took up the thread. "During the murder investigation, I learned that Jack had figured out Hill Rat's identity before he died. For several days, I considered it as a possible motive. Once I had a hunch Hill Rat might be Trevor, it was easier to eliminate him as a suspect."

Trevor smiled wryly. "Thank you, Kit, for that vote of

confidence. Although I might be an infamous blogger spilling the secrets of Washington, I am not a murderer."

Meg piped up, "But how did you figure out Trevor was Hill Rat?"

"It was an educated guess. Trevor seemed unusually interested in my progress on the case. That didn't make sense, since he had no strong connection to the victim or the accused. But the real evidence came from Geno."

Seeing their puzzled faces, I explained, "Geno works for the Architect of the Capitol as a craftsman in the Capitol basement. I talked with him to find out if the Speaker's gavels were made within one of the congressional buildings and how many were constructed at a time. Ultimately, I needed to determine where those extra gavels were kept and who had access to them."

Judy Talent broke in, "But what does this have to do with Hill Rat's identity?"

"I was just about to answer that question," I said. "When I talked to Geno about the gavels, he mentioned that a man had asked him earlier that morning about the Speaker's gavels. He thought it was strange that two people had inquired about the gavels in the same day. I showed him a photo of Gareth Pressler on my iPhone, but he wasn't the person who had talked to Geno."

Detective O'Halloran asked, "Wasn't that a clue Gareth wasn't the killer?"

I shrugged. "Sure, it was perplexing. At the time, I didn't think much of it."

Meg took a long sip of her drink and then raised her glass. "Maybe it's the Prosecco talking, but I'm still not following."

"It wasn't until after my kidnapping and the aftermath that I had time to mull over the entire series of events. How did Hill Rat know about the gavel as the weapon? I asked Detective O'Halloran if he'd leaked that detail to the press."

He shook his head. "Absolutely not."

"I knew Representative Dixon hadn't done it since that

detail emerging didn't help her case one bit. She wanted to keep information about the gavel out of the press as long as possible."

Maeve spoke up. "No way we wanted anyone to know about the murder weapon."

"That left a small number of people." I ticked each person's name off my fingers. "Doug, Meg, Dan, and Trevor."

Meg giggled. "Did you think I was Hill Rat?"

I smiled. "Not for a second. Doug was a no-brainer, as well."

Doug adjusted his glasses in apparent annoyance. "Why wasn't I considered as a possibility? Even briefly?"

Meg answered, "Doug, Hill Rat writes about contemporary politics, not about what happened two hundred years ago!"

After regaining the floor, I went on, "The only credible alternative to Trevor was Dan. When I thought about it, Dan made no sense as Hill Rat. First, he didn't know any of the people Hill Rat wrote about. Second, Dan is scared of his own shadow, and Hill Rat had guts. Lastly, Hill Rat, although nefarious, certainly understood how Capitol Hill operates. Unfortunately, Dan does not." I glanced at my boss when I said the last sentence. I hoped she wasn't offended by my dig at Dan. After all, he had served as her top aide during her first year in Congress. If she was annoyed, she didn't show it. She laughed along with everyone else.

Melinda said, "The only possibility was Trevor."

"Yes, although it was still only a strong hypothesis. I thought about the big clue Geno had provided. The person who spoke with him earlier that morning was either Hill Rat or the killer. Once I knew Trent was the murderer, I paid a visit to Geno and showed him photographs of Trent and Trevor. He easily identified Trevor as the person who'd asked about the gavels. Then I figured it out. After having breakfast with me at Pete's, Trevor immediately investigated to find out more information about the gavel, and then he wrote his blog post about the gavel as the murder weapon."

"But that post fingered me as the killer." Maeve pointed to herself. "Why would you write something accusatory like that when you were trying to help Kit find the real killer?"

Trevor rubbed his forehand nervously. "That's a fair question. I never thought you killed Jack, Representative Dixon. But my motives in helping Kit's informal investigation were more self-interested, I admit. Once Hill Rat's identity was revealed, I would be named a prime suspect—in that the police would think I killed Jack to silence him. Before my identity was compromised, it was imperative the case was solved. I figured releasing the information about the gavel would speed things up since there would be more pressure on Kit to find the guilty party."

Maeve gave Trevor a skeptical look. "That was a big gamble. It might have ruined my reputation in Washington."

"Temporarily, yes. But once the real killer was discovered, I believed you would rebound politically." Trevor smiled cautiously.

Maeve remained silent, but I could tell Trevor would not be a welcome guest in the office of Representative Maeve Dixon.

Judy took advantage of the lull in the conversation. "I read in the newspaper that Trent Roscoe was apprehended in the Cannon Tunnel and several of you helped catch him. Were you simply in the right place at the right time?"

With a considerable degree of sarcasm, Doug said, "Hardly."

Meg sat up straighter in her chair. "I can tell this part of the story!" With a dramatic gesture of my hand, I gave her the floor.

Meg smoothed her bob and smiled eagerly. "After Kit determined the spare gavel was missing, she ran off. Melinda tried to stop her but Kit was in too much of a hurry."

Melinda broke in, "I wanted her to examine the C-SPAN footage of the House floor on the night in question so we could see which staffers and members of Congress were on the dais. The camera angles might have prevented us from seeing the murderer swap the gavel, but we could have scanned the various shots to confirm who was close to the Speaker's desk around the time Representative Dixon presided over the chamber."

Meg gave a dismissive wave. "Kit didn't have time for more sleuthing. But our trusty press gallery friend had a hunch something wasn't right."

Melinda nodded. "After Kit left, I scanned the video online. It's simple to do if you know how to use the online C-SPAN search engine and there's a specific time of day you want to view. Sure enough, Gareth Pressler wasn't on the dais. But Trent Roscoe did appear in several shots."

Meg offered, "Melinda emailed Kit, but thought she'd also better reach out to someone else who could notify her."

Melinda continued the story. "The only person I knew connected to Kit was Professor Hollingsworth. Luckily, I still had his contact information in my phone. When I was a student in his class at Georgetown, I used to text him all the time with questions about assignments." She blushed, confirming the crush I already suspected.

Doug said, "When I got Melinda's message, I knew Kit was in trouble. If she accused the wrong person, it would only cast more suspicion on Representative Dixon. When my texts went unanswered, I contacted Meg. Luckily, I was already on the Hill that day due to Clarence's grooming appointment. The three of us agreed to meet in the Capitol."

Meg was so excited to tell her part of the story, she could hardly remain seated. "Once we found each other, we decided to head to Kit's office in Cannon." Meg paused briefly, allowing the suspense to build. "That's when we saw her charging down the tunnel, pointing at Trent."

Judy's eyes were wide with astonishment. Clearly impressed by the drama of the story, she asked, "Didn't I read that your dog had something to do with apprehending Trent?"

Doug chuckled. "That detail has made for good press fodder.

It was not Trent's evil nature but his general nastiness that ultimately cooked his goose. He stole Kit's snack after locking her up in the abandoned café. He was chomping on the cookies as he walked down the hallway. Clarence was already exuberant because he saw Kit running toward us. Given his healthy appetite, he lunged for the goodies. Classic Clarence, I'm afraid."

Meg pointed to herself with fingers from both hands. "And that gave me the opportunity to kick Trent right where it hurt. He folded like a house of cards!"

I laughed. "It was a lovely finishing touch. Couldn't you see the Capitol Hill Police behind me, though?"

Meg replied, "Sure, but why take chances? He deserved it."

Finishing off her wine, Judy donned her coat. "I've got to run. Now that the government shutdown is over, it's time to think about my new job on K Street. But I'm not the only one with a new job these days." Judy gave me a knowing smile.

"It's official. Can we let everyone know?" I directed my question toward my boss.

Rising, Representative Dixon said loudly, "Can I have everyone's attention?" Everyone quieted down immediately. Some people had the ability to command a room, and Maeve was one of them.

"For the rest of my political career and my life, for that matter, I will be grateful to Kit and those who helped solve Jack's murder. Because of your sleuthing, I have a future. Above all, I want to thank everyone for believing in me." She raised her glass, and the rest of the crowd followed suit.

She kept the floor. "I'm not done! The best thing to happen from this fiasco is that I'm honored to name Kit Marshall as my new chief of staff."

Cheers erupted from the crowd. Doug and Meg knew about the appointment, but I hadn't shared the news with anyone else.

Rising once again to my feet, I said, "Thank you,

Representative Dixon. I'm proud to work for you. I'm going to need a great deal of help as I begin my new position. I have two announcements in that regard. First, Judy Talent has agreed to serve as my mentor. Judy had a terrific career on Capitol Hill and she's going to teach me everything I need to know. Right, Judy?"

Judy was busy texting on her phone, but then, she was the consummate multitasker. "You got it, sister."

I grinned. "The other announcement also involves a talented female Capitol Hill staffer. Since I will assume the chief of staff role next week, Representative Dixon needs a new legislative director. I'm thrilled to name Meg Peters as our new LD for the office!"

This time, the cheers were even louder. People yelled "speech, speech" to persuade Meg to say a few words.

She wiped away several tears. "The United States Congress can be a tough place to work. But toiling away with a friend you trust makes the effort worthwhile. I didn't hesitate one moment when Kit offered me the job."

Only Trevor seemed skeptical. "You're leaving a professional committee staff position for this opportunity?"

Meg, never a Trevor fan, answered in a snippy tone. "Yes, I am. It turns out committee investigations weren't for me. And, by the way, I have an announcement, too."

"What news?" I asked.

"I broke up with Kyle last night. We got into another fight about my job. No relationship is worth that much heartache. The good news is that I'm a single woman again!"

Trevor rolled his eyes and muttered softly under his breath, "Head for the hills." I also saw Doug grimace. No doubt, he liked Meg better when she was attached. With a boyfriend in tow, she was more predictable and restrained. My favorite Capitol Hill flirt was back in business. Last time I checked, living vicariously wasn't a mortal sin.

I gave Meg a hug. "I'm sorry about Kyle."

She waved me off. "No worries. Besides, I can't be attached right now."

"Dare I ask why not?"

Meg leaned in and gave my arm a squeeze. "Because there can't be any restrictions on our next adventure!"

Chapter Twenty-Eight

After another hour of celebration, Doug and I exited the bar and breathed in the crisp air. The wind was still and the temperature didn't require gloves or hats, a welcome change from the dreariness that typically bookended January and February in Washington.

We strolled down Pennsylvania Avenue in contented silence. When we were about to turn left toward the Capitol South Metro, he grabbed my hand. "Let's keep strolling down First Street." With no work tomorrow and the Fahrenheit cooperating, I agreed.

We walked past the ornate Jefferson Building, the crown jewel of the Library of Congress, and Neptune's Fountain, the ornate statue that greeted visitors. Modeled after the Trevi Fountain in Rome, it wasn't quite as spectacular as the Italian masterpiece, but still provided a regal touch of classicism in harmony with the awesome splendor of the Capitol situated diagonally across the street.

Doug pulled me in the direction of the dome. After looking both ways, we crossed First Street to reach the east front of the Capitol. A large expanse of grass and concrete landscape separated the actual Capitol Building from the street. Doug led me down a pathway lit by rustic streetlamps. The shutdown having just ended, no tourists shared the grand expanse with us. They'd been deterred from visiting while the monuments and other attractions had been shuttered. Tomorrow, the bustle would return to Washington D.C., but for now, we relished the serenity.

With the steps of the Capitol directly ahead of us, Doug jerked me to the right. I asked, "What are you doing? I'd like to look at the dome at night for a moment. Isn't it beautiful when it's illuminated and the sky is clear behind it?"

Doug pulled us underneath a big tree. According to the metal marker on its trunk, it was an American beech as old as the Capitol itself. He turned to face me directly before he spoke. "I'm not interested in the Capitol Dome tonight."

I laughed uneasily. This wasn't like Doug. He was either laid-back or absentminded—take your pick—but rarely melodramatic.

He ignored my awkward laugh. "Kit, I know I've acted strangely the past couple of months. You've been incredibly busy with your job, but the whole time, I was preoccupied, too."

I gulped. I didn't like the sound of this. "What do you mean?"

"I was keeping a secret."

Terrific. I'd finally sorted out Jack's murder, my job, and the federal government shutdown. Now my boyfriend was about to unload something horrible. I braced myself, both mentally and physically, for his revelation.

"Go on. Don't keep me in suspense."

"You still don't get it, do you?"

"Actually, I don't. If you're going to break up with me, then let's not beat around the bush."

He smiled. "You've been working in the doom and gloom too long, Kit. This isn't about breaking up. This is about making our relationship permanent."

Doug knelt down on one knee and withdrew a black velvet box from his coat pocket.

I gasped. Then I covered my eyes with my hands in disbelief. "You're going to propose!"

Now it was Doug's turn to laugh. "Yes, Kit. For a detective, it took a lot of clues before you figured it out. I've been preoccupied because I've had the ring for a while, but there's never been a right time to give it to you. I decided tonight was it."

He opened up the box, and a beautiful diamond ring sparkled back at me. Instinctively, I reached for it, but Doug pulled it back.

"Not so fast. You didn't answer the question yet."

"What question?" Two could play at this game.

"Kit Marshall, congressional staffer extraordinaire and amateur sleuth, will you marry me?"

For once, I was speechless. I whispered "yes" before jumping into Doug's arms. Quite appropriately, the nighttime illumination of the Capitol caused my newly adorned ring finger to sparkle.

Photo by Glen Fuhrmeister,
GF Photography

Colleen J. Shogan is a senior executive at the Library of Congress. She is the former deputy director of the Congressional Research Service and previously served as a staffer in the United States Senate. A political scientist by training, Colleen has taught American government at Georgetown University, Penn, and George Mason.

Colleen is a native of Pittsburgh, Pennsylvania. She received her BA from Boston College and her doctorate from Yale. A member of Sisters in Crime, she lives in Arlington, Virginia, with her husband Rob Raffety and their rescue mutt, Conan.

For more information, please go to:
www.colleenshogan.com.

Book 1 in the Washington Whodunit series

Stabbing in the Senate

When Senate Staffer Kit Marshall stumbles upon her boss's dead body, she becomes the prime suspect in his murder. If she ever hopes to work on Capitol Hill again, she must prove she had nothing whatsoever to do with his death. And that means finding the real killer.

Made in the USA
Charleston, SC
14 October 2016